THE RETURN OF THE PSAMMEAD

THE
RETURN
~ OF THE ~
PSAMMEAD

HELEN CRESSWELL

Illustrated by John Holder

BBC BOOKS

The Publishers would like to thank Milton Primary School and
Ridley West for their help with the illustrations.

Published by BBC Books, a division of BBC Enterprises Limited
Woodlands, 80 Wood Lane, London W12 0TT

First published in hardback 1992
First published in paperback 1993
© Helen Cresswell 1992
The moral right of the author has been asserted
ISBN 0 563 36367 3 (Hardback)
ISBN 0 563 36766 0 (Paperback)

Illustrations by John Holder
Set in 13pt Caslon by Phoenix Photosetting, Chatham
Printed and bound in Great Britain by Redwood Press Ltd, Melksham
Colour separations by Dot Gradations, Chelmsford
Jacket printed by Belmont Press Ltd, Northampton

TO CAROLINE AND CANDIDA

My Lambs, you now are grown so tall
You do not read my books at all.
And yet I think you will be glad
To meet again the Psammead.
You loved it, in those far off days
When magic things could still amaze,
And wishes work, and dreams come true.
So here it is again – for you.

CONTENTS

LIST OF COLOUR ILLUSTRATIONS

Preface

There were once four children (five, if you count the baby) who spent their summer holidays in a white house, happily situated between a sand-pit and a chalk-pit. One day they had the good fortune to find in the sand-pit a strange creature. Its eyes were on long horns like a snail's eyes, and it could move them in and out like telescopes. It had ears like a bat's ears, and its tubby body was shaped like a spider's and covered with thick, soft fur – and it had hands and feet like a monkey's. It told the children – whose names were Cyril, Robert, Anthea and Jane – that it was a Psammead, or Sand-fairy. (Psammead is pronounced Sammyadd.) It was old, old, old, and its birthday was almost at the very beginning of everything. And it had been buried in the sand for thousands of years. But it still kept its fairylikeness, and part of this fairylikeness was its power to give people whatever they wished for. You know fairies have always been able to do this. Cyril, Robert, Anthea and Jane now found their wishes came true; but somehow, they never could think of just the right things to wish for, and their wishes sometimes turned out very oddly indeed. In the end their unwise wishings landed them in what Robert called 'a very tight place indeed', and the Psammead consented to help them out of it in return for their promise never, never to ask it to grant them any more wishes, and never to tell anyone about it, because it did not want to be bothered to give wishes to anyone ever any more . . .

The book about all this is called *Five Children and It*.

Chapter I

THE BEGINNING OF THINGS

And now read on . . .

When the Psammead had said that it never wanted to grant wishes again, it had only been talking out of a kind of general fed-upness – and in that mood, as you know, it is possible to say almost anything. It is fed-upness that makes grown-ups say things like 'That's the last time I ever take *you* on a picnic!' on Monday, and by Friday are merrily packing up a hamper for a whole day by the river. You must always make allowances for grown-ups, because life is a sore trial, and fed-upness is bound to creep in round the edges now and again.

The Psammead cannot be exactly described as a grown-up, even though it is thousands and thousands of years old, which beats any grown-up you might care to mention, including your Great Great Aunt Agatha, or even your parrot. Fairies are never properly grown-up, and they certainly do not wish to do business with anyone over the age of twelve, say, or thirteen at the very outside.

The Psammead, despite its grumpiness, had actually become rather fond of Cyril, Anthea, Robert and Jane (and baby), and if they had stayed at the White House would doubtless have changed its mind and let them have more wishes, after all. But once Father and Mother came back it was nearly the end of the holidays, and so the family had packed up and gone back to London, lock, stock and barrel.

There is another book, called *The Story of the Amulet*, where the Psammead met those same five children in London (and don't ask me to explain how. It is far too complicated, and if you wish to know you must read the book for yourself.). On this occasion they had amazing adventures all over the world, and even back in the past. By the end, the Psammead was again suffering from general fed-upness, and wished itself back into the past. Now you must understand that the Psammead was not able to wish things for itself. Luckily, a certain old gentleman made the wish for it, so back it went into the past.

At the time, it intended to stop there, but before long it was homesick for its own dear familiar sand-pit, and longed to go back there. It was then fortunate enough to meet a young Egyptian boy, who agreed to make that wish for it, in exchange for a wish of his own – wings to fly with. So back it went.

A sand-pit is a lonely place to be, especially if you are the last of your kind. So at sunset the solitary Psammead would sit and howl at the pale, rising disc of the moon. It would have cried, but did not for fear of wetting the top twelfth hair of its left whisker.

'A nice thing!' it would mutter, as it dug its way out of the sand day after day in the vain hope of seeing some children – *any* children.

'Here today and gone tomorrow! 'Tisn't manners!'

Hope deferred maketh the heart sick, so in the end the Psammead dug itself deep, deep, deep into the sand, and vowed to go to sleep for at least another thousand years. And that, no doubt, is where it would have stayed, if one day . . . but that is getting ahead of the story.

The real story starts a few years after the five children had left the

White House after a summer of adventures beyond their wildest dreams. It starts in a tall, putty-coloured brick house in Islington, which is a part of London, and again it is summer. It was one of those houses with a small front garden but a long one at the back — long enough, at any rate, for a decent game of French cricket, and with a tree big enough for a swing, or to be a mast in shipwrecks.

The house itself, as Mother was always telling Father, was bursting at the seams, because there were six children, and they were the kind of children who seemed to be everywhere at once and could do a very passable impression of there being at least a dozen of them. The eldest was George, and the next Ellen, who was called Ellie by the others, except in moments of high dudgeon and huff. Pip had once called her Ellen for a whole week after she had accidentally opened a matchbox containing Drake and Nelson, his pet spiders. The grateful creatures had then scampered off up a water spout, never to be seen again. Pip was next in age, and his real name was Philip.

Next came Lucy, who was a lover of fairytales and romance but could fly into a temper like anything. Likewise she could burst into tears at the drop of a hat despite having, or so she claimed, the heart of a lion. People said she was precocious, and perhaps she was. (You may have to look up precocious in a dictionary — it must on no account be confused with precious.)

Last of all came Edmund and Felix who were only six, and twins, and what Father called incorrigible. This is also a word you may have to look up, but I can give you a clue by saying that Bessie, the nurse, said they were trickier than a cartload of monkeys and she despaired of their ever mending their ways. Practically every month she threatened to give her notice on account of them, but they always said sorry so nicely, and swore to be such regular saints in the future, that she ended up forgiving them — till the next time. You may have noticed that the children who make most trouble for grown-ups often have the best manners. They need to have, to get them out of their scrapes. And if they happen to be six-year-old identical twins with golden hair and round blue eyes they are able to pass as angels, even to those who know them. Lady visitors, ignorant of their wayward ways, would fondly liken them to cherubs. (The author is not certain that ways can be wayward, but thinks the meaning is clear, which is the main thing in English prose.)

I shall not tell you any more about Edmund and Felix in case you become too fond of them – as I suspect some of you will be doing already. Because the twins, as it happened, were the reason for all the exciting adventures that were to follow. But they did not mean to be, and the sad thing is that they *missed* those adventures, which were the kind any self-respecting child would give its right arm for – or at any rate its pocket money for the next five years.

It started with Edmund and Felix both feeling what Bessie called 'off colour'. This meant their not wanting seconds of anything, even jam roly-poly, and their not feeling up to racketing about bothering the life out of the whole neighbourhood. Their brothers and sisters paid little heed, and even the grown-ups thankfully took it to be a passing ailment, possibly brought on by stuffing themselves at every meal, and over exercising their lungs.

Then, suddenly, everything changed. It was as if, as Ellie observed, a chill blight fell over the household. Suddenly Mother was looking pale and worried, and rushing up and down stairs to and from the room where the twins lay. Cook was everlastingly boiling up bones to make broth, and the savoury steam floated up from the basement and filled the whole house. Then the children were ordered to stay downstairs and on no account to go in to their brothers and to be as quiet as mice and to please, please try to be good. They promised to try.

They assembled in the best parlour, where they felt very uneasy among all the plush and the china ornaments. They felt so out of place that they half wondered if they should go and change into their best togs, though of course they didn't. No Garsington worthy of the name ever willingly got into its best things.

'What's up, d'you think?' Ellie wondered.

'Pigged themselves as usual,' said the heartless Pip, 'and got a bellyache.'

'They hardly ate a thing yesterday,' said Ellie reprovingly, 'and Mother doesn't like you to use that word.'

She carefully avoided using it herself.

'What – bellyache? What's wrong with it? If you're supposed to call a spade a spade you should call a bellyache a bellyache and – '

'Oh, stow it!' George told him, and shied a cushion from the sofa and Pip naturally shied one back and a regular fight began, with the girls shrieking and dancing and then, inevitably, a mighty crash.

An awesome silence followed. The four stared down at the hearth where lay the shattered remains of the pottery figure of Grace Darling, of which Mother was particularly fond.

'Oh crikey!' said the luckless Pip, for it was he who had shied the fateful cushion. '*Now* we're for it!'

Mother and Bessie came running, and the children braced themselves for all kinds of a row, but were not at all prepared for what happened.

'Oh, whatever . . . ? Oh no!' And Mother burst into tears.

This was a terrible thing. You can stand a good rowing, however uncomfortable, but the one thing that you simply can't stand is the sight of a grown-up in tears – especially if that person is your own dear Mother. The four were horrorstruck, they stared aghast, and Lucy burst out crying and ran forward sobbing, 'Mother, Mother, don't, don't! We're sorry, we're sorry!'

'We'll buy another!'

'We'll club our money!'

But Mother turned away and left the room, followed by the sobbing Lucy, and the remaining three were left to face the wrath of Bessie.

'*Now* look where your doggery's led to! And after all that was said at breakfast an' all them promises!'

The trio assiduously studied the pattern of the carpet. If there was one thing the young Garsingtons held dear it was their honour, and the faithful keeping of promises. They had on many occasions mingled blood and sworn to die for it (though the chances of this being necessary in leafy Islington were slight). On this occasion they had failed, and were bowed in shame.

'You ought to be ashamed of yourselves,' continued Bessie, with perfect truth. 'Your little brothers lying sick and your Pa away and your poor dear Ma near out of her mind with worry!'

'I say, they're not *really* sick, are they?' said George, to whom this thought had not occurred.

'Your Ma's sent for the doctor! They're as poorly as ever they know 'ow to be, bless their precious 'earts, I could weep to see 'em, I reelly could!'

This was serious news indeed. For Bessie to be as soppy about the twins as any lady visitor who did not know their wayward ways, boded ill.

'So you stop 'ere and make not one sound, d'you hear?'

They watched her go to the door, then turn.

'And not one of you sets foot up them stairs.' She lowered her voice. 'It might – it might be *fectious*!'

And with this awful warning she left. The trio were by now so stricken with guilt that they could hardly meet one another's eyes. And when they did speak, it was naturally in the merest whispers.

'I say, I hope it's not measles!' Pip was quite unnaturally white. 'I almost died of that!'

He knew this not because he remembered the occasion, being only three at the time, but because it was a well known piece of family lore. As a rule he was rather proud of it, and could listen endlessly to stories of how people had to sit up night after night bathing him with cold sponges to save his life. Today it seemed to strike rather too close to home.

'You can't get it twice, duffer!' George told him. 'Nor mumps either, thank goodness. Lor, how my jaw ached!'

'I think it's something much worse than either of them,' Ellie whispered.

'It can't be much worse than something you nearly died of,' pointed out Pip, nettled.

'Bubonic plague, or a mortal fever!' said George.

They lapsed into silence. The clock in the corner ticked loudly. This had a depressing effect on their spirits. They sat, sunk in gloom, each thinking its own dismal thoughts.

But there is a limit to how long perfectly ordinary healthy children can remain sunk in gloom. Presently George said, 'No one said we weren't to go outside.'

'That's true,' agreed Ellie. 'Only not to go upstairs.'

'On pain of death,' added Pip.

'We don't have to sit here and be quiet when we can perfectly well go outside and be quiet,' pointed out George, reasonably enough.

'Doing what?' enquired Pip. 'All outside games are rowdy.'

They pondered this undoubted truth. Ellie, however, while thinking of her own misfortune had tried, in time-honoured fashion, to cheer herself by thinking of others with worse misfortunes. It so happened that she had been reading *What Katy Did*, the pages of which had been liberally watered with her tears. When things were sad in books Ellie always cried, just as she would if they were in real life. And if there was one thing calculated to send her into a rage it was people laughing at her, or saying contemptuously, 'Fancy blubbing over a book! It's only a *story*, you know!' Ellie, despite her tender years, was one of those wise mortals who know that stories are just as real as anything else in life, and that all the best ones make you want to laugh or cry – or both.

As with all inspirations, this one came from two ideas coming together and fusing in a blinding flash of light. As Ellie was reminding herself how truly awful it must be to lie for weeks and months on end with your back hurting and knowing you might never walk again, her eye fell absently on Mother's workbox. From this was trailing a fine green thread.

'I know! I've thought of a game!'

Her brothers looked at her without enthusiasm. It is one thing for a game to be quiet, and quite another for it to be unmanly, fit only for milksops.

'That game out of *What Katy Did*!'

Neither of the boys had read this work, though Ellie had earnestly begged them to do so. The merest dip into it had convinced them that it was soppy, and distinctly lacking in brigands, pirates, highwaymen, sieges, shipwrecks or any other similar subject of interest. They had been horrorstruck to find that one of its heroines was called Clover. They had no intention, they said, of turning a single page to find out what happened to a girl with a name like that.

'Most girls' names are soppy,' George had said, 'including yours. No girls' names are even halfway decent. But *Clover*!'

At this point Lucy returned, very pink about the eyes and nose. She went straight to Ellie, who put her arms round her and said, 'Never mind, Lucy lamb, we'll club our money and buy Mother another. And listen, I've thought of a game we can play outside – a quiet one!'

She explained the game she had in mind.

'Though it's more a trick, really,' she said, and her brothers brightened somewhat at this.

First one found a trinket of some kind, bright enough to attract attention, but not too large – a bracelet, say. To this was tied a length of the finest possible grey thread, a grey that would be invisible on stone. The bracelet was then placed on the pavement as if it had been carelessly dropped. The children hid themselves, holding the other end of the thread, behind the garden gate or hedge. There they waited for an unsuspecting passer-by.

'Then, the minute someone bends to pick it up, you give the thread a little tug – not too hard, just enough to move it from under their fingers. If they try again, you give another tug, and if you want you can make the bracelet just glide away over the pavement as if it were alive! Can't you just see their faces?'

George and Pip agreed that they could. It was not, they said, the best trick they had ever heard of. It was in fact very tame, a real girl's trick. But given that it was at least quiet, in that any shrieking would be done by passers by, not themselves, they were willing to give it a shot.

'But we haven't got a bracelet. And we daren't go up to Mother's room to get one,' Lucy objected.

'What about your watch, Jaws?' suggested Pip.

Very small children find it quite difficult to say George, and when they try it comes out as something very like Jaws. And as George was eldest, all his younger brothers and sisters in turn had called him that, and, as often happens in families, it had stuck. And given that George was given to jawing, or so the others said, it rather suited, which is more than some nicknames do.

'My watch!' George now exclaimed in tones of horror.

This magnificent item had been presented to him by his parents on his last birthday, after years of pleading on his part. They said that they judged he was now old enough, being thirteen, and sensible enough to be entrusted with so valuable an object. And he had, indeed, been guarding it zealously up to this moment, removing it whenever a strenuous game was afoot, and absolutely forbidding any of the others to touch it, let alone wind it.

'You won't *lose* it, duffer!' said Pip, who was extremely jealous of the aforesaid watch.

'Oh let us use it, do!' begged Lucy, who was quite cheered by the prospect of this harmless game.

And so George reluctantly handed over his watch, and Ellie delved in the workbox for a suitable grey thread, and tied the watch to a good length of it. They went out on tiptoe and closed the front door quietly behind them. They had not been forbidden to go outside, but nor had they been given permission.

The front garden was bordered by a low brick wall. Along that grew rather straggly shrubs, sparse enough for the children to peer through, but ideal for the purpose of concealment.

As it was George's watch it was he who, first looking left and right, placed it carefully in the middle of the pavement and laid the thread through the gate and behind the wall. Lucy begged to be first to do the tugging, but George held grimly onto the thread.

Her eyes filled ominously at this rebuff, but Ellie said swiftly, 'You can be look-out, Lucy. Peer round the gate and tell us when someone's coming.'

So Lucy was scout, and did not have to wait long before the sighting of their first victim.

'Quick!' she hissed, darting from the gate and crouching beside the others. 'A lady with a big hat!'

They waited what seemed an eternity, breathing in the smells of soil and sooty hedge. Then they heard the click clack of heels, and stiffened. George peered forward, determined not to take his eyes off his watch. In his view, girls' games all too often misfired.

The heels stopped. The four held their breaths. They watched as the lady first stared downward, then looked quickly about her, then stooped. As her fingers were about to grasp the watch it moved – just out of reach.

'Oh!' they heard her gasp. Ellie and Lucy put their hands to their mouths to stifle giggles. The Hat had now straightened up but was still gazing, mystified, at the watch. Click clack, two tiny paces forward and again she glanced rapidly round to make sure no one was looking, and again stooped. Again the watch glided from under her fingers.

'Heavens above!'

The Hat was off now, click clack click clack at a very fast lick, and the children were rolling in mirth.

'She – she thinks it's bewitched!' gasped Lucy.

'Gone off to buy some specs, I should think,' said Pip.

'Did you see her face? Oh, do let's do it again!'

This time Lucy was allowed to creep out, replace the watch, then take the end of the thread.

'Do it like I did,' George instructed. 'Don't go getting excited and jerk it, you'll only scratch it. Gently does it.'

They had hardly settled themselves behind the hedge and were arguing who should be scout when there came the sound of a motor car being driven at what sounded like a very fast rate. The boys were about to stand, to observe this interesting phenomenon, when the sound stopped abruptly.

'The doctor!' Ellie whispered. 'It's Doctor Grey!'

'Oh lor,' groaned George. 'Don't let him see it!'

They watched helplessly as the doctor climbed briskly from his car, bag in hand, took two steps, saw the watch, stooped – and picked it up! The thread was whisked from Lucy's nerveless hand – at least, she said later that it was nerveless.

'Oh no!' gasped the four in unison. And there they crouched, thunderstruck at this turn of events, as the doctor strode right up the path, banged the knocker, then let himself in and shut the door firmly behind him.

I am sorry to say that the children did not then begin to lament for their poor little brothers, who were evidently so ill that the doctor had raced to the house in his motor car and let himself in without ceremony. They would feel sorry for the twins later, but at this particular moment were more concerned with the fate of the watch. Particularly George.

We will pass over the undignified row that followed. Recriminations flew. Ellie was accused of thinking of the silly trick in the first place, Pip of suggesting the watch as bait, Lucy of letting go the thread. Unfortunately, George himself had been strongly pressing his claim to be scout when the motor drove up. The other three rounded on him, pointing this out and claiming that the loss of the watch was his own silly fault.

'In any case, Dr Grey will give it back,' said Ellie. 'Doctors are men of honour.'

'Oh yes, and hand it straight over to Mother, I expect, and get me into the most fearful row. She'll never believe I was guarding that watch with my life now. She'll probably take it back and make me wait for it till I'm twenty-one!'

'And then we'll never know what the time is, thanks to you,' said Pip. 'And keep being late for dinner and tea, and miss our grub!'

In the end they decided their best hope was to wait in the garden and waylay the doctor on his way out.

'After all, he won't necessarily know it belongs to one of us,' Ellie said. 'So he might not give it to Mother at all. We must all cross our fingers and hope.'

Alas, their hoping was in vain. Dr Grey did show the watch to Mother, who instantly recognised it, and George did get into a row. But this was not such a bad one as he had feared, because other events came crowding in to take Mother's mind off anything so paltry as a watch. After the doctor's visit everyone's life was turned upside down in the twinkling of an eye.

The twins, it appeared, were very ill indeed with scarlet fever. This was, as Bessie had warned, highly infectious, and the rest of the children were to leave home immediately, that very day. They were to be sent to a person called Great Aunt Constance, who was not their aunt at all, but their father's, and lived in the country. Bessie was despatched to send a telegram.

'But what if she *hates* us?' wailed Lucy.

'And us her,' added George grimly.

'What if she turns out to be like that hateful Aunt Fortune in *The Wide Wide World*?' quavered Ellie. (She had wept over this book more copiously than most because its heroine shared her own name, though that virtuous child had no brothers or sisters and was never, ever called Ellie.)

'I'd rather stop and catch the beastly spots,' said Pip.

All their arguments and lamentations were to no avail. Mother was firm. Scarlet fever was a very serious business, she told them. She did not say that sometimes people died of it, because that was unthinkable, with Edmund and Felix stricken. But the children knew this. They knew also that you had to have your hair shaved and that all your skin peeled off, though they understood that it usually grew over again. They certainly hoped so, for the twins' sake.

Bessie came back and the children were ordered outside again while the packing was done.

'But *we* want to pack!' said Lucy. 'Nobody else knows what we want to take.'

'You can't take very much at all, I'm afraid,' said Mother. 'You'll be going on the train, and – '

'The train!'

'Hurray!'

'And then no doubt a cart will meet you at the station,' Mother continued. 'And I'd really rather you didn't go up to your rooms again – scarlet fever is dreadfully infectious.'

Everyone knows that a person has to do its own packing, especially if that person is a child. No one else can possibly know which objects are sacred and cannot be parted from.

'Then we'll have to make lists,' said Ellie. 'Else Bessie won't know what things we simply have to have with us.'

So this is what they did. George's list included his cricket bat, his book of Ancient Greek Myths and a stuffed owl in a glass case. This was a kind of oracle to George, and he consulted it in times of trouble.

'No owl, George,' said Mother firmly when she saw this. 'Certainly not on a train. Do try to be sensible, George.'

Ellie had a list of books as long as your arm, a box of watercolours, her Journal (which she wrote in conscientiously every day) and a Japanese parasol she had been given at Christmas and to which she was devoted. Pip wanted his Red Indian outfit and teepee, his Book of British Insects, his kite, his magnifying glass, his model fort and soldiers, his –

Even Ellie could see he was going too far.

'Do stop, Pip!' she begged, 'or there'll be no room left on the paper for Lucy!'

Lucy's list was even longer, and included a raftful of dolls, a teaset, her Noah's Ark and the entire contents of the dressing-up box.

'Fat chance of your taking that lot,' George told her. 'They'd have to lay on an extra train.'

'Try to think of *small* things, Lucy lamb,' said Ellie.

'Oooh!' Lucy's cheeks were suddenly pink. 'My magic thimble!'

The other groaned. This thimble was claimed to be silver, though it almost certainly was not, since it had come out of a cracker, a couple of Christmases ago. Lucy had been smitten by it from the moment it had flown out and rolled across the table. She credited it with limitless magic powers and would not be separated from it, even at night, when she slept with it underneath her pillow. Over the years it had been a sore trial to her family. If they were bowling along to the park to feed the ducks and she realised she had left it behind, she would howl until they had to turn back and fetch it. Now and again it went missing. On those occasions the entire house would have to be turned upside down until it was found. Matters were not helped by Lucy constantly hiding it in secret places for fear it would be stolen. As often as not she forgot where those secret places were. On one dreadful occasion the thimble had lain concealed in the toe of one of Lucy's best boots before it had been found. No one wished ever to live through three such days again.

'Where's the thimble now, Luce?' enquired Pip. 'In the teapot or up the chimney?'

'It's not either, piggy-wig,' she told him loftily. 'It's still under my pillow, as a matter of fact, guarding my dreams.'

The rest groaned again at the prospect of being accompanied to Great Aunt Constance's by the magic thimble, though they knew that Lucy would have to be dragged screaming from the house without it.

'Oh well,' said Pip, 'I s'pose the dratted thing'll have to go then. Pity some girls never grow up. Pity girls are such namby-pambies.'

'I'm not listening!'

She wasn't, either. Lucy promptly stuck her fingers in her ears, as she always did whenever things were being said that she would rather not hear. It is a useful trick, but very irritating to others.

The children's list was passed upstairs to Bessie, and they trooped into the kitchen to say goodbye to Cook and oversee the preparation of a food hamper for their journey. It was only then that they remembered Methusalah.

'Oh, Methusalah!' they cried as one. They were stricken with guilt that this venerable bird had not appeared on anyone's list.

'Oh darling Methusalah, we must take him!'

'What – take that bird on a *train?*' said Cook.

'We must, we must!'

'What if *he* catches scarlet fever!' said Lucy. 'What if all his feathers have to be chopped off!'

No one knew whether such a thing was a possibility. The idea of a featherless parrot was too awful to contemplate.

'Either he goes or we stay!' announced George, with a confidence he was far from feeling.

As it happened, Mother was quite willing for the parrot to go, though she did rather wonder what Great Aunt Constance would make of him.

'If she doesn't like him, you must keep him well out of her way,' she told them. 'And it goes without saying that I expect all of you to be on your very best behaviour.'

'We will,' they chorussed.

And then the luggage was being stowed on the wagon and it was time for the goodbyes, which are always horrid, and especially if you can see tears brimming in your mother's eyes. The four climbed aboard the wagon and waved furiously until they turned the corner and their house and their mother vanished.

Then each fell silent, and sank back in its seat and wondered what lay ahead. And it is safe to say that whatever their thoughts were, they could not possibly have included anything half so exciting and strange and wonderful as a Psammead.

Chapter II

A GLIMPSE OF MAGIC

Train journeys are exciting, but only when you yourself are having one, not when you hear about other people's. So I will pass over this one, and not even tell you about the fuss with the guard over the parrot. Suffice it to say that Methusalah behaved with impeccable dignity, but the guard did not.

When the train arrived at their station the children jumped down and looked about them for signs of their Great Aunt Constance. They did not know exactly what they were looking for, though Ellie said that she must be quite old if she was Father's aunt. But there were no ladies of any kind in sight, and presently a gloomy-looking man with whiskers and gaiters stepped forward.

'You for Miss Marchmont at the White 'Ouse?' and he looked at them as though he had just turned over a stone and found a particularly nasty collection of creepy crawlies.

Bessie agreed that they were, and apologised for the lateness of the train – though this was hardly her fault.

'Dobbs,' said the man. 'Come to fetch yer. There's never all *them* kiddies! Four on 'em!' He shook his head. 'The missis won't like it.'

He eyed the untidy heap of luggage.

'That stuff all yours?' He began to move it, grumbling.

''Undred years, you'd think yer'd come for!'

The children exchanged eyebrows, and tried to act invisible.

By the time the luggage had been unloaded from the train and reloaded on the cart the light was fading and the shadows were pulling out long and thin. They set off down the dim, leafy lanes, and the children were still dizzy from the motion of the train, and not at all their usual noisy selves. They also had a distinct sense of being unwelcome. Dobbs seemed a very silent kind of man, nor did he seem given to smiling.

As the cart went over a deep rut it swayed, and Ellie had to grab at Methusalah's cage to prevent it from sliding into the road. Timidly Bessie tapped Dobbs on the shoulder.

'If – if you was just to stop for a minute, if you please.'

Dobbs drew on the reins and they came to a standstill.

'I'm ever so sorry, but – that packing case, see. If we goes over another rut it'll tumble, I'm sure it will.'

Dobbs grunted. Without a word he climbed down and went to straighten the case. The children looked about them. They were out of the leafy tunnel of the lane now, and on one side lay what looked like sand dunes, though there was so sign of the sea. The sun was setting, and the sky was streaked with red and silver and the silence seemed uncanny. There was a hush that was so deep that when one of them did speak it was in a whisper, as if she were in church.

'Oh dear, I do wish he'd cheer up!'

No sooner had the words left Ellie's lips than a ripple of aliveness seemed to rush over those huddled figures in the cart.

They all of them felt it, and admitted it, later. And they certainly were not the only ones to feel it, because Dobbs, having secured the case, stepped back and beamed broadly up at the children.

'Bit of a rum go, you being packed down 'ere at the drop of a hat,' he said. 'And without your Ma, too.'

They were so startled by this sudden show of kindness that they could merely nod their agreement.

'And I expect your legs is cramped, sat on that train all day,' he went on. 'Meant to run about, kiddies is. Why don't you 'op down now, and 'ave a bit of a run round in all that sand?'

'Oh yes!' they chorussed eagerly, but Bessie said, 'Oughtn't we to get on, d'you think? Their aunt'll be expecting 'em.'

'Oh, 'er,' said Dobbs carelessly. 'Not at 'ome. Gorn off to London, before ever that telegram come.'

'She don't even know they're coming?'

'Not 'er. Not unless she seen it in 'er crystal ball. *Hout* you come, kiddies!'

They needed no second bidding. Down they clambered and were off, with whoops of joy, into the dunes, kicking up sand in showers.

'Sand!'

'We can build castles and all sorts!'

They scattered, because they were not playing a game, simply letting off the cooped-up feelings that came from spending hours on a train. They whooped and shouted because they had had to be quiet as mice at home for what seemed like ages.

And those shrieks, and the laughter of children, were like music to the ears of the Psammead, lone and lorn for years since those other children had disappeared. Because the Psammead was about, as you will have guessed. He was buried in the sand when the cart rolled by, but the Psammead has ears like a bat's. It can hear the flutter of moths' wings, and the worm turning and a thousand other sounds unknown to human ears. And when it heard Ellie's whisper it had thought, in its drowsiness, that it was the voice of Anthea it heard (and Anthea, it must be said, had been its favourite of the five children). Anthea, along with the others, had promised never to ask for any more wishes. But the Psammead, whatever its other faults, was not small-minded, and had instantly dug its way up through the sand and blown itself out to grant her wish. Dobbs, who had not cracked his face in a smile for years, smiled. If ever a leopard were to change its spots it would be at the wish of the Psammead.

It sat waiting, mightily pleased with itself, for Anthea to come running to the spot Cyril had marked so long ago with a ring of stones. When Ellie appeared instead it is hard to say which one had the biggest fright.

The Psammead stared at the strange girl, but it, at least, knew that it *was* a girl. For her part, Ellie simply could not believe her eyes. There, in the fading light, sat a furry creature that was not a fox or rat or monkey or even anything with a long Latin name in London Zoo. She rubbed her eyes. By the time she had done so all she could see was a tuft of fur and a furious whirl of sand.

She stood rooted, staring at the spot where the creature had been, and in that moment the sun set. Another ripple of magic went over the dunes, but this time it was felt only by Ellie. In the deep stillness she could hear the laughter and shouts of the others in the distance.

'What was it?' she whispered. 'Oh, I *do* wish it would come out again!'

She was not to know that any wish given by the Psammead disappears at sunset. And that *after* sunset you might as well wish upon a button, for all the good it would do. Ellie took a few steps forward, dropped to her knees, and was about to start scrabbling in the sand when there came a loud shout.

'Oy! Oy – you lot! Hout of there, the lot of you!'

It was Dobbs. Ellie sprang to her feet.

'So there you are. Where's them others? What's the game?'

'But – but you said – '

'*Oy!*' he yelled again. 'You get out of there, the 'ole pack of you, you 'ear me, afore I comes and fetches yer!'

Bessie appeared behind him.

'Come along, quickly, do!' she called.

George, Pip and Lucy came running from all sides.

'It's ripping!'

'Shall we be far from here?'

'Hat the double!' roared Dobbs. 'Hout of it!'

They filed meekly past him, but there was much strenuous pulling of faces.

'What's got into him?' whispered Pip, but Ellie groaned and helped Lucy into the cart, then climbed up herself.

'No better'n a pack of savages!' they heard Dobbs grumble as he drove off.

'You've not got sand all over you, I 'ope,' whispered poor Bessie, dusting Lucy furiously. She was always anxious for the children to make a good impression. It reflected on herself.

They almost immediately left the road and started up a long narrow lane between high trees. The children looked at the dense shrubbery and undergrowth, and could see how splendid it would be for playing Red Indians or bandits, or any other game with plenty of hiding and seeking.

A shot rang out, a sharp crack, quite close by. Bessie squealed and Lucy dived into Ellie's arms.

'Help! Murder!' screamed Bessie.

Gun shots are seldom heard in Islington.

Crack! Another shot.

'I say!' said George. 'Better keep your head down, Pip!'

Pip was already keeping his head as low as he could without being seen to be ducking.

'There's someone shooting at us!' Bessie's eyes were popping. 'Oh, go faster, can't you!'

'Sh-shooting?' came Lucy's muffled voice from Ellie's lap.

Only Dobbs seemed unperturbed. He sat, reins slack in his hands, letting the horse go at its own pace. Ellie, looking nervously about for signs of the shooter, saw a tumbledown cottage set back among the trees. She saw, too, the pale face of a small girl peering out from the window. For an instant the wide eyes were looking straight into her own, then the face vanished.

'A princess!' thought Ellie. 'Kidnapped and locked away in the woods. And her evil captor stalking the woods with a gun!'

A stay with Great Aunt Constance in the country had not seemed to promise much in the way of adventure, but already there was mystery afoot. Ellie, however, preferred her mystery without guns. The boys were trying to pretend that they were shot at every day of the week, but Lucy did not unbury her head until the cart drew up.

'I say!' said George. 'This isn't half bad!'

Nor was it. The house was white and rambling. The lawns rolled away into exciting distances, with trees and shrubbery. Red Indians and highwaymen were definitely on the agenda.

'Well!' said Bessie, adjusting her hat. 'Here we are, then!'

The long-faced Dobbs got down, and the front door opened.

'Mrs Dobbs,' said Dobbs, with a jerk of his head. ''Ousekeeper.'

Sometimes the dourest of men have jolly, smiling wives, but the children could see at a glance that this was not the case. Mrs Dobbs appeared every bit as sour as her husband. Their smiles faded.

'Well then,' said that lady. 'So *you're* the children. *Four* of you? The telegram never said anything about four. Two, I thought there'd be, and plenty at that!'

'Oh, they're ever so good,' said Bessie hastily, 'no trouble at all. I'm Bessie, ma'am, and I'll have the care of them.'

'Hmmph!' said that lady.

'How do you do, Mrs Dobbs.' George, as eldest, stepped forward. 'I'm George, and these are Ellen, Philip and Lucy.'

'Well, you'd best come in,' said Mrs Dobbs ungraciously. 'And get that luggage brought in, Dobbs.' Her eye then fell on Methusalah. 'And whatever's *that*? It's never a parrot! The telegram never said anything about a parrot!'

'It's only Methusalah and he's ever so good and hardly ever speaks!' gabbled Lucy.

This was true. The children had spent many a long hour trying to teach the bird the rudiments of the English language, but he remained stubbornly unconversational. Occasionally he said 'Hello' or 'Never mind, never mind!' but not much else. George had rather wondered whether the parrot's native language might be Latin, and had tried that, but the bird showed no interest at all in declining *amo*, *amas*, *amat* and could not even be brought to say '*Nil Desperandum*' which was more or less the family motto.

'We'll see what Miss Marchmont 'as to say about that!' observed Mrs Dobbs, and went back into the house.

There followed the bewilderment that always comes with arrival into a strange place, where there are doors that open into unfamiliar rooms and stairs whose number of steps have not yet been counted. And because only two children had been expected beds had to be made up in a hurry. The children tried to be helpful, as they had promised, but it was hard to know how, because they did not know where anything was, or what was wanted. They settled for hovering about the grown-ups, trying earnestly to *look* helpful, but then they were snapped at and accused of being under people's feet.

There was so much rushing to and fro with luggage and blankets that the matter of supper seemed to have been quite overlooked. Mrs Dobbs seemed to know nothing of children, and these particular ones were very much afraid that perhaps she did not know that they require feeding. At home, if a mealtime is delayed, you can always go to the kitchen and beg a few morsels from Cook. On this occasion they did not even know where the kitchen was, let alone whether it is manners to beg morsels from a strange Cook.

At last the rooms were ready and the bustle ceased. George was elected to corner Bessie and ask, 'What about supper?'

'You stop 'ere and be'ave yourselves,' she instructed, 'and I'll go down and ask,' and off she went.

'I don't think I'm going to like it here,' said Lucy in a small voice.

'Of course you are, Lucy lamb,' said Ellie, with a cheerfulness she was far from feeling.

'I don't like Dobbs and I don't like Mrs Dobbs. And they don't like us. And they think we should only be two, when there are four of us.'

'Definitely Foe,' agreed George. 'We shall just have to hope Great Aunt Constance turns out to be Friend.'

The young Garsingtons always divided grown-ups into Friend or Foe. 'And Cook,' said Pip. 'Keep your fingers crossed *she* turns out to be Friend.'

'But what about that murderer with the gun?' wailed Lucy. '*He* was Foe!'

'Fruminously Foe,' agreed George. 'That was a rum go, all right. And wasn't it queer the way Dobbs went from Foe to Friend, then straight back to Foe again?'

They all agreed that it was. Ellie did not mention the amazing furry creature she had glimpsed in the sand dunes. She said nothing, either, about the small girl in the cottage.

Lucy rummaged in her pocket, took out her thimble, and actually put it on her finger. She only ever did this in extremity, and it was always a bad sign.

'If that thimble *is* magic, I just hope it comes up with some supper,' said Pip.

'It doesn't have to be magic for *you*,' she told him crossly. 'And all you ever think about is grub!'

'If it's so magic, why don't you prove it? Go on – wish for something, and see what happens!'

'Oh, wouldn't it be wonderful if wishes *could* come true,' sighed Ellie, who had no idea that this very thing had happened only an hour ago.

'Go on,' said Pip. 'Show us!'

'I shan't then! It's *secretly* magic! And I think you're a beast!'

She started to cry again, and Ellie gave Pip a reproachful look.

'*I* can't stop her blubbing,' he said. 'She's a regular waterworks. We could try putting a key down her back, I suppose,' and he went over to the door and took out the key.

'That's for nosebleeds, idiot,' George told him.

'Could be for crying as well,' said Pip. 'It's worth a try – it'd be a scientific experiment.'

He advanced on Lucy with the key, and she shrieked 'Don't let him, don't let him!' and clung harder than ever to Ellie. It was fortunate that at this moment Bessie appeared, to announce supper, and this worked like a charm not only on the tears but on the general bad temper as well. Food, as you have probably noticed, is a great soother.

The food provided at this first meal was not of a high order. It consisted of thin soup with bread that Mrs Dobbs said 'wanted eating up'.

'And you may as well 'ave it as the birds,' she told them ungraciously. She was obviously much put out not only by finding there were four of them, but that they required feeding, into the bargain.

When the soup had disappeared and they were still hungry she allowed more bread, but said that they must choose between butter and jam to spread.

'Dobbs and me've no kiddies of our own, thank the Lord,' she said, 'but one thing I do know. They should be seen and not 'eard, and not give rich food to eat.'

After this cheerless repast the children were sent to bed, and this they thankfully did. Usually when the family went on holiday there would be a midnight feast on the first night, followed by a rip-roaring pillow fight. On this occasion they had neither the ingredients for the first nor the heart for the second. They turned in with spirits as low as any four children in England.

Lucy put her magic thimble under her pillow.

'I'm not going to like it here,' she said again. 'If Great Aunt Constance turns out as horrid as the others I shall write to Mother and ask her to fetch us home.'

'Stout heart,' Ellie told her. This was a saying the family had, and meant to try and be brave and stout-hearted in all circumstances, like the little tin soldier. It was a point of honour with them. No Garsington ever bowed before misfortune.

So Lucy nodded, and repeated 'Stout heart' rather wanly, and Ellie kissed her and climbed into her own bed.

'Never mind, tomorrow's another day,' she said, which is the sort of thing grown-ups say, and is perfectly obvious, when you think about it.

In the boys' room George was saying, 'That was a pretty average to rotten supper we had. Butter *or* jam, I ask you!'

'We'll end up skin and bones. I tell you what I'm going to do. I'm going to find the kitchen tomorrow, and get round the Cook. If we can get the Cook Friend, it won't matter about the beastly Dobbses.'

'That's not half a bad idea, Pips,' George told him. 'We'll all do it. And we'll go back and find that sandy place where old Dobbs let us off.'

'That was a rum go. Grumpy one minute, nice as pie the next, then back to a regular demon.'

'Must've had a brainstorm,' George agreed. 'Goodnight, old bird. Don't bother to reply.' He put the cover over Methusalah's cage and went to bed.

The next day the children woke up quite back to their usual selves and ready for anything. Straight after their porridge and toast they went off to the kitchen.

'Now mind, everyone, sweeten her up properly,' George instructed, but as it happened, they did not need to. It turned out that Cook doted on kiddies, had three of her own, grown up now, bless their hearts, and thought how nice it would be to have four of them at the White House.

'It'll liven the place up a treat,' she told them, then, lowering her voice, 'and don't you take notice of that Mrs Dobbs, my duckies – fair tartar she is, and no mistake.'

'She only let us have butter or jam,' said Pip, which whom this still rankled.

'The idea!' said Cook indignantly, rolling her eyes. 'You get 'ungry, you just pop in 'ere. I'll do a bit of extra baking, that I will. Like cookies, do you?'

They assured her, in an eager chorus, that they did.

'We're just off to the sand-pit, and I daresay we might get hungry before dinner,' said George, pushing his luck.

''Ere – you just put these in your pockets.' She took down a tin and doled out sugary biscuits. 'And mum's the word!'

'Mum's the word!' they promised.

It was lucky that Mrs Dobbs believed that children should be neither seen *nor* heard, if possible, because she made no objection at all to their going off for the morning. Bessie was to stay behind, so that she could be 'shown the ropes'.

'It's *two* 'ousekeepers'll be needed, if you ask me,' she observed sourly. ''Ow long'll they be stopping?'

Bessie did not know, and said so, but rather thought it might be several weeks.

'And you be'ave yourselves, you 'ear me?' she told her charges. 'And come back one sharp and with your 'ands and faces clean.'

'And you see a gel out there with dirty face and 'ands, don't you go talking to 'er,' added Mrs Dobbs. 'Nasty thieving varmints!'

No one but Ellie took particular notice of this remark. She fleetingly wondered whether it was the kidnapped princess in the cottage she meant, and why she was a thieving varmint.

The children escaped from the house and were free in the garden. Seen now in broad daylight it was as wide and wonderful as they had supposed last night.

'*This* knocks Islington to a cocked hat!'

'Trees to climb!'

'Look – a swing!'

'But whose? There aren't any children.'

They were not to know that a few summers ago, before Great Aunt Constance had moved back into the White House, there had been children – five of them, if you count the baby. Then George spotted the summer-house and there they found a store of riches. There were croquet mallets and hoops, bats and balls, buckets and spades. They fell on the latter with delight, and were off again, whooping down the leafy lane, and not one of them remembered the night before, and the gun shots.

They came to the cottage in the trees. A man was digging in the garden, and straightened to watch them.

'Morning!' they cried, and waved their spades. The small girl sitting in the doorway with a rag doll on her lap raised her arm and waved shyly back.

'See that?' said George. 'Were they the thieving varmints, d'you think?'

'Ssshh!' Ellie told him. 'They'll hear you.'

She did not mention that she had taken the girl to be a kidnapped princess, because now she herself thought the notion rather silly, and the others certainly would. She did, however, remember something.

'Listen, was that man the shooter, do you think?'

'Oooh, I'd forgotten that! Oh, we won't be shot at, will we?' Lucy clung to Ellie's sleeve.

'Don't be a ninny,' Pip told her. 'You're not a rabbit, even if you sometimes act like one!'

'It was round about here we heard the gun,' said George thoughtfully.

The four of them turned and looked back. The man was digging again and did not see them, but the girl was still watching. It was not an ordinary, careless kind of watching, but somehow fierce and pleading at the same time. It made them uncomfortable, though they couldn't tell why.

'Looks harmless enough,' said George, who as eldest felt bound to keep an eye on safety.

'Come *on*!' urged Pip, and so they did.

'I felt sorry for that girl,' said Ellie. 'Did you see the way she looked at us?'

'Oh you would,' said Pip. 'You're just a namby-pamby.'

'No I am not!'

'You are rather, you know,' George told her. 'For a Garsington.'

'I'm just as much a Garsington as you are!' she said, stung by this unjust remark. 'You can be soft-hearted *and* brave – Mother says so!'

'*Girls* might!' said Pip, and he set off at a run again. 'Come on – castles to build!'

George set off after him, and so, after a moment's hesitation, did Lucy. Ellie just kept walking and thinking her own rather disgruntled thoughts. When she had said 'I'm just as much a Garsington as you are!' she had not altogether believed it. She *was* softer-hearted than the others, in fact sometimes they seemed so heartless that she actually wondered whether they really were her brothers and sisters. Perhaps they were not, she would think. Perhaps she had been found, a little bundle abandoned in the snow, and had been taken in by her parents out of the kindness of their hearts. In that case she could be anyone, she thought – even a princess. Whenever the others were being particularly beastly she would dream about this, and comfort herself with the feeling of her own mysteriousness.

She had not told the others about her glimpse of the strange, furry beast the night before. She knew that they would simply not have believed her, and probably have laughed at her.

'But I didn't imagine it, I didn't!' she told herself. 'And what's more, I mean to find it again!'

By now she had reached the sandy place, and could hear shrieks and laughter in the distance. Otherwise the place was eerily silent, without even the singing of birds.

'Now where was it, I wonder?'

The trouble with sand is that it is all the same. There were humps and hollows, but they all looked the same, too. She simply did not know where to start.

'Like looking for a needle in a bottle of hay,' she thought. 'Oh, it's hopeless – just hopeless!'

But however difficult a task a start must be made somewhere, and so Ellie dropped to her knees and began to scrabble in the sand.

Deep, deep down the Psammead had heard the voices of children, and stirred in its sleep. It was tired of its long loneliness. And so when Ellie whispered to herself, 'Oh dear, I'll never find it, and I do so wish I could!' that whisper was heard, and that wish granted.

Ellie, sitting back on her heels to rest, saw first a fountain of sand, then furiously working furry arms and then – the Psammead itself! She gasped. It seemed too good to be true – as it always does when a wish is granted. Ellie, however, did not know that her wishing had brought the Psammead out of its hole. She did not even know that it was a Psammead.

It was looking at her now with its large eyes, and those eyes were so nearly human that she was not really surprised when it spoke.

'Well?'

She stared.

'Well – what?' she stammered.

'You wished me here,' it said, 'and so I suppose you want something. Folk usually do.'

'Oh, not really. Just to see you again,' she said.

'Hmmph!'

'Because – when I saw you last night, I couldn't – well, I couldn't really believe my eyes.'

'Not surprising,' said the creature. 'Psammeads don't exactly grow on trees.'

'I'm sure they don't,' agreed Ellie truthfully.

Its fur fairly puffed out with pride.

'I am a rare and wonderful beast. In fact, I may as well tell you, I am the last of the Psammeads!'

'How wonderful!' exclaimed Ellie, feeling that this was expected. And then, 'But how sad!'

'Sad?'

'Being alone, I mean. No mother and father or brothers and sisters.'

'Oh *them*!' said the Psammead scornfully. 'I've managed without them this last thousand years!'

'Thousand? Did you say *thousand*?'

'Give or take a century or two. I suppose *you* aren't thousands of years old?'

'Oh no, not nearly. None of us are.'

'None of whom? Explain yourself, child. You are talking in riddles. If anyone is to talk in riddles, it is I.'

'Well, there are four of us – six, really, but two are at home with scarlet fever, and – '

'Four . . .' murmured the Psammead. 'Just as before . . .'

He fixed Ellie with his fierce, bright eyes.

'If you have perfectly good brothers and sisters of your own, why are you not with them, pray, instead of here, bothering me?'

'They were being hateful, and calling me a ninny!'

'And *are* you a ninny?'

'No I'm not! It's just that they don't understand me. I sometimes wonder if they're my real brothers and sisters at all. The ones at home are twins. It must be lovely to be a twin, and have somebody who knows your most secret and inmost thoughts before you even speak them. Don't you think so?'

'No,' replied the Psammead, 'I most certainly do not. I prefer to be singular, thank you. One of me is quite sufficient. I find myself excellent company.'

'Oh, so would I, if I were *you*,' Ellie assured it hastily. 'But I'm not, I'm just ordinary, and I honestly do wish I was twins!'

The Psammead made no reply but began, to her astonishment, to huff and puff in a most extraordinary way. And the huffing and puffing made its hairy chest blow out like a balloon, and then, just as she was sure it was about to burst before her very eyes, it let all the breath out again with a long, shuddering gasp.

'Are you all right?' she enquired anxiously. 'You must have swallowed the wrong way. Shall I pat your back – it often helps.'

'*Swallowed* the wrong way?' repeated the Psammead in withering tones. 'Pat me on the back? Which one of you, pray?'

'Which – what?'

She looked about her to see whom he could possibly mean, and found herself looking straight – into her own eyes!

'Oh!' she gasped, and felt quite giddy. She knew that she could not possibly be seeing what she thought she was seeing, so very sensibly she shut her eyes, then opened them again.

'Still there!'

Her self looked back at her. It was the queerest thing in the world. It was as if she had been looking into a full length mirror, and then her own reflection had stepped out of the glass to meet her.

'*Is* it a reflection?'

She decided to test this theory. She put out her left arm – her other self did not move, merely smiled, faintly mocking. Then she scratched her head. Not a sign from that strange but familiar self. She turned back to the Psammead, which was looking from one to the other of them in some interest.

'*That* came off well,' it observed smugly. 'Particularly as I was rather out of practice.'

'Oh – but I didn't mean it, not really! And – and it's rather scary. Make it go away, can't you? Please?'

'Didn't *mean* it? Then you should think before you speak, child, and not come bothering me with wishes you don't want.'

'Oh, I'm sorry! I didn't realise. Oh please – '

'I'm going back to sand now, and don't wish to be disturbed. Good day!'

And to her horror it began a furious digging and disappeared in a shower of sand.

Chapter III

A FIGMENT OF THE IMAGINATION

Ellie gazed for a moment at the spot where it had been, then slowly, fearfully, moved her eyes upwards and sideways.

'Still there!'

You may imagine for yourself the eeriness of the sensations she then felt. You are looking at your very own self, and that self is looking back at you with your own eyes – and yet not your eyes at all. And this is happening, not in a dream, from which you can wake up thankfully at any moment, but in real true life. Ellie was fairly frozen with fright.

'Well!' said that other self. 'This is jolly! I never really thought I'd ever be anything but a Figment of your Imagination. Thank you!'

'But – but who are you?'

'Don't you know? You dreamed me up enough times. I've even got a name you gave me.'

'Harriet!' exclaimed Ellie in wonderment.

The other nodded.

'Harry for short. Because I'm rather a tomboy, and not half so nicey-picey as you!'

'You're always getting into trouble . . .'

'Of course. Because *I* do all the things you'd like to do, but don't dare. I'm a regular demon!'

'Oh don't be!' begged Ellie.

'I can't help it,' replied Harry (for that is what we had better call her). 'It's what *you* decided. I told you – I'm a Figment of your Imagination. I expect I'll get into all kinds of scrapes.'

She said this with a dangerous satisfaction, and Ellie remembered that they could not stay here in the sand-pit all day. They would have to go back to the White House for dinner, and what then?

'Ellie! Ellie!'

The others were calling her. She clapped her hand to her mouth.

'The others! Oh – hide, can't you?'

'Hurray! You've told me so much about them – I'm longing to meet them!'

They were coming at a run.

'Oh, do just stand behind me – just till I can explain. Oh, poor little Lucy – she'll die of fright!'

'That would be rather fun,' agreed Harry. 'Stand behind you – then suddenly step out and see their faces! Oh my!'

And so she stood behind Ellie, and that unfortunate girl wished herself invisible or a thousand miles away. But no amount of wishing would serve her now.

'Where've you been?'

'We're making a ripping fort!'

Then, 'Oooooh!' screamed Lucy, 'who's that behind you?'

And at these words the Figment of Ellie's Imagination stepped out. The faces of those three young Garsingtons were a sight to see. One reads in books of jaws dropping and eyes popping, but very rarely sees such phenomena in real life. On this occasion jaws were dropping and eyes popping like anything. Each of them stared, blinked, then shut its eyes and opened them again – just as Ellie herself had done.

'Must be dreaming!' said George. 'Pinch me, somebody!'

'Oooh, there's two of her,' wailed Lucy. 'She's gone double!'

'Can't all be dreaming the same thing at the same time,' said Pip. 'It's not scientific.'

It was almost unbearable for poor Ellie to see her own brothers and sister looking at her with such horror and suspicion.

'Are they *both* her?' muttered George to Pip. 'Or just one of them?'

'And which is which?'

'Oh it's horrible, horrible! I want Ellie!' Lucy looked fit to burst into tears.

'Oh don't, Lucy lamb!' Ellie stepped forward. 'Don't be frightened – it's only me!'

'And me,' added Harry. She looked with satisfaction at her new found brothers and sisters. 'Hello, all – I'm Harry!'

'And who's Harry, when she's at home?' demanded George, rather rudely, it must be said.

'I'm the twin that Ellie's always longed for. What do you think?' She twirled about for inspection. 'Peas in a pod?'

'You're that, all right,' said Pip with feeling. 'Or maggots in a jar!'

'Look here,' said George, 'what's going off, exactly?'

'Oh you'll never believe me but it's all true,' said Ellie. 'I met a Sammyadd, and it looks as if it can give wishes – but it's gone now, and I don't know what to do!'

'Sammyadd?' repeated George.

'Gone where?' demanded Pip, looking about at the deserted dunes. 'A Sammy *what*?'

'Is she *real*?' asked Lucy in awed tones. She crept forward, very cautiously, and gingerly touched the Figment on the hand. She leapt back as if stung.

'Oh!' *they heard her gasp.*

They set off down the dim leafy lane . . .

'She *is* real! Oh – remind me again which is which!'

'I am Ellie,' said Ellie firmly.

'But what shall we say to Mother, when she sees there's two of you?'

'Not to mention Bessie, and Ma Dobbs,' agreed George. 'Look here, Ellie, you can't go on with this fooling. Get rid of it, can't you?'

'*She*, not it, if you don't mind,' said Harry sharply. 'And I'm not going anywhere. I'm enjoying myself, for the first time in my life.'

Ellie said, 'I don't think I can. The Sammyadd did it and I expect it's the only one who can *un*do it.'

'I suppose this Sammyadd thing's another Figment of your Imagination,' George told her coldly. 'You've gone too far over the moon this time, old thing.'

'It's reading all those rubbishy books that's done it,' added Pip.

'It's not, it's not! It's real. I'll show you!'

She did not know whether or not the Psammead would respond, but she dropped to her knees, and called,

'Sammyadd! Dear Sammyadd – I wish you'd come out again!'

There was a short pause during which George and Pip exchanged rolled up eyes, and George tapped his forehead with his finger and shook his head ruefully.

'I'm *not* mad! Oh, I wish, I wish!' gabbled Ellie in desperation.

And then it happened. With jaws dropping and eyes popping all over again, they all saw that spurting fountain of sand, those skinny arms, and finally the cross, bewhiskered face of the Psammead itself.

'Oh my sainted!' said George faintly.

'There! I told you!' Ellie was triumphant.

'Now what?' snapped the Psammead. 'And who are all these? I'm not a public freak show!'

'They're George and Pip and Lucy, and they don't like me being twins, and I don't, either. I thought I would, but I don't.'

'Too bad,' said the Psammead. 'You've wished it now.'

Lucy, ever since the Psammead had come whirling out of the sand, had been staring in wonder.

'You really and truly can give wishes?' she asked.

'Naturally! It would be a poor sort of fairy that couldn't grant wishes.'

'I thought you said it was a Sammyadd, or whatever it was,' said George to Ellie.

'You evidently don't know Greek,' said the Psammead. 'Psammead is Greek for Sand-fairy. I hope you are not going to turn out to be duffers.'

'But dear, kind Sammyadd, if you can *give* wishes, surely you can take them away?' begged Ellie.

The Psammead heaved a weary sigh.

'I suppose I shall have to explain,' it said. 'You had better listen carefully, as I shan't tell you twice. I can give you any wish you ask for – '

'Oh rapture!' breathed Lucy, and it shot her a sharp look.

'– but I'd rather not give more than one a day because it's bad for my health. And any wish I do give, lasts only till sunset.'

'Hurray!' cried Harry, kicking up the sand. 'That means I've got hours yet!'

'I've already given three wishes today, and I'm quite worn out,' said the Psammead. 'I'm going back to sand. But I must warn you of one thing.'

They all looked at it.

'You must on no account come near me with anything wet. If a Sand-fairy gets wet, it catches cold, and dies. I lost my whole family like that.'

The children murmured their sympathy and assurances.

'Once my poor top twelfth left whisker got wet, and no one knows what I suffered, no one knows . . .'

No one did, but they all put on suitable expressions of sympathy and Lucy said, 'Oh, you poor thing!'

'Goodbye!' said the Psammead abruptly, and whirled out of view.

Chapter IV

SEEING DOUBLE

'Jiminy!' exclaimed George. 'I'll eat my hat, if you like, Ellie!'

'Just think – wishes!' said Lucy. 'Even magicker magic than my thimble!'

'Just wait, *I'll* think of some wishes, won't I just!' said Pip.

'It's all very well for you,' said Ellie, 'What about me?'

'And me,' put in Harry. 'You can't just wish me away – you heard it.'

'You *look* like Ellie, but I don't like you,' Lucy said, and she took Ellie's hand. 'Why don't you just go away and play on your own till sunset?'

'No fear!' said Harry, and she executed a perfect cartwheel, which was something Ellie had always longed to be able to do without tumbling over sideways.

'Let's all give her a good prod, just to make sure she *is* real,' suggested Pip.

'You never know, with Figments of the Imagination,' George agreed. 'We'd better pinch her.'

They advanced on Ellie's double, but she shrieked and ran off to a safe distance.

'You needn't think you've got rid of me!' she yelled.

'Perhaps we shouldn't really be unkind,' said Ellie doubtfully. She was bound to feel a certain sympathy for someone so absolutely her spitting image.

'We've got to get rid of her before dinner,' Pip pointed out.

'I heard you!' came Harry's voice. '*I* want some dinner, I'm starving!'

'Look here, Ellie-bobs,' said George. 'You wished her here. You'd better work it out between the two of you.'

'There's no reason why we should miss *our* grub,' Pip said. 'Come on – back to the ramparts!'

He and George raced off, and Lucy let go Ellie's hand.

'Don't worry, it'll all come right in the end,' she said comfortingly. She then ran after the others, taking good care to give the Figment a very wide berth indeed.

Alone again, Ellie started to walk slowly towards her double.

'*Pax*!' she called.

Harry nodded and came to meet her.

'Pity you don't like me now you've wished for me,' she said, rather wistfully.

'I think I'm beginning to get used to you now,' Ellie told her. 'But you're so much like me, it is rather spooky.'

'But think of the fun we can have, teasing people,' said Harry. 'You've often thought that.'

This was true. Ellie realised that this girl not only was her mirror image, but knew all her thoughts, too.

'Now's the time to test it out,' suggested Harry. 'If we work it out, we can *both* have dinner. Think what fun it'll be, fooling everyone!'

Ellie nodded slowly. After all, she *had* often longed for a twin, and now she had one – at least for the day. It would be feeble not to make the most of it.

And so the pair of them worked out various plans.

'The main thing is for both of us never to be seen at the same time,' Ellie said.

'So if one of us is in a room, the other'll be under the table – '

'Or behind the curtains – '

'Or in the wardrobe – '

'Or – up the chimney!'

Soon they were hooting with mirth, and Ellie even began to think what a shame it was that she should have a twin only till sunset.

'Perhaps I could wish for her again tomorrow,' she thought.

'Oh no, you couldn't,' said Harry. Ellie was startled. Her thoughts were no longer her own. 'The others'll want to wish for all kinds of things.'

'And the Sammyadd was fearfully strict about only one wish a day.'

'So I really am here today – gone tomorrow!'

'Like a dragonfly!'

At dinner time the five of them went back to the White House.

'The absolute main thing is to be sure Bessie doesn't see us both at once,' Ellie instructed.

'And if Ma Dobbs catches sight of you both, the rest of us pretend we haven't noticed anything,' said George.

'She'll think she's going off her nut!'

'Oh dear, I hope I don't giggle,' said Lucy.

As they went up the drive they saw no sign of anyone at the cottage. But once they came near the house, there was Dobbs, digging one of the flowerbeds.

'Look out!' said Ellie. 'Now what?'

'I vote we just carry on,' said Pip. 'He won't notice.'

'He's just the sort not to notice the difference between four and five,' agreed George. 'Come on!'

As they passed, Dobbs paused for a moment in his digging, and Ellie, for one, tried to act invisible. He gave them a look fit to turn the cream sour, but evidently noticed nothing amiss. Safely in the porch, they all breathed sighs of relief. Ellie whispered to her twin,

'You go on in with the others. I'll come in when the coast's clear.'

This was a noble gesture. For all she knew, it might cost her her dinner.

'Oh, there you all are!' she heard Mrs Dobbs say. 'Get yourselves cleaned and tidied, dinner's ready.'

'Where's Bessie?' asked Lucy's voice.

'Gone to the village, for some shopping.'

'Oh hurray!' breathed the listening Ellie. 'That's one less to notice!'

Bessie's sharp eyes were the ones most to be feared. And she was used to twins and their pranks.

Ellie pushed the door and peered cautiously in. No one was about. She started to move swiftly towards the dining room, but Mrs Dobbs appeared, carrying a tray.

''Ere!' she said sharply. 'I thought I told you to get yourself cleaned up!'

'Oh – sorry!'

Ellie fled upstairs, to meet the others, hastily tidied, about to descend.

'Oh – I ran straight into Mrs Dobbs!' she gasped.

'I don't think you've got the nerve for this,' her twin told her. 'You'd better go down with the others. I'll do all the dodging and hiding.'

So Ellie hastily arranged her hair and smoothed her pinafore.

'Do be careful!' she begged. Ellie was not a mouse, but did not really have the heart for this kind of escapade – which is exactly why she had so often wished for a twin who *did*.

They sat down for their dinner and Mrs Dobbs stood, arms folded, watching. After a moment or two she went out, then almost at once they heard her exclaim,

''Ere! Whatever? I've just this minute – '

'Quick!'

Ellie snatched a bread roll and dived under the table. From behind the cloth she heard the scene above.

'Well you get sat straight down again!' she heard Mrs Dobbs order. 'I don't know! I could've sworn . . .'

'Perhaps you should get your eyes tested?' she heard Harry say innocently.

Ellie winced.

'I want no sauce from you, miss! You just sit and get them greens ate up!'

'But I don't like greens!'

'You get them ate!'

'I shouldn't think *you* eat things you hate,' said Harry. 'Grown-ups never do.'

'Oh eat them, do,' said Lucy anxiously.

'I shan't!' said Harry. 'Even if I put them in my mouth, I shan't be able to swallow them. Look!'

There was a short silence, and then the unmistakable sound of food being violently spat out.

'Well!' came the outraged tones of Mrs Dobbs. 'Drat your impudence, miss! And there was me thinking you looked the quietest of the pack of you! Off to your room this minute!'

'But I haven't had my chops and potatoes. And what about puds?'

'Puds? I'll give you puds, and I'll give you something else as well, if you – '

Here Ellie heard a chair being scraped back, feet running, the slam of the door.

'And don't you slam doors in your tantrums!'

Ellie had certainly wished for a twin who would liven things up rather, but now wondered if things were not going too far.

'The rest of you, you sit and get that ate up, every bit of it!' she heard Mrs Dobbs say. 'When I get back, I want to see clean plates!'

Again the door opened and shut. Immediately the tablecloth was lifted on all sides.

'Quick!'

'Crikey!'

'She's certainly got some nerve!' said Pip admiringly.

Ellie scrambled back into her place and stared down at her plate.

'Ugh! There's her horrible spat out cabbage!'

'Well, if you're not hungry, don't eat!'

But Ellie was hungry, and after carefully pushing the cabbage to the very rim of the plate, she set to on the chops and potatoes. She wolfed it at such a rate that when the door suddenly opened and there stood Mrs Dobbs again, her cheeks were bulging.

She stared in horror at Mrs Dobbs, and Mrs Dobbs gaped back.

'Well! I never – '

She did not finish the sentence. She was gaping at something beyond the children, then back at Ellie, and her mouth was working, but no sound coming out. The children turned and saw, at the window, the Figment herself, pulling the most horrible faces and waggling her fingers. Mrs Dobbs looked from Ellie to Harry, then back, then back again.

'Eeeech!' she screamed, and crash! – the tray fell to the floor. She turned then and ran from the room.

'Oooh, 'orrible, 'orrible!' they heard her scream. ''Elp!'

'Come on! Quick!' said George.

The children bolted, pausing only to grab up fistfuls of chocolate sponge from the carpet and cram them into their mouths. Cook had come up trumps, but rather in vain on this occasion. They ran out of the house and yelled 'Come on! Quick!' to Harry, who was convulsed in helpless mirth, and the five of them ran helter skelter down the drive.

'Look out!'

There, ahead, was the familiar figure of Bessie, carrying two laden baskets.

'Hide! Quick!'

George pushed the Figment unceremoniously behind a bush.

'Oh Bessie!'

'Now, what's all this?'

'There's been the most fearful shindig, but it wasn't our fault!'

'That Dobbs is a beast!'

'She'll tell you the most frightful tales about me,' said Ellie, 'but they're not true, they're not!'

'I don't understand a word you're saying,' said Bessie. 'But I just 'ope you 'aven't been acting up!'

They assured her fervently that they had not.

'You'd best take yourselves off out her way, then,' said Bessie, who most fortunately did not see Ellie's double grinning from behind her bush. Nor did she notice Ellie's warning frowns and shakes of the head.

Bessie picked up her baskets again.

'And mind what you promised your Ma!' she told them. 'Good as gold – though I daresay that *was* asking too much.'

'Oh we will, we will!' and thankfully they watched her go.

'And don't be late for supper, mind!'

'We won't!'

'Depends whether supper's before or after sunset,' George pointed out. 'I don't much fancy that charade again.'

'I just hope that beastly Mrs Dobbs gives her notice, that's all,' said Pip. 'At least then it'll have done some good. That scrumptious choccy sponge!'

They spent the afternoon in games of tag and hide-and-seek in the woods. The latter was not made easier by there being two of Ellie, and there being some doubt at times about who was hiding and who seeking.

Naturally, as the sun began to set, they felt pangs of hunger.

'If you were a sport, you'd offer to stop here and just disappear on your own!' Pip told the Figment.

'Oh, but I want to *see* her disappear,' said Lucy. 'It'll be the magickest magic ever!'

'How do you know I shall disappear?' said Harry. 'I might rise up into the air, or go up in a puff of smoke, or be turned to stone!'

Here she was nearer the truth than she knew. In the early days, thousands and thousands of years ago, all Psammeads' wishes *were* turned to stone at sunset. Ellie thought it might be rather nice to have a statue of herself, but the rest feared it might go to her head, and she would get above herself.

'Only important people have statues made of them,' Pip told her. 'Generals and queens and such. Not namby-pamby girls from Islington.'

'Aren't you a tiny bit scared of only lasting till sunset?' Ellie asked her twin. '*I* would be.' She shuddered feelingly. 'I can't even imagine it!'

'I'll still be here in a way,' said Harry. 'I'll still be a Figment of your Imagination, remember.'

'Let's go right back near the house,' George suggested. 'Then, when you've done your vanishing trick, we can go straight in for supper.'

This was generally agreed to be a sound idea. As they walked back through the woods the sunset was beginning to glow red through the trees, and the echoing whistle of the birds sounded mournful, to Ellie at least. She was beginning to feel how unbearably sad it was for a child to have only one single day on earth. She thought of all the splendid things the Figment would never know, like flying kites on a windy day, steak and kidney pudding, going to the pantomime on Boxing Day, or holding a sandcastle against the sea. (She naturally did not think of the unpleasant things, like the dentist, having mumps, being dragged round London by Bessie to buy boots, and being landed in a desert of boredom without a book to read.) Then she thought of what Harry had just said about her still living on as a Figment of her own Imagination. And she made a silent vow, there and then, to try to think of Harry at least once every day, and talk to her.

She really did think it amazingly fearless of Harry to be so offhand about her fate. She readily admitted to herself that if it were she who had only a few more minutes in the world, she would be in a frightful funk.

'Look,' she said. 'I want to give you something to remember me by. Take this – it's quite clean.'

And she took her handkerchief from her pinafore pocket and gave it to Harry.

'We'll *exchange* hankies,' said the Figment. 'It'll be a new kind of ceremony, like exchanging rings,' and she handed over her own, which was distinctly grubby, but was nevertheless rapturously received by Ellie.

'I'll keep it forever!' she promised.

'You'll be saying next you'll wear it next to your heart,' said Pip disgustedly. He was impatient with all this girlish soppiness, and eager to get on with the vanishing, and supper.

'It must be on the very edge of sunset!' said Lucy, surveying the red disc behind the trees. 'The witching hour is at hand!'

Just then Mrs Dobbs emerged from the house and set off at a brisk rate towards where the children were huddling at the edge of the drive. She saw them and stopped. It was too late for Harry to hide even if she wished to – and she didn't.

'Oooh, there's still two of one of 'em!' they heard her say. 'I *am* seeing double!'

'Here's my chance!' said Harry.

She stepped forward, arms outspread, and chanted in ringing tones, 'I am a Figment of the Imagination. Look upon me well, you may never see my like again!'

The other four stared with mixed admiration and consternation, and Mrs Dobbs was evidently struck dumb.

Then the sun set, and so it was that all five of them actually saw Ellie's double fade into the air, quietly and smoothly as smoke dwindling from an autumn bonfire.

'Crikey!' exclaimed George.

'Strewth!' Pip had just witnessed something he knew to be thoroughly unscientific, but could not deny without denying the witness of his own eyes.

The four of them had at least been expecting this vanishing. Mrs Dobbs had not. She gave a sort of strangled moan, then fled, past them and on down the drive, never to be seen again.

Chapter V

THE QUEST

Mrs Dobbs had not herself vanished in the same way as the Figment had. When I say that she was never to be seen again, that means only for the purposes of this story. I believe she consulted her doctor, who nodded gravely and prescribed a complete rest, and she went off for a long stay with her sister in Margate. This was a wholly satisfactory outcome for the young Garsingtons, and one for which they were ever grateful to the Figment.

What also vanished was the handkerchief given to Ellie – it melted in her palm so swiftly that she did not even feel it go. It seemed that not only the wish disappeared at sunset, but everything else connected with it.

When they got in for their supper that night they had a wigging from Bessie, but only an average more or less everyday one, for being late. Bessie was convinced that Mrs Dobbs had taken leave of her senses.

'You never 'eard such twaddle,' she told them. 'On and on about there being two of one of you – two of *you*, Miss Ellie, would you believe?'

Miss Ellie would believe, but wisely did not say so.

'One of her's plenty,' said Pip, mouth full of the delicious cheese pudding served by the Friendly cook.

'And you spitting out your greens, Miss Ellie, as if you ever would!' went on Bessie. 'Any'ow, she's going to give in 'er notice, she says, directly Miss Marchmont gets back from London. Going to see the doctor, any'ow – that's where she was just off to.'

'I don't somehow think she'll be back,' said George.

'Well, I can't put my 'and on my 'eart and say I'm sorry,' said Bessie. 'Because I'm not. I daresay we shall all breathe easier for 'er 'aving gone.'

They all agreed fervently that this was so.

'*Not*,' she added, 'that I don't know 'ow aggravating you can be, when you puts your minds to it.'

'We're just high-spirited,' said Lucy. 'Father says so.'

'You call it 'igh-spirited or you can call it plain down-right naughty, but I want you on your best be'aviours. Your aunt's coming back from London tomorrow.'

It appeared that Dobbs was going to fetch her from the station in time for dinner. Next morning Bessie insisted that the children stay indoors.

'Where you can keep yourselves clean and tidy, and I can give eye to you,' she told them.

They were naturally longing to return to the sand-pit, and the Psammead, so this was a sore trial. However, there had been so much toing and froing on the night of their arrival that they had had no chance to explore the house thoroughly. The boys went up to the top of the house to look for attics. These are excellent places for secret games, and for hiding from the grown-ups. They also often contain all kinds of in-teresting things that are disused, but thought too good to give or throw away.

The girls went into the room that Mrs Dobbs had described as Miss Marchmont's sitting room. This was rather like their own parlour at home, but much bigger. There was a musty smell, like a mixture of dust and apples and mothballs, as though the windows were never opened.

There were a good many tapestry cushions and chair backs, and a half finished piece lay neatly folded on the table.

'She does a lot of tapestry,' observed Lucy. 'I expect she sits hour after hour, weaving, like the *Lady of Shalott*.'

'She left the web, she left the loom

She took three paces through the room,'
supplied Ellie obligingly. 'Except she's bound to be ancient and silvery-haired. I think she'll be more like Miss Havisham.'

'There's no cobwebs and no wedding cake. In any case, Miss Havisham didn't go to London on the train. She just sat, year in year out, with the dust settling about her, dreaming of her lost happiness . . .'

'Look – books!' Ellie eagerly explored the shelves.

'She must have been a regular Sunday School prig,' said Lucy. 'Look at all her prizes!'

'The trouble with Sunday School books is that they're so improving. The children in them are always learning to mend their ways.'

'Or dying,' Lucy reminded her. 'A lot of them die, and go to heaven. If we died, should we go to heaven, do you think?'

'Oh, I expect so,' murmured Ellie absently. She was now scanning the pictures, which were mainly of Biblical subjects or of Highland cattle in mist.

'Look at this!'

It was a sampler, neatly edged with houses and flowers, and what looked like sheep. (Animals are extremely difficult to achieve in cross-stitch.)

'It's hers! Constance Mabel Marchmont, her work, aged nine years. 1860. We can work out how old she is! What's sixty take away nine?'

'Fifty-one,' said Lucy, after the merest pause.

They then worked out a hundred minus fifty-one, which is, of course, forty-nine, and then added on eight, the year they were now in being 1908.

'Fifty-seven!' exclaimed Lucy triumphantly. 'My hat – ancient!'

The boys then returned in high good humour to report finding excellent attics.

'We didn't explore much, because of getting dirty,' explained Pip virtuously.

'But there's loads of stuff up there, even toys – I s'pose they must've been hers.'

'We've worked out how old she is,' Lucy told them with some pride. 'Fifty-seven.'

'Jiminy – ancient!' exclaimed George.

'And unused to the ways of children . . .!'

'Unused to *our* ways, anyhow!' and they all giggled.

The rest of the morning passed quite pleasantly. They constructed two wigwams, using shawls, a fireguard and a clothes-horse, and Lucy allowed herself to be tied to a table leg in order to be rescued by the intrepid Pip. She declined, however, to allow her favourite doll to be burned at the stake as a martyr, but fortunately as tempers began to fray dinner was announced.

At half past twelve they were lined up for inspection by Bessie, anxious as always that her charges should do her credit.

'You can be as decent and mannerly as any other children, when you try,' she told them. 'And first impressions is the ones that counts. Oooh – 'ere she is now!'

'Should we curtsey, do you think?' asked Lucy, and was told not to be so silly, and to look sharp and rub that speck off her cheek.

Great Aunt Constance did not fulfil anybody's dreams of what she might be like, because no one had troubled to dream about her. They had vaguely hoped that she would be of the sweet, rosy-cheeked variety of old lady who is always giving children shillings for treats, and saying what dears they are.

Any such hopes were dashed the instant they set eyes on Great Aunt Constance. She was small and thin and straight as a ramrod, and dressed entirely in black. Ellie said later that she reminded her of Mr Murdstone, in Mr Charles Dickens' book *David Copperfield*, but George objected to this, saying that you can't have a lady reminding you of a man. Ellie argued that the insides of ladies' heads could be exactly the same as those of men, and Lucy rather agreed, and something of a row developed. This, however, was later.

'So *these* are the children!' said Great Aunt Constance, after a long, hard stare.

'I'm Bessie, ma'am, and I do trus' you 'ad a good journey and ain't too fatigued,' gushed Bessie. 'And these are Miss Ellie and Miss Lucy, and this is Master George and Master Philip.'

Each of the children held out its hand and murmured 'How d'you do, Great Aunt Constance,' but she rudely ignored this, and marched straight on past them. It is amazing what bad manners grown-ups are allowed to get away with (particularly as it is they who make the rules in the first place). They sometimes seem to think that the laws of common courtesy do not apply to themselves, whereas they are tirelessly drumming these into children. It is doubtful whether Great Aunt Constance had troubled to straighten her jacket or rub a smudge from her cheek before meeting her great-nephews and nieces. She seemed to care not a jot for first impressions.

They followed into the hall, exchanging glum looks. Everyone's worst fears were being realised. Mrs Dobbs was to be replaced by Great Aunt Constance, and they were out of the fat and into the fire, it seemed. She stopped and turned so abruptly that they all jumped.

'I gather that Mrs Dobbs has been ordered a rest by her doctor,' she said. 'And I gather from Dobbs that her indisposition is not entirely unconnected with yourselves.'

'We didn't do anything, really we didn't!' cried Lucy. 'Please don't be cross, Great Aunt Constance!'

'She just seemed to start seeing double,' Pip explained.

Great Aunt Constance held up a quelling hand.

'Silence! Hold your tongues! And kindly do not address me as Great Aunt Constance. It is virtually a sentence in itself. Nor does it trip lightly off the tongue.'

This they had already discovered for themselves. Repeated fast, it was as good a tongue twister as any they knew. You may try it for yourself.

'Shall we call you just plain Aunt Constance, then?' asked Pip.

'No, you shall not,' that lady replied. 'It is an absurd familiarity from children I have never even met until now. You will call me Aunt Marchmont. Is that understood?'

'Yes, Aunt Marchmont,' they said in chorus.

'Great heavens, look at you all, slouching and poking your heads! Hold yourselves straight!'

They stiffened themselves to guardsman attention, and George, at least, resisted a temptation to salute and snap 'Yus m'am!'. Even poor Bessie stood rigid as a poker.

'Character and deportment go hand in hand,' she stated. 'Sloppiness in dress and manner lead to sloppiness in action. Your poor Papa never held himself properly, I recall.'

The children were made indignant by this slight on their father, and judged it both unfair and very bad manners. They had been taught that it is extremely rude to make personal remarks. In their observation, grown-ups all too often did. They had all, in their time, been subject to such remarks as, 'Oh – hasn't she grown – not going to be a beanpole, I hope?' Or 'Oh dear – all those freckles! Don't you make him wear a hat when he goes out in the sun?' Or 'Oh dear – I'm afraid that's poor grandfather's nose he's got!' None of these remarks were calculated to cheer those of whom they were said. People are very fond of saying 'Sticks and stones may break your bones, but words can hurt you never,' but this is ridiculous, as I expect you have found out for yourselves. (These same people will sometimes also observe that 'the pen is mightier than the sword', without in the least bothering that they are directly contradicting themselves.)

Aunt Marchmont went on to say that a special room would be set aside for the children as playroom.

'I suppose you do play,' she said. 'Most children seem to. And at least I shall know exactly where you are. You'll see to that – Betty, did you say your name was?'

'Yes, 'm,' said Bessie meekly. 'And Bessie, please, 'm.'

Aunt Marchmont's next words were more welcome, though they could not have been intended to be so.

'You will play in there only when it rains,' she said. 'On all other occasions you will go outside, and as far as possible from the house. Children should be seen and not heard.'

'Yes, Aunt Marchmont,' they chorussed, mightily relieved, though careful not to show it. Each was thinking of that wide, mysterious sandy place, and the strange beast with the power to grant wishes. And the mere thought gave them the warm glow of the promise of good things to come.

'You will take your breakfast, tea and supper in your own room. At luncheon you will sit with me in the dining room. I should warn you that I am not accustomed to fidgeting and chattering with my food, and shall not expect it.'

'No, Aunt Marchmont.'

'However, I do have a duty to your parents. They would doubtless not wish to have you return as savages. What a pity there are so many of you!'

With these dismissive words she swept off, saying to Bessie over her shoulder, 'Wait ten minutes, then ring the gong for lunch.'

'What cheek, saying that about father!' whispered Ellie. 'And after that time he told us to make her a special Christmas card, because he was sorry for her being so lone and lorn!'

'Hst! She'll hear you!' said Bessie with a frown. 'Oh dear, I 'ope she's not going to be a tartar!'

'She's that, all right,' said Pip glumly. 'A double dyed one.'

'Definitely Foe,' George agreed.

We will pass over lunch with Aunt Marchmont, and will not even give this meal that title hereafter. The meal in the middle of the day with meat and vegetables, and spotted dick to follow, with luck, is called dinner, so far as children are concerned. We will pass over all future mealtimes unless they are of special importance, and will not report that the children ate, any more than that they washed their faces and hands and brushed their teeth. Such details are tiresome to reader and author alike, and may be taken for granted. On this occasion I shall mention only that there was roast pork with stuffing and tremendous crackling, followed by gooseberry tart, and that such conversation as there was was overly polite and stilted. Aunt Marchmont asked the girls whether they enjoyed embroidery, and they replied that they did not, but that they very much admired what they had seen of her own work. She then hoped that Felix and Edmund (she did not call them that, she said 'The other two') would soon recover. This seems a kind enough remark, but the way it was said gave the impression that her real concern was to have the 'other four' from under her roof as soon as possible.

The only significant thing that happened during this meal was that it started to rain. Ellie noticed it first, slanting on the windows, and frowned and nudged George. They all exchanged looks of despair. They had planned to go down to the sand-pit and try to find the Psammead again. Now they were doomed to stay in. They gathered in their playroom.

'What beastly rotten luck!' said George.

'Playroom!' said Pip in disgust. 'Not a toy in sight!'

'I bet she never played with toys. I should think she used to sit all day sewing cushion covers and doilies. A real little Sunday School prig.'

'Still is,' said Lucy.

'Listen,' Ellie said, 'I've got something to tell you. I went down to see Cook this morning, and – '

'Sneak!' said Pip indignantly. 'You mean to say you went cadging without us?'

'No, I did not. I went to ask her something. You know that little cottage in the trees down the drive? Where we heard the gun, remember?'

'And saw that man digging yesterday?'

'Yes, and the little girl. And what Mrs Dobbs said about thieving varmints? Well, they're starving – nearly starving, anyway, and it's all Aunt Marchmont's fault!'

'I shouldn't be surprised,' said George.

'It's terribly sad. The man – his name's Dawkins – his wife died, and he's bringing the little girl up all on his own and her name's Lily – little Lil, Cook called her – and she's poorly, and needs all kinds of good food to build her up. And her father used to work for Aunt Marchmont and now she's dismissed him!'

'For stealing?' Pip asked.

'It wasn't stealing. All he did was shoot some rabbits and pheasants to feed his poor starving child.'

'But he's still shooting them – we heard him.'

'Aunt Marchmont was away, remember. And Cook says you might as well be hanged for a sheep as a lamb. But listen, the worst's to come!'

They waited expectantly.

'She's turning them out of the cottage at the end of the month! They'll be homeless. Cook says it's a crying shame, and I do, too!'

'She's got a heart of stone,' said Lucy. 'Oh – but the Sammyadd! We could wish her to have a heart of gold!'

'No good, silly,' Pip told her. 'The wishes only last till sunset, remember.'

'Hearts of stone can be melted . . .' said Ellie.

'Not hers!' said Pip with feeling. 'Stone can't be melted, anyway, it's unscientific.'

'But they can! Remember Little Lord Fauntleroy!'

'Yes, but that was in a book,' George pointed out. 'Things always come out right in the end in books.'

'Yes, but in the book there was only Cedric to melt his grandfather's heart of stone with his winning ways. And there are four of us!'

'But we haven't *got* winning ways,' Pip objected.

They pondered this undoubted truth. Winning ways were something they had never hankered after, or even given much thought.

'Do you want that poor little girl and her father to be thrown out onto the streets without even a crust of bread?' demanded Ellie.

They were bound to say that they did not. They did not wish to see this happen to anyone at all.

'Well, then! Are we going to be absolute rabbits and just sit and watch it happen? Oh Pip, do stop that beastly row!'

Her brother had a comb and piece of paper, and had been blowing tunelessly on it while the above discussions were taking place. It is quite fun to do this yourself, but it is extremely irritating to the listener.

'I think we should have a Campaign,' announced Ellie. 'A sort of Quest.'

'To save little Lil!' said Lucy. 'Oh do let's!'

'We can't give him his job back, and so our only hope is to soften Aunt Marchmont's heart. We *can* do it, I tell you! Look – every day, each one of us is to do a Good Deed.'

'A *Golden* Deed,' said Lucy eagerly, 'that sounds more noble.'

'All right, a Golden Deed.'

'Like what?'

'Like – like taking her bunches of flowers, and offering to do things, and sitting and talking to her.'

'I don't think I'm going to be much good at Golden Deeds,' Pip said.

'Well at any rate you can try not to do any bad ones,' Ellie told him.

'It's all very well for children in *books* to go around having winning ways and doing Golden Deeds, but – '

'Pity about her name,' George said. 'If it's true, it bodes ill. Constancy means *not* changing. Pity she's not Hope.'

'Or Charity,' supplied Lucy.

'Or Pity,' said Ellie, 'except that I don't think people do get called that. Imagine if Mother had called *you* that, Lucy – Pity Garsington!'

'Well, I vote we do it – the Quest, I mean,' said George. 'I don't think the honour of the Garsingtons will let them stand by and watch people turned onto the streets to starve.'

'Hurray!' cried the girls.

'Oh all right,' said Pip. 'And now – how about going up to the attics to see what we can find?'

So this is what they did. The attics were marvellously wide and dim and shadowy, perfect for all kinds of games. As George pointed out, any noise they made up there was far less likely to be heard by Aunt Marchmont than if they were in their own room. He said that playing up there would practically be a Golden Deed in itself. They found heaps of clothes for dressing up, including a yellowing wedding dress of satin and lace.

'I can be Miss Havisham,' said Ellie, 'and you can be Pip, Pip!'

Then there were boxes of toys – dolls, bricks, bowling hoops, a fort and a box of tin soldiers.

'Hers? Did *she* play with tin soldiers?'

'I can't imagine it,' said Ellie. 'In fact, I can't imagine her ever being a child at all, though I suppose she must have been.'

This is a curious fact. You must have noticed that the world is full of very boring grown-ups – boring, tiresome and sometimes downright disagreeable. You simply cannot imagine them ever having been a child, and climbing trees and tearing their clothes and scrumping apples. And yet, of course, they must have been, once. So the mystery is – what happened to them? The author has a theory about this, which you may take or leave as you please. It is simply that this sort of person did not read enough stories as a child, and the sad consequence of this is that they simply have no imagination. This is a dreadful fate, and the author solemnly warns you to read plenty of stories, especially fairy-tales and adventures, if you wish to escape a similar one. (It is a good idea to have a secret place to do it, one where the grown-ups cannot find you and tell you to find something useful to do.)

The afternoon passed as happily as you can expect any wet afternoon to do, and after supper the children decided to take the first steps in their Quest. They scrubbed their faces and hands and brushed their hair as if for church. Then they knocked on the door of Aunt Marchmont's sitting room.

'Enter!'

They trooped in and stood in a line before her, looking so outstandingly clean and docile that their own mother would scarcely have recognised them. George, as eldest, cleared his throat and spoke first.

'We have come to say goodnight, Aunt Marchmont, and to thank you very, very much for having us here.'

'We must have come as a bit of a shock,' added Pip.

'We didn't have chance to thank you properly this morning, but we are eternally grateful,' said Ellie.

'We think you must have a heart of gold!' said Lucy, who had been

'There! I told you!' Ellie was triumphant.

'Eeeech!' she screamed, and crash! – the tray fell to the floor.
She turned and ran from the room.

warned by the others not to say this, but said it anyway.

Their aunt certainly looked startled by the suggestion.

'We shall try not to be too much of a bother to you.' said George.

'Or eat too much,' said Pip nobly.

'We would've gone and picked you some flowers, but it's too wet,' said Lucy.

'But we will tomorrow,' added Ellie.

There was a pause. The children had run out of honeyed words. Aunt Marchmont eyed them suspiciously, and sniffed.

'Words are fine things. It is actions that count. And what is this I hear about a parrot?'

'It's only Methusalah and he's silent as the grave!' said Lucy.

'He doesn't even squawk, let alone talk,' Pip said.

'That had better be the case,' said Aunt Marchmont. 'Otherwise, he will be posted straight back home. Goodnight!'

They said goodnight, and after a hissed reminder from Ellie they gave their aunt such sudden and radiant smiles that one could have counted their teeth.

Chapter VI

INTO THE FUTURE

Next morning the children wondered whether perhaps they had rather overdone their act of cheerfulness and helpfulness.

'Your aunt wants you to run into the village for 'er,' Bessie told them. 'There's letters for posting, and she wants a skein of blue wool, and one of green.'

Pip groaned, but Ellie gave him a hard look and whispered, 'Golden Deeds, remember!'

'Need we bring them straight back, or will it do at dinner time?' asked George, who was as anxious as anyone to see the Psammead again.

'Dinner time'll do,' she said. ''Ere's the money. Your aunt's out for the day visiting a friend. But you be back one o'clock sharp, you 'ear me?'

'Yes, Bessie,' they chorussed.

They set off straight after breakfast with pockets full of biscuits and hearts full of hope.

'D'you think we should give little Lil some of our biscuits, if she's starving?' asked Lucy as they skipped off down the lane.

'No,' said Ellie, who had thought about this. 'Poor people don't like charity. They're usually poor but proud.'

'*I'm* not poor, and I wouldn't mind a biscuit!' said Pip, and promptly took one from his pocket and ate it.

'The only way for Dawkins to redeem himself with honour is for him to get his job back,' Ellie said.

'Let's hope he hasn't got wind of the sainted aunt being out, and doesn't start shooting again,' said George, who was of a practical nature.

They rounded a bend in the lane and there was Dawkins, dog at his heel and gun under his arm. They stopped dead. Seen close to Dawkins looked not at all a murderer or a thieving varmint. He grinned.

'Morning!'

They wished him the same.

'You the kiddies stopping at the house?'

They nodded.

'Ain't exactly full of the milk of 'uman kindness, is she?'

'Not exactly,' said George.

'But she soon will be!' piped up Lucy. 'Don't despair!'

He seemed rather puzzled by this.

'It's very nice to meet you, Mr Dawkins,' said Ellie hastily. 'What a nice dog!'

She moved forward to pat it and the dog, which had looked fearsome enough in the first place, bared its teeth and snarled.

'Oh!' she dropped rapidly back several paces, and so did the others. Dawkins laughed.

''E ain't no namby-pamby lap dog, miss,' he said. ''Unter, 'e is, ain't yer, Tiger?'

Tiger showed his teeth again.

'Tiger by name, tiger by nature,' said Dawkins. 'Come on!' And off he went among the trees, whistling.

'Good!' said Ellie. 'Now we can talk to Lily.'

She was there, as usual, sitting in the doorway with her rag doll.

'Look, there are rather many of us. We don't want to scare her. You boys go on, and Lucy and me'll talk to her.'

They nodded, and walked on. As the girls drew close they saw how thin the child was and how pale, and her eyes were wide and fearful.

'Hello,' said Ellie gently. 'Are you Lily?'

The child nodded.

'I'm Ellie, and this is Lucy. We're stopping up at the White House.'

No reply. She looked from one to the other of them. She coughed, a hollow, racking cough.

'Miss Marchmont, she don't like me and my Pa,' she said in a tiny voice.

'We know. Don't worry, she's not here. She's away for the day.'

'If she knowed you'd spoke to me she'd tan your backsides, I daresay.'

'Do you stop here by yourself all the time?' asked Ellie.

'Can't play. This cough, see, and I gets tired.'

'It must be dreadfully lonely,' Lucy said. 'Like Rapunzel in the tower.'

'I just sits and thinks,' said little Lil. 'And sometimes I gets my Pa's tea for 'im.' She paused. 'Are you rich?'

The girls were fairly bowled by this question, which was not one they had ever considered.

'I've got eleven shillings and sixpence ha'penny,' said Lucy.

''Ave you got a Pa *and* a Ma?'

They admitted that they had, and Ellie said, 'We were dreadfully sorry to hear about your mother. You must miss her very much,' and saw, to her horror, tears rolling down Lily's thin cheeks. 'Oh don't! Don't cry!'

She dropped to her knees and hugged the skinny child exactly as she would with Lucy.

'Here – use this,' and she gave Lily her handkerchief. 'You've got us now, we're your friends.'

'Yes we are, and we're on a Quest and doing Golden Deeds and – '

'That's pretty,' said Lily wistfully, looking at the handkerchief which was embroidered with flowers.

'Keep it!' said Ellie impulsively.

'Oooh, can I?'

'Of course. And we'll come every day and see you – every day we can, anyhow.'

Little Lil started to sniff again.

'Shan't – shan't be 'ere much longer, miss.'

'I think you will,' said Ellie firmly. 'I think the powers of light will triumph over darkness . . .'

'. . . and hearts of stone will melt . . .'

'It's secret, and we can't tell you yet – '

'But everyone will live happily ever after!' concluded Lucy triumphantly.

Lily, bewildered, looked at them both, clutching her handkerchief.

'We must go now,' Ellie told her. 'But we'll be back.'

'Try wishing!' Lucy called as they walked away. 'It works, you know!'

They soon caught up with the boys, and told them about the encounter.

'It's just a crying shame!' said Ellie. 'I can't bear to think of people as poor and miserable as that!'

'When I grow up, I'm going to reform the world,' George said. 'Just see if I don't!'

'And me. I'm going to do millions of scientific inventions,' said Pip.

'I wonder if one day the world *will* be perfect,' George mused. 'I'd give a lot to know. You know, be able to see into the future . . .'

Then they reached the village. They went to buy stamps and post the letters, then into the little shop for the wool.

'I know jus' the wool Miss Marchmont is after,' the woman told them. 'Trouble is, I've run out, for now. But you come back in a couple of hours, and I'll 'ave it for you.'

'That's a nuisance,' said George as they left the shop.

'Oh never mind,' said Pip impatiently. 'Come on – the Sammyadd!'

And soon they were back in the strange, sandy place which always seemed deserted yet *not* deserted – which is hardly surprising.

'Now look,' said George, 'I've got a wish, a really first class one. Leave it up to me.'

'But *I* want one,' wailed Lucy.

'It'll be your turn tomorrow,' he told her. 'Anyway, you'll be in on this wish, we all will. Now – where are those stones . . . ?'

Without knowing it, George had done exactly what Cyril had done years before – marked the spot where the Psammead appeared with a pile of stones.

'Here!'

They all dropped to their knees.

'Right!' George started to scrabble at the sand, rather gingerly, it must be admitted, because the idea that his fingers might actually encounter that fairy creature was rather daunting. But almost at once the sand started to spurt as if of its own accord. The Psammead emerged, shaking the sand off its whiskers.

'Good morning,' said Ellie. 'I hope you are well?'

'As well as can be expected. All that nasty rain!'

'Of course – your poor top left eleventh whisker!'

'Twelfth!' corrected the Psammead sharply. 'Twelfth whisker!'

'Of course – twelfth,' said George soothingly. 'Er – are you game for a wish?'

'Game?' repeated the Psammead. 'It's no *game*, granting wishes. It's a very serious business, and you'd better look out!'

'Yesterday's wish came off well – got rid of that beastly Mrs Dobbs,' said Pip.

'Who this Mrs Dobbs is I neither know nor care,' returned the

Psammead. 'And whether wishes come off well is your affair, not mine!'

'Go on then – wish!' hissed Pip, nudging George.

The Psammead fixed him with a cold glare.

'No whispering – it's not manners! And there's no need to fall over yourselves to wish in that rude way. It's not much of a life, you know, being the last of the Psammeads. I should have thought the least I could hope for was a little polite conversation.'

'Oh, we do like talking to you,' Lucy assured it eagerly. 'We like talking to you better than to anyone else in the whole world.'

'Hmph! Well,' said the Psammead, somewhat mollified. He looked from one to the other. 'Well? I'm waiting . . .'

'Er – this wish I've thought of,' George said. 'It's to do with time.'

'Time,' said the Psammead loftily, 'does not exist. It is merely a Mode of Thought.'

'I see,' said George.

'No you don't!' it told him. (He didn't, either.)

'Time and space are both only Modes of Thought.'

'I'm sure you're right,' murmured Ellie politely.

'Of course I'm right!' it snapped. 'I'm just warning you about meddling with things you don't understand. And there are plenty of *those*, I daresay.'

'Anyway, what I was thinking,' said George, picking his words as carefully as he could, 'is that it would be absolutely splendid to be able to see into the future – '

'Oh yes!' cried Lucy.

' – and even better to actually *go* into the future!'

'Oh no!' cried Lucy. 'No, I don't want to!'

'That's not such a dusty idea, Jaws,' Pip told him. 'Just think – I'd be able to see some of my own scientific inventions, and – '

'But what if we couldn't get back again, and never saw Mother and

Father again! Oh, I'm not going to listen, I'm not!' and Lucy clapped both hands over her ears in the annoying way she had of shutting out anything disagreeable.

'What a silly, vexing child,' observed the Psammead. 'Is she always like this?'

'No,' said Ellie, and 'As often as not,' said Pip, both at once.

'We shall have to go without her, then,' George said.

'We can't! You know we can't!'

'Then you had better try and persuade her. Because *I'm* going.'

'And so am I,' said Pip. 'If she doesn't like it, she can jolly well do the other thing!'

'Dear me!' said the Psammead, who had been watching this minor squabble as if it were a tennis match, turning its head from side to side. 'What a bad tempered lot you are. Rude, too. I have yet to hear a single word of thanks to myself.'

'Thank you, thank you!' George, Ellie and Pip cried at once.

Lucy, of course, had not heard him.

'That's better. The odd token of esteem would not come amiss, either. However. What time do you want to go to? A couple of hundred years on? A thousand?'

'No! I want to see what it'll be like in my own lifetime,' said George. 'After all, there weren't even motor cars when Father was a boy, he says.'

'Yes – then I could see all my own scientific inventions,' said Pip eagerly.

'And whether people are still thrown out on the streets without a penny to their name,' added Ellie.

'Which is the eldest of you?' enquired the Psammead. 'We shall have to do a little arithmetic, I fear.'

'I am. I'm thirteen,' said George.

'And what age do you expect to live to?'

George was momentarily baffled.

'Not *my* age, naturally,' said the Psammead.

'Well – say ninety.'

'Not an awful lot of people do,' pointed out Pip.

'I'm going to. I was born in 1895, so that'll take us to . . .'

'1985,' said Pip. 'I say, he won't actually *be* ninety will he? And us all ancient, without teeth and such?'

'Certainly not,' replied the Psammead. 'No one can meddle with time like that, not even myself.'

'Thank heaven for that!'

'You will simply be visitors. Look upon it as a day outing. I've been there myself, as a matter of fact – or thereabouts, given a decade or so.'

'Crikey!'

'You're in for some shocks,' it said. 'I shouldn't think you've imagined yourself flying in the air, like birds?'

'*I* have!' This was from Lucy, who had unstopped her ears just in time to hear this tantalising titbit. 'Oh, I've dreamed and dreamed of it! Can they really, in the future?'

'Certainly. And you'd better go and look for yourselves, if that's what you've decided to do. I haven't got all day.'

Ellie looked hopefully at Lucy, who nodded, took a deep breath and held tightly on to Ellie's hand.

'It's – it's dreadfully *doomy*,' she whispered.

'Right!' George himself took a deep breath. 'I wish we were all in 1985!'

'It is a difficult wish,' said the Psammead, 'and will require the most tremendous effort. But I'll do it!'

Then it began to blow itself up. The only one of the children who had seen this before was Ellie, and she had thought at the time it was having some kind of choking fit. It was clearly enormously hard work. The children stared, fascinated.

'Oh dear, is it all right?' whispered Lucy.

'It'll *bust!*' whispered Pip.

As before, it let out all its breath in a long, shuddering gasp, and as it did so, warned 'Better shut your eyes!'

The children squeezed their eyes tight. They had no idea what it might be like to travel through time, but it seemed very likely that it might make a person giddy, even the kind of person who travels quite comfortably in trains. As it was, they felt no sensation at all – which is not to say that they would not have done if they had not obeyed the Psammead. (The author does not know – regretfully, she has never done this.)

'Are we there, d'you think?'

'Is it safe to open them?'

They did so. Their shock and disappointment was at first great. There lay the wide, sandy dunes and tufted grass, exactly as when last seen.

'We're still there!'

'The beastly thing's tricked us!'

'I knew it couldn't really do it! Future, my elbow!'

Whoosh! The children turned, startled. Whooosh! On the self same road along which they had travelled on Mr Dobbs' cart from the station, were strange, shiny shapes. They sped past in both directions faster than anything the children had ever seen before – faster than anything they had ever dreamed of. Pip understood from his researches that the fastest moving thing on earth was a cheetah. He had never seen one of these creatures, but felt certain these were not they. And evolution in the next eighty years or so could surely not have produced animals which appeared to be of multicoloured metals, and on wheels? Light dawned.

'They're motor cars!'

'Jiminy!' Just look at 'em go!'

'I'll have one of them, won't I just!'

They stood watching the shining beasts go roaring to and fro. Then they became aware of another sound, overhead this time. Looking up they saw a huge, silvery bird with wide, featherless wings.

'Swelp me!' breathed Pip, who as a scientist was in very heaven. 'They *are* flying!'

'Are there people inside? But I thought the Sammyadd meant for people to *really* fly!'

' You never thought you'd see dozens of people up there flapping wings, duffer!' said Pip.

'Well I *did*, then! And I've been tricked and I don't think I'm going to like it here.'

'That's what you always say,' Pip told her. 'Come on – let's go and see what the future's really like! We've only got till sunset!'

He set off towards the road and George followed.

'Careful!' screamed Lucy, running after them.

There began the most dreadful journey back to the village. The road was much wider than when they had last seen it, but there were no pavements. The motor cars and even larger vehicles went roaring past, and each time the children flinched, and Lucy put her hands over her ears. Some of the cars had piercing hooters, and the people inside them waved and stared.

This was confusing enough, but only as the children approached the village did they realise how far from home they were – not in space, but in time.

'It this it?' said Pip dubiously.

Where there had once been a few houses and cottages, here and there among the trees, there were now rows of them on either hand. And from the main street ran other streets, and the children could see more houses, close together, more like those at home in Islington. And these houses looked strange and different – they all had roofs and doors and windows, of course, but they were not at all like the houses the children knew.

'Look!' George pointed. 'They've been chopped in half!'

Sure enough, there were houses with roofs low down, so that there could not possibly be bedrooms, let alone attics.

'P'raps they're for dwarfs, like in *Snow White*,' suggested Lucy, and rather hoped so.

Standing by the kerb was a long red motor car, and the boys eagerly ran towards it, and walked all round it, admiring and peering inside at the dashboard with its bewildering array of dials and knobs.

'Here!' came a man's voice. 'What d'you think you're doing?'

'Oh – we're just looking, thank you,' said George politely. 'It's absolutely ripping, sir.'

The man stared.

'I could even have invented it myself!' said Pip. 'In fact, I think I will! How fast does it go? Twenty? Thirty?'

'Now look here – you clear off and leave it alone. And don't let me catch you at it again or I'll call the police.'

Lucy screamed.

'Oh quick, quick, we'll all be sent to prison!'

She started to run, and the others had to as well, to catch up.

'Don't be such a goose,' George told her. 'The Law of England can't send you to prison for *looking*.'

'Are we really in the village?' Ellie looked ahead and was well and truly puzzled. Gone were the tiny cottages and little post office and shop. Ahead lay an even wider street, and buildings with huge, gleaming windows, like the shops in London.

'Where's the shop that sells wool?'

'Gone, silly,' Pip told her. 'You weren't thinking of collecting *that*? The woman said two hours, not eighty years.'

It was only then that the true enormity of what they had done dawned on the children. The world as they knew it had vanished, and another, quite other world lay in its place. It dawned on them, too, that the people looked different. They had arms and legs and eyes and noses, of course, but still were hardly recognisable.

'Look!' Lucy tugged at Ellie's sleeve. 'Ladies with legs!'

'And wearing trousers!' Ellie stared. 'Those *are* ladies, aren't they?'

The trouble was, people were staring at them, too. Some merely glanced, others nudged their companions, pointed and laughed. Others downright stared.

'Pity you didn't think of wishing us to be dressed right,' Pip told George. 'I feel like a circus freak.'

'Or invisible, then we could've seen them, but not them us,' added Ellie.

A girl nearby called 'Hey, where's the fancy dress?'

'Cheek!' said Pip.

'Did you see – she's wearing trousers!'

'Look at those bicycles – lor, they've come on a bit!'

Everyone was looking everywhere at once, because every single thing was exciting and strange, but at the same time a little frightening.

'I'm hungry,' Pip announced.

'Me too,' said George. 'Come on, let's buy some grub.'

'How much've you got?' Pip asked. 'I'm not exactly flush of chink.'

'Wait!' Ellie told them. 'Look!'

They were level with a wide, open area where stood row upon row of gleaming motor cars. Here and there were people pushing large trolleys made of wire, piled high with boxes and tins and packets of buns and biscuits. These they then pushed to one of the cars, opened up a kind of flap at the back, and began to load the food in.

'Look – that's where they're getting it!'

Pip pointed, and sure enough the trolleys were being pushed out of a large, glass fronted building, with a sign saying 'Supermarket'.

'They're just going in, filling up trolleys and wheeling them away!'

'Helping themselves!' exclaimed George. 'Look – I can see them – they're just picking things off the shelves!'

'Oh wonderful!' cried Ellie, overjoyed. 'So the world *is* a better place! Now, no one can ever starve. I wish Dawkins and little Lil could see it!'

'Come on,' said Pip, 'let's grab some grub! What a wheeze!'

They followed the crowd in through the wide glass door and George, copying the rest, pulled out a trolley and wheeled it in.

'Just look!' gasped Lucy. 'It's like Aladdin's cave! Can we really help ourselves to anything?'

'It's what everyone else is doing,' Pip told her.

'Glad you came now?' asked George.

There began the most tremendous fun. It was like a dream come true. For children, who have to save every penny even to buy such necessities as sweets and chocolate, to be able to help themselves to anything in sight was very heaven. It was better than Christmas.

Items were taken from the racks and tossed into the trolley at an amazing rate. Oranges, apples, pears and tomatoes were followed by bread rolls wrapped in see-through paper, butter and cheese. Then they discovered slices of pink ham in shiny packets.

'No tins,' George warned. 'We shan't be able to open them.'

'I don't think we should be too greedy,' said Ellie, eyeing the mounting pile of food. 'We can't take anything back with us, remember.'

'More's the pity. Just look at those biscuits!'

Pip took several packets of his favourites, intending to eat them all before sunset or bust.

Then they saw row upon multicoloured row of drinks in bottles – orange, lime, lemonade.

'Better take one each,' George said. 'It's thirsty work, being in the future.'

So four large bottles joined the other things in the trolley. It was now beginning to look quite full.

'Remember we shall have to carry it, as well as eat it,' Ellie said. 'And I'm sure we'll never eat all that.'

'If there's any left over we can always give it to a beggar,' Pip argued.

'But there won't *be* any. How can anyone possibly starve when all they've got to do is help themselves?'

They found themselves in a line of people waiting to go out. A woman behind the counter was working some strange machine that made odd squeaking noises. The customer in front of them was writing something in a little book. She then tore it out and handed it to the woman, who seemed to put it into her machine.

'Next?'

Shyly the children wheeled their trolley forward. Ellie hoped anxiously that the woman would not think them greedy.

'I know there seems an awful lot,' she explained confidingly, 'but there are four of us, and we shall need tea as well as dinner.'

The woman stared. 'Come on, then!' she said.

George, who had seen what was happening in the next line, started piling the goodies on to the counter.

'Look, the counter's moving!' whispered Lucy.

So it was. As if by magic the packets and cartons went gliding away, and as they did, bleep bleep went the little machine. It was amazing. At last the trolley was empty.

'Nine pounds forty-three, please,' the woman said. 'Here – get them put in this, you're holding folk up.'

She passed a shiny carrier bag to Ellie, who obediently began packing the food, helped by Lucy.

'Thank you,' said Ellie, smiling. 'I couldn't think how we were going to carry it.'

They seemed to have thought of everything in this wonderful new world, where food was yours for the taking.

'Nine pounds forty-three,' repeated the woman sharply, looking at George.

'I – beg your pardon?'

'The money. Come along, look sharp!'

'But – but we didn't think you had to pay,' he stammered. He went bright red right to the roots of his hair in the unfortunate way he had. 'We thought people were just helping themselves.'

'Is this some kind of silly joke, or what?' the woman demanded. 'What are you all dressed up like that for?'

'Ah, well. This is how you *do* dress, where we come from.'

'Well, whatever you thought or didn't think, it's nine pounds forty-three, if you please.'

'But – we haven't got nearly that much!' Pip dug his hand in his pocket and fished out a few coppers and a florin. The woman peered forward.

'Them's foreign,' she said. 'No they ain't – what's that – a farthing?'

'I know there's not much,' said Pip humbly.

'Watch them girls don't make off with them bags, miss,' said a man behind George.

'You should send for the police, if you ask me,' said a woman.

At this Lucy shrieked. The woman behind the counter nodded, pressed a bell and raised her arm in the air, as if in a signal. That was enough for the frightened children.

'Better bunk!' muttered George to Pip. Lucy was already tugging Ellie's arm, and begging, 'Please let's go! The police will come and we'll be sent to prison!'

George took a deep breath and made up his mind. A Garsington did not usually take to its heels in times of danger, but if ever there were an exception to a rule, this seemed to be it.

'Right – run!' he commanded.

The four ran, their bulging bags abandoned on the counter, and followed by a chorus of outraged voices. They ran out into the street, weaving in and out of shoppers, and all the time expecting the shrill sound of a police whistle, and arrest.

Chapter VII

CAPTURED

The children eventually collapsed panting onto a seat outside a building whose stone lintel announced it to be the library.

'Dressing up as children from books, are you?' a woman asked them, smiling. 'Let me guess – *The Railway Children*!'

They looked blankly back at her.

'You'll win, I shouldn't wonder,' she told them, and went off, her books under her arm.

'Oh dear, I wish we hadn't come,' said Lucy. 'I never wanted to.'

'Oh whiney-piney!' said Pip, and pulled a face. 'You haven't been burned at the stake yet.'

She gave a little shriek and clapped both hands over her ears.

'I'm still hungry,' he said glumly. 'Ravenous.'

'We could *buy* food. I saw a little baker's shop.'

'Using what exactly for tin?' enquired Pip. 'You heard what she said – ours is no good.'

They sat gloomily considering the cheerless prospect of a day without dinner, or even tea.

'Now we know how Dawkins and little Lil feel,' Ellie said. 'Starving.'

'I know,' said George. 'Let's go back to the White House.'

'If it's still there,' Pip said.

Lucy, who had just removed her hands from her ears, gave another squeal and clapped them back again.

'The thing is this. Remember what the Sammyadd said about time being a Mode of Thought?'

'Whatever that means,' put in Pip.

'Well, I don't know exactly what it meant, but I suppose it might mean that the past is still going on, somewhere. And in the village we didn't see anyone we knew from the past, because we don't know anyone round here. But if we go back to the house, the past – our present, that is – might still be going on, even if we are in the future.'

'I don't quite follow you, Jaws,' Pip told him.

'Nor me,' said Ellie. 'But do let's go back to the house. I hate it when all the people point and stare.'

'Come to think, there might be strawberries or raspberries in the garden,' Pip said. 'Let's go!'

'I'll tell you what, we'll split into pairs,' George said. 'Then we won't attract so much attention. And if the police *are* looking for us, they'll be looking for four children, not two.'

'Good thinking, Jaws,' Pip told him. 'You and me'll go first. You girls wait five minutes, then follow.'

'See you back at the house,' George called over his shoulder as they went.

'I thought having wishes come true would be fun,' said Lucy dolefully. 'I don't like this one bit.'

'You will when it's over, and you look back on it,' Ellie told her encouragingly. 'Just think – you've visited the future! You'll be able to tell your grandchildren about it.'

'We will get back, won't we?'

'Of course we will. The minute it's sunset.'

'It's all terribly complicated. I wish they taught you magic at school, like history and arithmetic.'

'The trouble is, most grown-ups don't believe in magic.'

'I do. I did even before we met the Sammyadd. Oooh!' Her face suddenly crumpled. 'My thimble! My magic thimble! I left it under my pillow.'

'It'll still be there tonight,' Ellie said. 'And I can't think what use it would be now. It would take more than a magic thimble to get us out of this.'

'But the Sammyadd could,' said Lucy, her face brightening. 'I know — let's go and see it on the way home, and ask it to wish us back to the past — the present, I mean.'

'I suppose we could try,' said Ellie dubiously.

'Oh let's, do let's!'

And so, when their five minutes were up (or as nearly as they could judge without a watch) the girls made their way back through the village that was now more like a town. And when they reached the outskirts they went, not up the lane to the White House, but back towards the sand-pit. When they reached it they were strangely comforted by how exactly the same it looked as it had before.

'It's just the same as it was this morning,' Lucy said.

'As if time had stood still . . .' murmured Ellie.

'I suppose it's just that you can't change things like sand and grass,' Lucy said. 'I expect it'd be just the same even in a thousand years, let alone eighty.'

'And I don't suppose the Sammyadd will have changed, either,' Ellie said. She stared down at the heap of stones.

'You ask it to come out, Ellie-bobs,' said Lucy. 'I think it likes you best.'

So Ellie dropped to her knees and called softly, 'Sammyadd! Sammyadd!'

They waited. Nothing happened, there was not the least stir of the sand. She called again, louder this time.

'Oh – what if it's moved house!' wailed Lucy.

'I do *wish* you'd come out! said Ellie desperately.

It worked. The sand sprayed out in all directions, followed by the furry form of the Sand Fairy.

'Oh Sammyadd!' cried both girls together.

'Now what?' it demanded crossly. 'I've barely been to sand five minutes, and here you are bothering me again.'

The children, you see, might have moved eighty years forward in time, but the Psammead had continued in its own time, and so was annoyed at having its nap so rudely interrupted.

'One wish a day, that's the rule,' it said. 'You can't think how all this wishing hurts my poor whisker.'

'Oh we're sorry, truly we are,' said Ellie. 'But you see we're hungry, ravenous, and we can't get any food till we get back to our own time.'

'You should have thought of that,' it told her. 'I warned you about meddling with things you don't understand.'

'Yes, you did,' admitted Ellie humbly.

'It's no good making wishes and just giving up when they don't suit you,' it continued. 'Think before you wish!'

'Oh, we will next time,' promised Lucy. 'But please, please dear Sammyadd, couldn't you just wish us back home now?'

'No I could not,' replied the Psammead. 'You can't go unwishing wishes at the drop of a hat.'

'I was afraid not,' said Ellie sadly.

'There have to be some rules, you know, even in magic.'

'I suppose so. But it's a comfort you're still here, dear Sammyadd.'

'Of course I am!' it snapped. 'I was here before you, and I'll be here after. I'm the oldest living thing on the face of the earth, I may as well tell you.'

'Oh, I'm sure you are,' said Ellie. 'You're a wonderful and fabulous beast!'

'A radiating dream!' added Lucy.

The Psammead was evidently pleased by this flattery, and assumed an expression of sublime smugness.

'I don't boast,' it said, 'but I am rather, aren't I?'

'Oh yes!' and 'Indeed you are!' the girls agreed at once.

It beamed benignly at them, and for a moment they thought it might relent, and grant their wish, after all. Then its expression changed.

'But that doesn't mean to say I'm going to unwish wishes for silly noodles who don't think before they wish! I wish you good day!'

And before the girls had chance to utter their pleas for it to stay it had whisked itself away and out of sight in a shower of sand.

'Bother!' said Lucy, and 'Drat!' said Ellie, their one hope of rescue now gone.

'Back to the White House now, I suppose,' said Ellie. 'Never mind, Lucy lamb, only till sunset. Stout heart.'

'Stout heart, I s'pose,' said Lucy with a sigh.

The boys, meanwhile, had not hit upon the idea of visiting the sand-pit, but made their way back to the White House – or rather, to where they hoped the house still stood.

The first change they noticed was when they turned up the lane. It was dimmer and greener than ever, because the tall trees had grown higher and spread wider over the years. But where once Dawkins' tumbledown cottage had stood, was now a neat, trim little place with new thatch, white door with gleaming brass knocker, and pretty garden with roses and delphiniums.

'That's Dawkins' cottage!'

The boys stood and stared. It was Dawkins' cottage, all right, but patched up and painted almost beyond recognition.

'Well, at least it's still there. Keep your fingers crossed'

It is unlikely that the crossing of two boys' rather grubby fingers affected the unrolling of the years, but the fact is that when they rounded the last bend in the lane the White House *was* still there, and looking almost exactly as when they had left it nearly eighty years ago – straight after breakfast.

'Phew!' George let out his breath.

'Looks just the same.'

'Does – practically.'

'*Is* it the same, d'you think? You know – all that stuff you were spouting about our time still going on?'

'There's only one way to find out,' said George. 'Come on!'

He judged it prudent to proceed with caution. The door looked pretty much the same to him, but appearances can be deceptive, and there was no denying the fact that Dawkins' cottage had changed. Surely they could not have stepped over an invisible line somewhere in the lane, and were now back in their own time? He turned the handle slowly and pushed open the door. Pip, behind him, peered past him, and both boys knew at a glance that this was not home. The hatstand had gone and the picture of Elijah being fed by the ravens, and the floor was covered from wall to wall by a plain blue carpet.

The boys held a whispered consultation.

'Had we better go in? We don't exactly live here now.'

'We do! And we know where the kitchen is. We might find some eats.'

George nodded. To go in through a door you have come out of that very morning does not seem a very serious crime. And curiosity is a very strong instinct, particularly in the young. (It also, of course, killed the cat.) Both George and Pip badly wanted to see what changes had taken place in the White House. This was probably the only chance they would ever have to visit the future, and it would be feeble to waste it by kicking their heels in the garden till the sun set.

So they crept in and tiptoed across the hall, though the carpet was so wonderfully soft under their feet that they scarcely needed to. They were halfway across when all at once a terrible hullaballoo set up in Aunt Marchmont's sitting room. One moment the whole house had seemed as quiet as the grave, and the next it sounded as if a whole army was in there.

The boys froze for an instant, then bolted back the way they had come, with no nonsense about tiptoeing this time.

'Jiminy! What happened?'

'It sounds like dozens of them!'

'Sssh! Listen!'

Through the half open door they still heard voices from the strange visitors in what had been Aunt Marchmont's sitting room. They heard something else, too.

'Music!'

'There's a whole orchestra in there!'

The gleaming motor cars, the moving counter, the lopped off houses, all paled into insignificance compared with this new phenomenon.

'They didn't go in by the door, we'd have seen them.'

'The *window?*'

It seemed unlikely that all these people, including a full orchestra with its fiddles, trumpets and drums, had actually entered the house by the window, when there were several perfectly good doors. However, to peer in at the window and see exactly who was in there, and what they were doing, seemed a sensible plan. They crept among the shrubbery along the wall and looked in, scarcely daring to imagine what would meet their eyes.

'So these are the children!' said Great Aunt Constance,
after a long hard stare.

'Better take one of each,' George said. 'It's thirsty work, being in the future.'

Whatever they might have seen could scarcely have been a greater shock than what they did see.

They still heard the voices, and the music, but at first glance the room seemed empty – of people and horses, that is. There was plenty of strange furniture, including the most comfortable looking chairs and sofas, but no sign of the orchestra, or anyone else.

'Are they *invisible?*' This was a scientific development Pip had never imagined in his wildest dreams.

'What's that?' whispered George, pointing.

'Jiminy!'

Facing them was a large box with a glass front, and in that box were moving pictures, and even from that distance they could see them quite clearly.

'Cowboys!'

'And Indians!'

There, in Aunt Marchmont's sitting room, an epic battle was taking place. Horses thundered by, guns cracked, dust flew. The boys fairly boggled. It was as if all the stories they had ever read were coming to life before their eyes.

'How did they get there?'

'Blowed if I know!'

'D'you think they – help!'

The pictures vanished. The voices and music stopped abruptly, cut off short. It was then that they saw the girl. She was a girl, with long fair hair, but was wearing the blue trousers that so many people in the village seemed to have, as if it were a uniform. She rose from one of the big chairs and left the room. The boys stared at the now empty box.

'What happened?'

'Red Indians? In *England?*'

'But where did they *go?*'

'Get down!'

George pushed Pip unceremoniously behind a shrub, and they watched the girl who had just come out wander off over the lawn in the direction of the summerhouse – or at least, where the summerhouse had been.

'Coast's clear!'

They crept back into the house again. The door of Aunt Marchmont's sitting room had been left open. They exchanged eyebrows, nodded, and cautiously went in. There stood the magic box, still and silent. They went slowly over and examined it, scarcely able to believe that only minutes earlier it had been filled with galloping horses, cowboys and Indians.

'What *is* it?'

'I don't know,' said Pip. 'But I'm going to invent it. It's prime!'

'Come on – the kitchen!'

The kitchen was unrecognisable, except by the view from the window, which had hardly changed. It seemed as if the world itself did not change, only the things in it.

'Is this it?'

Gone was Cook's cosy domain, with its blazing fire and fender, its burnished copper pans, hams hanging from the beams, jars of pickles and salted beans.

'But there's no fire!'

'Or oven!'

'How do they cook things?'

'Look!' George pointed.

Perched in a cage was a parrot, a parrot that looked oddly familiar, with his tilted head and leather-lidded eyes.

'The dead spit of Methusalah!'

Pip poked a finger into the cage.

'Methusalah! Who's a pretty boy, then?'

The parrot made no reply to this pleasantry, nor did they expect it to.

'*Could* it be . . .' George murmured. 'But how?'

Pip shrugged.

'Says in the Bible Methusalah lived to be nine hundred and sixty-nine, but I call that bunk. Not scientific. Listen — what's that?'

There was a faint humming sound, that seemed to come from a tall, white cabinet behind the door. Pip went over to it.

'Cupboards can't hum!'

'Careful!' warned George, who did not exactly believe that a horde of Red Indians would come whooping out, but would not have been altogether surprised if they had.

'Crikey!' said Pip, opening the door, 'it's winter in there!'

Gingerly he touched the packets and bags that were stacked on the shelves.

'Frozen solid!'

'But how?'

'Search me. A sort of indoors icehouse.'

'But why should they want their grub frozen? You mean to say they eat it frozen instead of cooked?'

'Course not, duffer. It's to preserve it. It's scientific.'

'Oh,' said George, who was not so well up on things scientific as his brother, despite being older. (You either have a scientific brain or you don't. It is rather like having brown eyes or not, something you are born with.)

'We'll never get our teeth in that, and it might take a week to thaw out,' George said, trying to be practical, if not scientific. 'There must be some proper food somewhere, and we'd better find it quick, before that girl gets back.'

The girls meanwhile had already passed Dawkins' transmogrified cottage, and were nervously wondering what would meet their eyes when they reached the end of the lane. It is very unsettling to have your whole safe, cosy world disappear, and feel like strangers on the face of the earth.

'I know,' said Lucy, 'let's see if the summerhouse is still there. At least it would be somewhere to hide.' (Lucy was still in rather a funk. Her great dread was to be arrested by the police and sent to prison, where she might end her days in a dank cell, or at least spend as long there as the Father of the Marshalsea in Mr Charles Dickens' book *Little Dorrit*.)

So they left the lane and went in among the trees, which was a thankful thing because at least they were still green and leafy and filled with birds. Then, ahead, they glimpsed the wide lawns of the White House, and the summerhouse itself.

'It *is* still there!' Lucy pointed, and both girls cried 'Hurray!' because truth be told, Ellie herself did not much like the idea of entering the White House if it were, indeed, in the future.

'We could stop here, and then the boys bring food out to us,' she said.

They hurried towards the summerhouse and opened its door and were met with its fusty dusty smell that seemed also the smell of time itself, and that was when they saw the girl. They stared. She stared. It is hard to say who stared the harder. Had it been a competition, the judges would have been hard put to to award the prize.

'Who are you?' demanded the girl.

'I'm Ellie and this is Lucy, but I think we'd better be going. Come on Lucy.'

'No, don't go! I'm Stella. It means "star" but it's a horrible name and I hate it.'

'I quite like mine,' Lucy said. 'It's from the Latin *lux*, and it means "light".'

'What are you dressed up like that for?'

The girls felt that they might very well have asked her the same thing.

'It's how you do dress, where we come from,' said Ellie primly, eyeing Stella's blue trousers and queer chunky shoes.

'You mean – ? You can't possibly be – are you *ghosts*?'

'Certainly not,' replied Ellie stiffly.

'What a rude question!' said Lucy.

'But you just said – people dressed like that *ages* ago – I've seen them in films.'

'Well, we're not ghosts,' said Lucy, indignant at the very idea. 'We're just on a day outing and if anyone's a ghost it's *you*!'

'Oh *yes* – you can see right through me, I suppose? Go on – pinch me, then you'll see if I'm real or not!'

'I shan't pinch you,' said Ellie distantly, 'but I'll shake hands, if you like.'

She half regretted the offer as soon as she had made it. Perhaps this girl was a sort of ghost, only back to front – from the future instead of the past, like in *The Christmas Carol*. Gingerly she stretched out her hand. The girl took it and 'How d'you do?' said Ellie politely, and 'You *are* real!' exclaimed Stella.

'You really are from the past?'

'No, we're not – it's you that's in the future,' Ellie told her.

'We came here on a wish,' piped up Lucy. 'But we'll be back home by sunset and don't I just wish it'd come quick!'

Just then Ellie spied the boys advancing rapidly over the lawn. Stella saw them too.

'There's more of you?'

'Only two,' said Lucy. The others are at home with scarlet fever.'

'Come on,' they heard George say, 'we'll leave the grub here then go and find the girls.'

Their shock at finding the girl from the future in the summerhouse was not so great as that of their sisters, because they had already seen her. It was, however, a dreadful embarrassment, laden as they were with food from her kitchen. It had not felt like stealing at the time, and in any case Pip had said that to take food when you were starving was not a crime, but every human being's right.

'It's more like a lion killing its prey,' he had explained. 'It's a basic instinct.'

Now, pockets bulging with fruit and biscuits, and carrying hunks of bread and cheese, they felt not at all like lions with their prey, but just plain ordinary caught out. George's face went into sunset flame.

'We nicked it from your larder, but only out of direst need,' he explained.

'You do talk funny!' Stella said. 'And that's all right – no one's going to miss that. I say, I can't believe that this is really happening!'

She was to say this several more times during the course of the day, to the irritation of the children. It is not altogether flattering to be considered unbelievable.

They picnicked merrily enough in the summerhouse. They learned that Stella had no brothers and sisters and was staying at the White House with her grandparents. She referred to them as 'the wrinklies', which rather shocked the others, and said that they were stuffy old sticks and that she was bored stiff.

'Till you came,' she said, 'but how did you *get* here?'

'We met this sort of furry – ' began Lucy, but the others were frowning and shaking their heads, so she broke off and said simply, 'We just wished to be here.'

'But you can't just wish things and then they happen,' said Stella. 'I've wished millions of times, but it's never any good.'

She looked hard from one to another of them, but they remained mute. They had not actually promised the Psammead to keep it secret, but they superstitiously felt that all magic is secret. In any case, this girl could go straight to the sand-pit and start wishing things herself. They did not care for the idea of this at all.

'Though come to think,' said Stella thoughtfully, '*you're* a bit of a wish come true. I get lonely here, stuck with the wrinklies. I've – I've even got an imaginary friend!'

'Oh!' Ellie was interested. 'I've got an imaginary twin!'

'Not so imaginary, either!' said Pip. 'Look here – we've come to find out about the future, not sit round spouting silly girls' stuff!'

He kept up a relentless scientific enquiry. He wanted to know how the pictures of Indians and horses appeared out of thin air in Aunt Marchmont's sitting room, and how the food was kept frozen solid.

'I'll show you, if you like,' she offered. 'The wrinklies have gone to town and won't be back for ages. In any case, I can always hide you.'

They did not altogether like the way she said this, as if they were objects, toys rather than real flesh and blood.

There followed a guided tour of the White House, which might have looked almost exactly the same on the outside, but turned out to be a truly magical box of tricks. Gone were the old gas mantels. Now, by the flick of a switch, lights went on and off without even a match to light them. Stella showed off like anything. She worked the machine in the sitting room, which she called the 'telly'. Our heroes and heroines were transfixed as she conjured up living pictures by the mere touch of buttons, and without going anywhere near the box.

In the end they spent nearly the whole afternoon watching it, and time flew (though whose time it really was, was a mystery). When the story they were watching was over, Stella showed Lucy how to press the button to switch it off.

'I still can't believe you're real,' said Stella, eyeing her guests. 'It's the best thing that ever happened to me.'

'And us,' said Pip gallantly. It was true in a way, but he did not altogether care for Stella, and he found himself thinking that he was glad she was not his sister. She had small eyes, which is something a person cannot help, of course, but he did not much like the way she looked with them.

'The wrinklies'll be back soon,' she told them. 'I tell you what – you go back to the summerhouse and I'll bring you some food.'

At this Pip modified his opinion of her somewhat. They waited for what seemed like ages in the summerhouse. They heard a motor car drive up, and voices, and then everything went quiet again, except for the birds. The shadows started to lengthen. The children fell quiet, each thinking its own thoughts, which it did not voice for fear of frightening the others.

'I've been thinking . . .' said Lucy at last in a small voice. They all looked at her. 'It's all very well saying the wishes wear off at sunset, but *our* sunset's already gone.'

'I see what you mean,' said George slowly. 'This is a future sunset.'

'So if our sunset's already gone, how do we know we'll ever get back?'

Everyone's brain was racing as it tried to work this out. There was an uncomfortable logic in Lucy's words. They remembered the Psammead's warning about meddling with things they didn't understand – and they certainly didn't understand this. Even Pip's scientific brain was baffled.

'I'm sure we will,' said Ellie, but more to stop Lucy from crying than because she really believed it.

'But I've had a truly dreadful thought,' said Lucy. 'What if sunset comes and we stop here but we don't stay how we are – children, I mean.'

'Phew!' George whistled. 'I see what you mean. Me ninety, and you all eighty-something.'

'Oh don't say it, don't! It's horrible! We don't even know *how* to be grown up!'

'Let alone old,' said Pip. 'Positively ancient, in fact. Rip van Winkle!'

Lucy clapped her hands over her ears, and for once the others sympathised with her. Luckily, before they had time to ponder this dreadful possibility, 'Here she is!' said George, and Stella appeared.

'Here we are.'

She passed over the food, and stood in the doorway watching the children as they opened up the various packages. Ellie, glancing up, caught a curious expression on Stella's face, and felt a fleeting alarm.

'You'll be all right tonight,' Stella said. 'I'll see you in the morning!'

And with that she slammed shut the door and the children heard the unmistakable sound of a key being turned in the lock. They jumped to their feet as one.

'What's the game?' demanded George.

'I'm keeping you!' came Stella's voice.

'You can't, you can't!' screamed Lucy.

'Now look here,' said George, 'it's not exactly cricket, you know.'

'Who cares!'

'We trusted you,' said Ellie bitterly.

Chapter VIII

ITNAPPED

'Oh do please let us out!' begged Lucy.

'Sorry,' came Stella's voice. 'But you don't know how awful and lonely it is here with old Gran and Grandpa Dawkins.'

'With *who*?' repeated George incredulously, as everyone stretched its eyes wide.

'The wrinklies.'

'But what did you say their name was?'

'Dawkins. So's mine. Oh – there's Grandpa calling – got to go – see you tomorrow!'

Her voice was fading as she spoke, and already she was beyond entreaty.

'Well,' said George, as the true awfulness of what was happening dawned on them all. 'This is a pretty decent ghastly sort of a mess!'

'We could be here forever,' said Pip in hollow tones.

'Don't say it!' begged Ellie.

'I want to go home!' wailed Lucy.

George, who would usually have told her to stow it, and not be such a whiney-piney baby, realised that this was an occasion when he was called upon to play the part of eldest, and be wise and calm. The trouble was, he did not feel it. He was, after all, only thirteen, and it is difficult to be wise and calm when you realise that you might be cut adrift in a sea of time and never ever return to your old, familiar life. The Garsingtons had faced many an adversity before with fortitude, but now their courage was being tested to the utmost.

'Don't worry, Lucy lamb,' he told her, and was horrified to hear his own voice coming out as a croak.

'If we do have to stop here, we'll be orphans!'

'Eighty-year-old orphans,' said Pip morosely.

George, feeling bound to do something, rattled the handle of the summerhouse door again.

'It's locked, all right.'

'She's going to keep us like animals in a zoo! Did you see her face when she looked at us – as if she owned us!'

'Oh, I wish I'd got my thimble!'

'Fat lot of good wishing now,' Pip told her.

'Look here,' said George, with a great effort at firmness and wisdom, 'we still don't know exactly what's happening with time, and whether when sunset comes, it'll be our sunset or hers. Or both. Right?'

'Right,' they nodded, their eyes fixed hopefully on his face.

'There's only one single thing in the whole world we can count on – on being in our time, I mean, *and* this.'

'The Sammyadd!' exclaimed Ellie.

'Exactly. Well, those pictures in the box we saw this afternoon, Stella said they'd travelled through the air. So if pictures can do that, why shouldn't wishes?'

'It's not exactly scientific,' said Pip dubiously.

'*Wishes* aren't scientific,' Ellie told him. '*You* never believed in them till we met the Sammyadd.'

'So I vote that we all shut our eyes and wish hard. Think of the Sammyadd, and wish!'

'I suppose we could try . . . it's nearly sunset now, anyway,' said Ellie.

'I'll think of my thimble *and* the Sammyadd,' Lucy said.

'I s'pose it'd be a kind of experiment,' said Pip reluctantly.

'Right. So altogether, when I say go. And no one to open its eyes till I say so. Think of the Sammyadd and *wish*, wish like one o'clock! Ready, steady – go!'

At the word all four closed their eyes tight and thought of that curious and ancient beast with its sandy fur and whiskers, and wished harder than they'd ever wished in their lives before. They wished to be back in their own time, where Mother and Father and the twins were, and they even wished to see Aunt Marchmont again, because when you are lost, any familiar face is welcome, even one you are not usually glad to see. They wished so hard that they even feared that they might burst, as they feared the Psammead might when it blew itself up to wish.

If only they had known it, they need not have troubled. The Psammead was a beast of its word, and when it said that wishes wore off at sunset, that is exactly what they did, and it made not a jot of difference which sunset it was. It so happened that while the children had their eyes squeezed tight shut, the sun dropped behind the rim of the hill beyond the garden, and they went whirling back through time as smoothly and easily as they had travelled forward that morning.

'Right!' said George. He cleared his throat. 'Now open them!'

They peered at one another anxiously in the dusty dimness.

'I don't feel any different.' said Lucy wanly.

Then, welcome as a passing ship to a marooned sailor, a familiar voice was heard far off in the dusky distance.

'Master George! Miss Ellie!'

'Bessie!' George seized the handle of the door. 'It's open!'

And the children rushed out into the twilit garden, laughing and crying at the same time, and they raced to Bessie and hugged her and pranced about her till they almost knocked her off her feet.

'What's all this?' cried the startled Bessie, who had been looking out for the children since one o'clock, and calling them this past two hours.

'Oh Bessie, darling ducky Bessie!'

'Oh, we do love you!'

'Is it really you?'

The children's faces were so shining, and their hugs so heartfelt, that Bessie's ill temper was quite dissolved. It is hard to be cross with people when they are laughing and so glad to see you.

'But where you *been?*' she cried.

A silence fell.

'Er – we were – lost.'

'Sort of.'

'Then don't you go wandering off again where you can get lost, you 'ear me?'

'We'll never go *there* again!' said Lucy with feeling.

So they all went indoors and supper was waiting with soup, dripping toast and stewed fruit. The kitchen was snug and cosy in the lamplight, and the boys thought of the cold white cabinets and humming machines, and even Pip was glad to be still in 1908.

'I'm still as cross with you as can be,' Bessie told them, ladling out the soup. 'Anywhere, you could've been!'

'We were!' muttered Pip, but George frowned.

'We were only round the garden and in the summerhouse most of the time,' Ellie said.

'Then why didn't you 'ear me screeching for you? And I'd looked in that summer'ouse, not half an hour since! Could've knocked me over with a feather when you all come tumbling out!'

'Er – is Aunt Marchmont back?' asked George hastily.

'Yes she is. Not that *she* cares if kiddies is lost and can't be found and it getting dark and folks shooting off guns. "But Betty," she says – and if she can't learn to call me Bessie I shall scream, I swear I shall – "but Betty, what about my wool?"'

The children stared at one another, horrorstruck. In all the terror and excitement of being in the future, they had clear forgotten Aunt Marchmont's green and blue wool. Their Golden Deed had turned to Lead.

'Wool, I ask you,' went on Bessie scornfully. 'As if wool wouldn't wait!'

She stopped, struck by the unusual silence, and saw their stricken faces.

'You've never forgot it!'

'I'm – I'm afraid we have,' said Ellie, her eyes lowered. No one could have been sorrier than she. The Golden Deeds and the Quest had been her idea, and the fate of Dawkins and little Lil depended on them.

'Then it's the last straw, I declare!' said Bessie. 'I never did know such harum scarums.'

'We'll go back tomorrow, first thing,' said George.

'Oh no you won't! she told him. 'Leastways, I might let one of you go. The rest of you'll stop 'ere where I can keep an eye.'

'Oh no!' the children groaned, and pulled faces of despair at one another.

'You go not one step further than the end of the lane.'

The sand-pit was beyond the lane, and the Psammead. The children, who had never before even dreamed that their every wish might be granted, had already come to expect a wish a day.

At bedtime, rather quaking in their shoes, the children tapped on the door of their aunt's room. To George and Pip, at least, it was a queer feeling to see it again, back to its usual self. Aunt Marchmont was sewing as if her life depended on it.

'Goodnight, Aunt Marchmont.'

'We hope you enjoyed your visit.'

'Your sewing is simply beautiful.'

'It's really not half bad – for sewing.'

'Do you *always* carry on like this?' she interrupted, fixing them with a hard gaze. 'You sound like tinkers trying to sell a patent medicine. Plain "Goodnight, Aunt Marchmont," will do.'

'Goodnight, Aunt Marchmont,' they chorussed obediently.

'"Buttering up" is what it is called, I believe,' she went on. 'Now why should I require buttering up, I wonder?'

George, who could blush, blushed. The others merely felt as if they were blushing, but without actually turning a bright tomato red.

'Could it be that you have forgotten the wool I sent you for?'

'We're dreadfully sorry, Aunt Marchmont,' Ellie said, and this was not buttering up, but plain truthfulness.

'We did go back, but the shop had vanished,' said Lucy.

Luckily Aunt Marchmont appeared not to have heard this.

'Do you know,' said Aunt Marchmont thoughtfully, 'I believe I shall survive the night without wool.'

'We'll get it first thing in the morning, honour bright,' Pip said.

'And so I forgive you,' said Aunt Marchmont surprisingly. 'And in future, perhaps you'll come straight to the point, without all this "buttering up".'

'Yes, Aunt Marchmont,' in a meek chorus.

'Goodnight, then.'

'Goodnight, Aunt Marchmont.'

'Remind me again of your names.'

'George.'

'Ellen.'

'Phillip.'

'Lucy.'

'I daresay I shall remember them, eventually.'

'Er – and Bessie's name's Bessie,' Lucy said timidly. But Aunt Marchmont had gone back to her sewing.

As the girls were getting ready for bed Lucy said, 'I don't think Aunt Marchmont's quite such a gorgon as we thought. Or p'raps her heart of stone's already melting with our winning ways.'

'Just unused to the ways of children,' Ellie said. 'Listen – I've just remembered! Stella said her name was Dawkins. There were Dawkins living here!'

'Not *were* – will be,' Lucy corrected her. 'But how, I wonder – how could they possibly? Oh – here's my darling thimble! Thank you, thimble!'

Ellie opened her mouth to say that their getting back to their own time was almost certainly nothing to do with a Christmas cracker thimble, but wisely closed it again. When you are eleven and nearly twelve you have still not entirely forgotten how it feels to be eight. Instead, she said 'It's a sign, and omen! Our Quest will succeed!'

In the boys' room, George was saying, 'That was a day and a half, Pipsqueak – I'm surprised it hasn't turned our hair grey. And I say, that was a rum go, it turning out that girl was called Dawkins.'

Pip was not really listening.

'I tell you what I think,' he said, 'I think we should ask Bessie if we can't have supper at sunset. Otherwise we shall keep getting into all sorts of rows.

'Not such a dusty notion,' agreed George. 'And listen, that parrot . . .' he gazed at that uncommunicative bird, hunched on his perch and giving not the least sign that he was the subject of discussion. 'Tell you what, old bird, we saw your spitting double today!'

The parrot merely flickered his hooded eyes. George dropped the cover over the cage.

'We were jolly lucky it turned out to be *our* sunset in the summer-house,' Pip said.

'This time and future business is fearfully muddling. *Was* it the future, really, d'you think? Or could it've been a kind of dream?'

'I've told you, you can't have people having the same dream at the same time – it's not scientific.'

'Nor's the Sammyadd!' retorted George, who occasionally became sick of his younger brother's lordly pronouncements. 'So much for science!'

There was no answer to this that Pip could conveniently think of, and so he got into bed and pulled up the blankets and George, for once, had the last word.

Next morning George won the argument about who should go back to the village to fetch the wool. The girls declared their intention of visiting little Lil, as they had promised, and Pip said that he would put up the croquet hoops.

No sooner had George set off down the drive when the rest, about to scatter on their own business, heard a loud shout.

''Ere! You!'

They turned to see Dobbs advancing, and holding aloft a delphinium as if it were a flag.

'Which one of you's done this?' he demanded.

'Not me!' said all three promptly.

'Snapped clean off!'

'It could have done it of its own accord,' suggested Ellie.

'Or the wind or rain,' added Pip.

'Don't give me no lip!' growled Dobbs. 'Warned yer off my flowerbeds, yer little 'eathens. We'll see what Miss Marchmont's got to say about this!'

He tramped off, delphinium waving.

'Bad tempered old curmudgeon!' said Lucy, reasonably enough. Delphiniums *do* sometimes snap off in the course of nature, and are not necessarily the victims of thoughtless children. Dobbs, as gardener, should have known this.

'Oh dear,' sighed Ellie, watching him go. '*That* won't count as a Golden Deed . . .'

George was relieved to see the village back to its ordinary sleepy self, and the old woman still in the shop. He purchased the wool and made back home at a leisurely pace. Just where the lane turned off he met Dawkins, gun under his arm and dog at his heels. They exchanged greetings, and George felt bound to warn Dawkins that the aunt was at home. It was no earthly good, he reasoned, their doing Golden Deeds until they were blue in the face, if Dawkins carried on poaching.

'Er – the aunt's about,' he said.

Dawkins grinned.

'Not where I'm a going,' he replied. 'She don't own England, you know. They reckons there's rabbits in that there sand-pit, and if there is, Tiger'll dig 'em out!'

'In – in the sand-pit?' repeated George faintly. 'Oh – I don't think there are, Mr Dawkins. We've been playing there and we haven't seen any, not a single one!'

'Best rabbiter in England, that dog is,' said Dawkins, as if he had not heard.

George imagined the fearsome Tiger down at the sand-pit, and the poor Psammead snoozing peacefully in its burrow and Dawkins waiting, gun cocked.

'Excuse me – just remembered – got to go!' and he started to run, not up the lane but towards the sand-pit. He was under strict orders to go straight to the village and back, but he did not think even Bessie would wish to see the demise of the last of the Psammeads.

He dropped breathlessly to his knees by the heap of stones.

'Sammyadd, Sammyadd!' he called urgently. There was no response. The sand lay bare and quiet, and all the while Dawkins was advancing with dog and gun.

'Oh Sammyadd, I *wish* you'd come out, please!'

The wish was heard and granted. The sand spurted and next minute there was the Psammead.

'Good morning,' it said. 'Where are the rest of you?'

'Oh Sammyadd, you've got to get out of here! There's a man coming and he thinks you're a rabbit and he's got a gun and this terrible dog!'

'Rabbit?' repeated the Psammead, hugely affronted. 'Takes *me* for a *rabbit?*'

'Yes. And oh please do be quick – run!'

'I never run,' replied the Psammead grandly. It sat there preening its whiskers and cool as a cucumber, without the least idea of the danger it was in.

'You must, you must!'

'Never,' it said.

'Come with me, then!' pleaded George, and he stretched out a hand, but the Psammead drew itself up and snapped 'Get away from me, you rude boy!'

'But you don't understand – '

'If you come near me I'll bite! I can, you know!'

But George was desperate. He drew a deep breath, grasped hold of the Psammead's furry form, thrust it under his jacket, and ran.

'Let go! You let me go!'

He heard its furious, muffled voice and felt it squirming. He met Dawkins almost head on, and the dog growled and began to run after him, snapping at his heels and barking furiously.

'Oh lor, he's got its scent!'

But most fortunately for George and the Psammead Dawkins called his dog off. 'Tiger! Here, sir! heel!'

The dog gave a final bark and went back to its master, but George kept running. He did not even stop as he passed the cottage where he could see his sisters with little Lil, he did not stop until he reached the summer-house. He dived through the open door, saw a hamper, lifted the lid and thrust the Psammead inside. Then he slammed down the lid and stood panting, filled with a huge relief that his own daring act had saved the last of the Psammeads.

That beast was far from grateful to its deliverer. It scrabbled and fought to get out till the hamper fairly rocked.

'You let me out, you let me out!'

'I can't, I daren't!'

Then Ellie and Lucy appeared, also breathless.

'What's happening?'

'The Sammyadd! It's in there!' he jerked his head towards the basket. 'And it's jolly lucky to be alive – the beastly thing threatened to bite me!'

'I can hear you,' came the Psammead's voice. 'Don't think because I can't see you I can't hear you!'

'It *is* in there!' gasped Lucy.

'Dawkins thought it was a rabbit and was going after it with his gun and that brute of a dog!'

'I don't like it in here.' The Psammead's tone had changed now to a plaintive whine. 'There's no sand. I shall die without sand.'

'Oh, you won't really, will you?' cried Ellie, dismayed.

'I'm a *Sand*-Fairy. Oh, oh, it's too cruel!'

'Oh, don't die, don't die!' cried Lucy.

'Here!' Ellie snatched up a couple of buckets and thrust them into George's hands. 'Fetch it some sand, quick!'

George hesitated, nodded, and ran off again through the trees. Lucy patted the hamper as if it were a dog.

'There, there,' she said soothingly. 'You'll soon be better. Oh, I've always wanted a pet!'

'Pet? The last of the Psammeads a *pet*?'

It had evidently quickly been restored to health by the promise of sand.

Ellie frowned at Lucy.

'We are honoured to have you as our guest, oh mighty Sammyadd,' she said. 'We – er – we salute you!'

There was a pause.

'That's better!' came the voice from the hamper. 'Now, open the lid, do!'

Ellie and Lucy exchanged uneasy glances. If they obeyed, for all they knew the Psammead would jump out and go scuttling back to the sand-pit, at the mercy of Dawkins and his dog and gun. The thought of it ending up in the cooking pot, like any common rabbit, was too awful to contemplate.

'If we do, will you promise not to run away?' asked Ellie.

'I never run. When have you ever seen me so much as stir, let alone run?'

'Well – never,' she admitted.

'Precisely. I have spent thousands of years, thousands and thousands, just – sitting. And I shall stay here sitting till that rude, violent boy takes me back where I belong. It is a pity more people don't spend their lives just sitting. There'd be a lot less muddle and fuss.'

The girls exchanged glances again and nodded. Ellie lifted the lid of the hamper.

'There!'

They gazed down and saw that the Psammead was presently sitting on a heap of clothes for dressing up. It looked so forlorn and out of place away from its own kingdom of the sand-pit that they felt a pang.

'Things have come to a pretty pass,' it said. 'The last of the Psammeads in an old basket! It's not fitting, no it's not.'

'We know,' agreed Ellie, 'but it's direst need.'

'And without sand!'

'It's coming, dear Sammyadd, George won't be long.'

'It's to be hoped it comes in time to save me!' The Psammead heaved several deep sighs, and the girls watched in alarm, fearful that these might be its last gasps.

'There – that's done – now for the mallets and – ?' Pip, who had rushed in without their noticing his coming, stopped dead. He stared.

'Jiminy! Crikey! What the – ?'

'If people are going to stare in that rude manner I'll have the lid shut again, if you please,' said the Psammead.

'Are you coming to live with us?'

'It's hiding from Dawkins – he's down at the sand-pit with his gun!'

'I never hide,' said the Psammead loftily. 'As a matter of fact, I was itnapped.'

'Itnapped?' Pip echoed.

'It means kidnapped,' Lucy whispered, but she might as well have shouted. Those bat's ears could hear the rustle of moths' wings, let alone a human whisper.

'*It*napped!' it repeated loudly. 'Kid indeed!'

'James! Eleanor!' A voice was calling from quite nearby.

'Help – quick!' gasped Ellie, and unceremoniously slammed down the lid.

'Ah, there you are!'

Aunt Marchmont appeared at the door of the summerhouse. She looked around it, as if half recognising it, and sighed.

'Oh, the hours I spent in here . . .' she murmured.

'You?' said Lucy. 'Those buckets and spades and things – they're yours?'

'Oh – there's my bow and arrow and – the old hampers – and my dressing-up clothes!'

She moved towards the hamper containing the Psammead, but Ellie and Lucy hastily arranged themselves so as to block her way.

'I don't think there's anything much in there now,' said Ellie.

'The moths have eaten them,' added Lucy helpfully.

Aunt Marchmont lifted the lid of the other hamper and lifted redskins' headgear and brigands' masks and actually stroked them, as if they were faithful pets.

'You have been putting in the croquet hoops, I see, Felix,' she said.

'Philip, actually. Yes, I hope you don't mind, Aunt Marchmont.'

'The memories!' she sighed again. 'I was sent away from here, you know, when I was nine years old. They rented out the house.'

'How sad!' said Ellie.

'I sometimes feel I never had a childhood at all.'

The children simply did not know what to say.

'Yet I was happy here, that I do remember. I think I lived in a world of – make believe.'

Still they watched her, partly for fear that she might decide to open the other hamper, and partly because they realised that she was talking to herself, rather than to them.

'Do you know, I really wish I could remember how it felt to be a child!'

In the silence that followed there came a faint, but unmistakable sound from the hamper behind Ellie and Lucy. The Psammead was blowing itself up, not to grant any wish of theirs, but Aunt Marchmont's.

'Oh no!' gasped Ellie.

'What is that strange sound?'

Aunt Marchmont peered into the dim recesses of the summerhouse. Then there came that final, triumphant gasp that meant a wish had been successfully granted. The children, awestruck at what the consequences might be, gazed in horror at their aunt. Would she shrink under their very eyes, like Alice in Wonderland when she drank from the little bottle? If so, Pip thought, he might have to abandon his scientific career altogether – it was already becoming rather ragged at the edges.

But Aunt Marchmont did not shrink. (Pip, in an effort to put some kind of reasonableness into things, later pointed out that she had not wished to *be* a child, only to remember how it felt.) But Aunt Marchmont did change under their very eyes. It was the strangest thing. Her whole face seemed to dissolve and melt, and her usually stern expression changed into one of sheer impishness and glee. She looked, as George said later, as if she were ready for anything. She grinned. The shock was so great that the children could not for the life of them grin back.

'I'm famished!' she announced. 'Anyone got a bikky?'

Dumbly Pip produced one from his pocket and she snatched and crunched it happily. Still the children stared. Under that dull black bombazine and that wrinkled face, could there really be a child? And if so – how old?

'I'm sick of that beastly sewing,' she said. 'Stitch stitch stitch from morning till night!'

'It – it is rather boring,' ventured Ellie nervously. 'Er – do you feel quite well, Aunt Marchmont?'

Her aunt stared, then burst into laughter.

'Aunt – ? Oooh, that's rich – playing Happy Families, are we? Soppy game – let's play something exciting!'

She reached out, picked up a croquet mallet and twirled it so wildly that

'Crikey!' said Pip, opening the door, 'it's winter in there!'

He drew a deep breath, grasped hold of the Psammead's furry form,
thrust it under his jacket, and ran.

the children jumped back and nearly tipped over the hidden Psammead's basket.

'Let's have a whack! Come on!'

At this moment George arrived back, staggering under the weight of two buckets of sand.

'Got it!' he puffed. 'Is it – oh!'

George, who could not possibly know that Aunt Marchmont had been translated, gasped with horror. The others, who could not possibly tell him what had happened in his absence, could try to convey it only by their expressions. The grimaces and gestures of his brother and sisters were clearly trying to tell him something, but he could not for the life of him tell what. He saw with relief that the lid of the hamper was down. The secret of the Psammead was so far safe, he guessed.

'Er – good morning, Aunt Marchmont,' he said politely.

Aunt Marchmont shrieked again with laughter.

'Oh Georgy Porgy, you are a card!'

George gaped at her, then at the others, shaking heads and grimacing. The whole pack of them had gone stark, staring mad, he decided. He dropped the buckets.

'What's the sand for, Georgy Porgy?'

George opened and shut his mouth, but nothing came out.

'Going to make sandy-wandy pies, diddums?'

All at once she seemed to be looking at something beyond him, and her face changed.

'Look out! Grown-up!'

Advancing towards the summerhouse, basket on arm, was Bessie. The children groaned.

Chapter IX

AN ACCIDENTAL WISH

Aunt Marchmont scrambled past the four children into the farthest recesses of the summerhouse, where there lay a great heap of netting. She burrowed her way into it, pulling its folds over her in a shower of dust.

'Mum's the word!' they heard her muffled voice.

'Master Pip! Miss Ellie!'

The children, with one accord, moved out of the summerhouse so fast that they almost jammed in the doorway.

'Oh, Master George, you're back. Got that wool, 'ave you?'

George nodded. From behind them they heard 'Bother wool! Bother beastly sewing!'

Pip, fearful that Bessie might hear, began loudly and tunelessly to sing *John Brown's Body*, and Ellie, anxious as always to help, struck up *London's Burning*.

Bessie looked at them rather oddly, and said, 'Now you all just be'ave while I nips down the lane for a minute.'

'Are you going to the village? You can be as long as you like, we'll be good as gold, honour bright!'

'No, I ain't. There's a little gel in that cottage, Cook says, as poorly as can be, and 'ardly a bite to eat.'

'Little Lil!' exclaimed Lucy.

'And I can't go letting 'elpless kiddies starve and nor would your Ma want me to, never mind what 'er royal 'ighness says!'

They winced at the knowledge that this reference was being overheard by its subject, and Pip sang the louder, in the vain hope of drowning it.

'Singing is 'armless enough,' she remarked, 'as long as it's in *toon*,' and she went off, bearing her covered basket of goodies for little Lil.

'Phew!' Pip stopped singing as abruptly as he had started.

'That was a shaver!'

'What's going *on*?' demanded George.

'Ssshh!' hissed the others in unison, looking meaningly at the summerhouse.

'What's up?' he whispered. 'Has she gone off her chump?'

'She wished,' Ellie whispered back.

'Has she gone?' demanded Aunt Marchmont's voice, still well and truly muffled by the netting.

'Gone!' called Ellie. Then 'Humour her!' she hissed to George.

'And don't call her Aunt Marchmont!' whispered Pip.

George, bewildered, shook his head. As eldest, he could not help feeling that if he had stopped behind he could have prevented from happening whatever it was that *had* happened in his absence. (This is what is known as being wise after the event.)

'Cor, I'm stifled in here!'

The figure of Aunt Marchmont appeared, still shaking itself free from the toils of netting. Her face was grimed and streaked with dust, her hair awry and cobwebby.

'Oh crikey!' George muttered under his breath. 'She *has* gone off her chump!'

'Grown-ups should be seen and not heard!' pronounced Aunt Marchmont, and giggled. 'And they should wash their hands and stand up straight and mind their manners!'

The others could not help giggling too. The child inside their aunt would at some stage in its growing up change its mind about all that, as they knew to their cost.

'Now, who's for a whack?' She seized again the dropped croquet mallet.

'I'm game!' Pip picked up another. 'Come on, everyone!'

Ellie and Lucy followed suit, but George said, 'In a sec!' and looked meaningfully towards the Psammead's basket. He watched the others go, then went to the hamper.

'Sammyadd!'

'Ooooh, oooh, I'm dying! Sand, sand!'

'I've got it!' George lifted the lid and met the reproachful eyes of the Psammead, hunched miserably in one corner.

'You've nearly done for me!' it said faintly. 'Sand, sand . . .'

George siezed one bucket and tipped its contents into the hamper. The Psammead stirred and brightened. In went the other bucketful. The Psammead made burrowing movements with its monkey arms and the sand flew.

'Steady on! You'll chuck it all out!' George warned.

'There's not enough to burrow – how shall I ever get to sleep if I can't go to sand?'

'We'll get some more,' George promised. 'But – Sammyadd, what's been going off?'

'Going off?' repeated the Psammead. 'What an inelegant turn of phrase! The English language is not what it was, I fear.'

'Did someone wish? Did Aunt Marchmont?'

'Certainly she did, and very inconsiderate too!' said the Psammead. 'You can't think what it cost to make that ridiculous wish.'

'But what – what did she wish?'

'She wished she could remember how it feels to be a child. So now she does, and she's as silly as the rest of you.'

'Phew!' George whistled softly. All now became clear. He looked through the open door and saw his aunt, her skirts tucked right up, wielding her mallet and cracking the ball like one o'clock.

'You mean you can give anyone wishes – not just us?'

'Of course. Why else do you think I live in a sand-pit, where nobody ever goes? I'd be giving wishes from morning till night and worn to a frazzle.'

'There's someone there now, all right. Dawkins and that dog – digging like fury.'

George was rather hoping for some gratitude from the Psammead for his daring rescue.

'Pooh!' said the Psammead contemptuously. 'Dog! Have you ever met a Pterodactyl?'

'Er – no,' admitted George.

'Or a Brontosaurus?'

George shook his head.

'Then don't talk to me about dogs!' it snapped. 'Now kindly shut my lid. I'm tired of talking to nincompoops!'

Obediently George closed the lid, gave it a comforting pat, murmured 'Sweet dreams, old thing!' and went out to join the others.

'Here's Georgy Porgy!' shrieked Aunt Marchmont. 'Where's your mallet?'

'You can have mine,' offered Ellie, and passed it to him.

'Connie's ever so good at it,' she said meaningly.

'C- C- ?' spluttered George.

'Look out!' yelled Aunt Marchmont, and a ball came straight towards him.

'You shouldn't do that, Connie,' said Lucy reprovingly. 'You might have hurt him.'

'Hurt, fiddlesticks!' said that incorrigible lady. She let out another shriek. 'Here's that beastly grown-up again!'

They all turned and saw, horrorstruck, Bessie advancing fast with her empty basket.

'Oh help!' said Pip faintly. 'Now what?'

'Hide, Connie!' urged Lucy. Inside her aunt might be a child, but to all outward appearances she was still the same stiff and starchy Miss Marchmont — except that now her skirts were hitched up in a very unladylike way, her hair tumbling everywhere, her face smutty, and heaven only knew what she might come out with. Already Lucy thought she could see a look of shock and disbelief on Bessie's face.

'Hide!' she urged again. 'She's bound to notice you!'

'Pooh!' responded Aunt Marchmont defiantly, whirling her mallet.

Lucy had an inspiration. She was rather more used to making wishes than the others, as proud possessor of a magic thimble. She knew that only a wish could save them now.

'Oh, I *wish* she wouldn't notice you!'

The Psammead was deep in its hamper inside the summerhouse, and so none of them heard the laborious huffing and puffing that went into the granting of that wish. And George, Pip and Ellie had not even heard the wish being made, not having ears like bats' themselves. They waited, transfixed, to see what Bessie would say and do, confronted by the transmogrified Aunt Marchmont. The look of slight puzzlement on her face as she approached did not seem to fit the case at all.

'That's funny!' they heard her mutter.

'W-what is, Bessie?' asked Ellie.

'I could've — I could've swore I saw your aunt with you.' She shook her head, as if to clear it. 'And with 'er skirts 'itched right up over 'er knees!'

'B-but –' George, bewildered, looked from Bessie to his aunt and back again.

'Better get your eyes tested!' said Aunt Marchmont rudely.

The children cringed. But only Lucy was not surprised by the fact that Bessie seemed not even to hear this.

'Oh thank you, Sammyadd,' she whispered.

'I'll 'ave to get me eyes looked at,' Bessie went on. She laughed. 'The very idea – 'er, playing croquet!'

Thwack! A ball came straight at her, struck by Aunt Marchmont's mallet.

''Oo did that?' she demanded.

'Not me!' chorussed the children as one. Then, as the look of puzzlement came over her face again, 'I did!' volunteered Pip nobly, and the others cast him grateful glances.

'I might 'ave known, Master Pip,' she said reprovingly. 'One of your scientific speriments, I s'pose!'

'Come *on*!' demanded Aunt Marchmont. 'Are we playing or not?'

'I'd best be getting back,' Bessie said. 'Dinner in ten minutes, mind. Cook's day off, so it's cold. But your aunt's 'ere, remember, so you come in and get yourselves tidied first.'

She went off, and the children breathed huge sighs of relief.

'She didn't see her!' exclaimed George.

'Or hear,' added Pip.

'That's because I wished,' announced Lucy proudly. 'I saved the day!'

The rest looked at her in amazement. She was, after all, younger than any of them, and they would not, in all honesty, have thought she had it in her.

'Oh, you clever little thing!' Ellie hugged her, and Lucy beamed.

'Well done, Luce!' said George generously, and 'You certainly saved our bacon,' admitted Pip.

Lucy, who was used to having her wishes treated with contempt, beamed the more. This wish, unlike previous ones, had been addressed not to a magic silver thimble, but to the last of the Psammeads, and it had worked.

Aunt Marchmont had been looking from one to the other of them during this exchange with extreme bafflement.

'I'm sick of this!' she announced, and flung down her mallet. 'Rude thing – she never even spoke to me. But did she say something about grub?'

'Well. yes,' admitted George. 'But you see, she doesn't know about you.'

'Got eyes in her head, hasn't she?'

The children exchanged anguished glances. However were they to explain that Bessie could not see her at all, without telling about the Psammead?

'Er – excuse us a sec, er – Connie,' George said. 'We need to talk about something.'

'You talk,' retorted Connie. 'I'm going to find a tree to climb!'

She ran off, and at once the children went into a huddle.

'How are we to tell her Bessie can't see her?'

'Or hear her?'

'We *can't* tell about the Sammyadd.'

'Don't forget she's a grown-up, really – and a pretty waxy one, at that!'

'She might stop us going to the sand-pit, once she's back to being Aunt Marchmont.'

'Or worse!' said George in sepulchral tones.

'*I* know!' cried Lucy. 'Let's tell her we wished it on my magic silver thimble!'

As a rule the others would have dismissed this ridiculous suggestion out of hand. Everyone knows that Christmas cracker thimbles cannot give wishes. On the other hand Aunt Marchmont – or Connie – did not know that the thimble came out of a cracker.

'Would she swallow it, d'you think?'

'Would she swallow the *Sammyadd*, even if we told her? I know jolly well *I* wouldn't have, if anyone had told me,' said Pip.

'True . . .' murmured George. 'All right – the thimble.'

'After all, she'll soon find out that Bessie can't see or hear her.' said Ellie.

'Thanks to me,' said Lucy.

'So she'll have to believe it!' concluded Ellie triumphantly.

'Right! Now, where's she gone?'

They looked all about them but could see no sign of her.

'Yooee! Yooee!'

They looked in the direction of the voice and saw Aunt Marchmont perched in a nearby tree like some great, improbable bird. She waved wildly and the children waved rather feebly back.

'Thought you said she spent her whole childhood sewing samplers,' Pip said.

'She's a real sport!' said George admiringly.

The children coaxed the new born Connie out of the tree and they set off to the house for dinner, not without some trepidation. They tried to explain about Lucy's magic thimble, and Bessie not being able to notice Connie.

'Magic thimble?' she repeated, staring at that object as it lay winking in Lucy's palm. 'Magic, my elbow!'

'It *is* then!' said Lucy, stung. 'Why else do you think Bessie couldn't see or hear you?'

'Hmmm . . . true . . .' then, without warning, she stretched forward and snatched the thimble. Lucy shrieked and all three raced in pursuit of Aunt Marchmont to the house. She ran straight past Bessie who had come to the door to look for them, and disappeared.

'Come along, quick – you'll only aggravate your aunt!' Bessie scolded.

They ran upstairs and went through the motions of washing and tidying themselves, though knew very well there would be no Aunt Marchmont to inspect them on this occasion.

They were in the dining room and sitting down at the table just as the clock in the hall struck one. They sat, hands folded primly in their laps, not betraying for one moment that they knew beyond a shadow of a doubt there would be no Aunt Marchmont.

'Not like 'er to be late,' said Bessie. 'Proper stickler, she is.' No one spoke. 'I'd best go and tap on 'er door.'
She went out.

'Where *is* she?' Lucy whispered. 'She's got my thimble!'

'She'll turn up for grub, never fear,' said Pip (who, like most of us, usually judged others by himself).

Bessie came back in.

'Not there,' she said, puzzled. 'I don't rightly know what we should do . . .'

'I think we should begin,' said George. 'You said yourself she likes meals on time.'

'That's true . . .' she murmured. 'Go on, then, you'd best begin. You 'elp yourselves and I'll get this pork pie cut.'

They set to with a will, and perhaps it was the clatter of knives and forks that brought Aunt Marchmont in and straight to the table. She had torn her dress in the tree, was now wearing a large, feathered headdress and the rest of her person was so downright mucky that Aunt Marchmont would certainly have sent her straight upstairs to bath and change her clothes. But this *was* Aunt Marchmont.

The children stared at her in horror. She had certainly been in the summerhouse to fetch that headdress and they could only hope that she had not made any more wishes in the Psammead's hearing. Bessie was mercifully too busily engaged in dishing out the food to notice their expressions.

'I do think it's funny, 'er not being 'ere,' she said again.

'Oh ripping – porky pies!' cried Aunt Marchmont, and picked a piece from almost under Bessie's nose. Bessie, startled, stopped carving, and the children held their breath. But she merely shook her head, and carried on.

'That poor little gel at the cottage, she's all skin and bone,' she said. 'I shall take 'er a piece of this.'

'If there's any left!' spluttered Aunt Marchmont, her mouth cramful, and already stretching out for another slice.

'And 'er Pa – as fine upstanding a fellow as ever I see,' continued Bessie. 'As if any father wouldn't want to see 'is poor child fed!'

'I know,' agreed Ellie. 'We think it's a shame.'

'And so it is. 'Eart of stone, she must 'ave!'

This was so exactly the children's own opinion of the case that they were quite startled at hearing it put into words by their nurse. Bessie lowered her voice.

'If Cook's to be believed, it's them Dobbses as put the missis against 'im! Miss Marchmont'd never 'ave noticed a few rabbits, she says. It was them Dobbses as told on 'im!'

'I'm not surprised,' said George.

'But at least *she's* gone,' said Ellie, 'thanks to my – ' and here she had to stop herself suddenly, because she had been going to say 'twin' as you will have guessed. Bessie knew nothing of the Figment, nor would she ever. She knew nothing, either, of the existence of Connie, who all the time was making darting snatches at the food and gobbling it up like any savage.

'It's a pity 'er old man don't go after 'er,' said Bessie darkly. 'Cross-grained old badger!'

The children giggled.

'Now . . . where's that trifle Cook left . . .?' She went to the side-board, stopped and stared. 'Whatever . . .? Ooo's . . .? Now which of you's done this – and where's my spoon?'

Aunt Marchmont was at that very moment licking that very spoon, having made a thorough attack upon the trifle. She then, with a wink at the gasping children, dropped that spoon back into the dish behind Bessie's back.

'Er . . . what spoon, Bessie?' enquired Pip innocently.

'Why, the one as I'd left . . .' her voice tailed off. '*This* one!' she cried, seizing it. 'But it . . . ooh, that's twice today I've thought I've seen things that I ain't!'

'Perhaps you've just had a funny turn,' suggested Ellie, who knew that servants suffered a good deal from this mysterious complaint.

'Oooh, I dunno . . . I just 'ope I'm not going to be liable to it, that's all!'

The children, who were genuinely fond of Bessie, began to think that Connie was going too far with her tricks. Each one of them, when it saw its chance, shook its head at her and frowned.

'It's no use your shaking your heads at me!' she told them. '*You* might be milksops!' and she ran forward and tugged hard at one of Bessie's apron strings, and Bessie clapped a hand behind her and let out a long, piercing shriek . . .

After dinner Bessie announced her intention of going to have a lie down.

'My nerves is all to pieces,' she said.

'Don't worry, Bessie, it'll wear off,' George told her. 'And – er – we've decided we don't want our supper till sunset, from now on.'

'Till *when*? What sort of time's that for a decent body – sunset?'

'It's just a phase we're going through,' explained Ellie.

'A sort of scientific experiment.'

'Oh please, Bessie!'

'Oh, go on, then,' she said. 'Now, you be quiet, mind. There's no telling where that aunt of yours might be.'

The children, of course, knew very well where their aunt was, and once they were safely out of doors reproached her for tormenting Bessie.

'She's not just any old grown-up, you know,' George told her. 'She's a real brick.'

'Half one, anyway,' said Pip.

'She's better than *my* nurse!' Aunt Marchmont said. 'Norah, she's called. Mean old thing. Stitch stitch stitch from morning till night!'

'Do you work samplers, then?' enquired Ellie, already knowing the answer.

'Dozens of 'em. Finished one only yesterday, *and* framed it. Oh lor, if only she knew!'

She threw herself on the ground and rolled in uncontrollable mirth.

'What?' they demanded. 'Knew what?'

'On the back!' she spluttered. 'I got some fine thread, and I sewed something else on the back!'

'But what?'

'I sewed . . .' giggle giggle, 'I sewed a pink pig with a curly tail, and I sewed "Norah's a cross-eyed piggywiggy!"'

'*Is* she cross-eyed?' asked Lucy with interest.

'And just think – it'll be there for ever and ever! And they've hung it in the drawing room and they don't even know!'

She stuffed the hem of her frock into her mouth and rolled until her bloomers showed. Then she sat up abruptly and said, 'Wish you were always here. I get sick of being on my own with only Norah and that horrible governess. *Now* what shall we do? I know. Let's go down to that sand-pit!'

'We can't,' said Ellie promptly.

'Out of bounds today,' George explained.

'Why d'you want to go, anyway?' asked Pip, who wondered if the aunt had discovered the Psammead herself during her childhood.

'Build castles of course, idiot!' she told him. 'Anyway, it's sort of doomy and spooky.'

'Spooky?'

'You know – haunted.'

'P'raps a fairy lives there?' suggested Pip slyly.

'Fairy? Who believes in fairies?' she said scornfully, and jumped onto the swing and worked it furiously, standing up.

The rest exchanged glances and wisely held their peace. They did not know how far they could trust this childhood version of their aunt, nor what she might be able to remember after sunset.

'Right, then – let's go to the village!' Aunt Marchmont leapt off the swing and was off through the trees.

Chapter X

THE PLOT THICKENS

'After her!' ordered George.

'But Bessie said we weren't to go out!' cried Ellie.

'We can't let her out on her own like this,' George pointed out. 'She might *act* like a child, but she still looks the same.'

'And people might think she's gone mad, and then she'll be locked up,' added Pip.

'Oh don't!' shrieked Lucy.

'Come on!' George set off after the fast vanishing figure of their aunt, and the rest followed. They were caught between the devil and the deep blue sea – or on the horns of a dilemma. (This means you have no real choice, that you are in the wrong, whatever you do. These children did not usually disobey their nurse, except in small matters. They had not even considered going against her orders to visit the Psammead. But if their aunt was going to play madcap Connie in the village, while looking like ordinary, grown up Aunt Marchmont, they knew they must be there to protect her. If she were certified insane and locked away, it would certainly be their fault.)

They did not catch her up till she had reached the village. Young Aunt

Marchmont was a surprisingly fast runner. George, having the longest legs, was there first.

'Come on, Connie,' he panted, 'be a sport! Come back with us. We'll get into all sorts of a row if we're caught!'

'Pooh!' she returned. 'And anyway, no one told *me* not to go out!' – which was perfectly true.

'Oh do come back home,' begged Ellie. 'We'll play bandits and you can be the robber king!'

'We'll play *anything*!' cried Lucy. 'But do come away before you get locked up!'

'Locked up? Fiddlesticks! I'm after some tuck! Got sixpence – look! Come on!'

She linked her arm companionably with that of the luckless Ellie and swept her along.

'Sing a song of sixpence, a pocket full of rye!' she started to sing. The rest, after a moment's hesitation, joined in, largely hoping to drown their aunt's voice. They knew little of her everyday habits, but felt sure these could not include marching through the village singing at the top of her voice. They saw advancing two perfectly neat and proper elderly ladies, and braced themselves for what might come. At first they seemed to notice little amiss.

'Oh, good afternoon, Miss Marchmont,' they said, nodding and smiling, and pausing for a civil word – about the weather, perhaps, or the Ladies' Sewing Circle.

The children held their breath. Their aunt was staring at the ladies in bafflement.

'How are you getting along with your embroidery for the church bazaar, I wonder?' enquired one pleasantly.

'Embroidery?' echoed Aunt Marchmont in disgust. 'Embroidery, my eye!'

The children winced and the ladies looked startled.

'And – er – who are these?' asked the other, meaning the children, who smiled at her with a desperate politeness.

'We're relatives,' said Ellie swiftly.

'Come on a visit.'

'She's our aunt!'

Aunt Marchmont let out a derisive hoot.

'Oh Georgy Porgy, you are a card! Playing Happy Families again, are we?'

'How very nice,' said the lady nervously, plucking at her friend's arm.

'We'll see you on Wednesday then, Miss Marchmont, at the Sewing Bee. Come, Ethel!'

'You'll see me at a Sewing Bee,' said Connie dangerously, 'my elbow!'

The ladies gaped.

'Boo!' yelled Connie suddenly, poking forward her head.

The ladies fled. They didn't run, but tottered off with little short steps and taking scared backward glances over their shoulders.

'Oh lor!' groaned George. 'She *will* get locked up!'

Their journey to the shop for Connie's tuck was a jumpy business, what with gentlemen doffing their caps to Aunt Marchmont and her rudely pretending to doff hers back, and a particularly fraught moment when she was invited to admire a new baby. The children, who had not the least interest in babies, peered into the perambulator and cooed and exclaimed on the baby's hair and eyes and general look of promise. This was in the vain effort to drown out Connie's own remarks, which were mercifully pretty well inaudible, but certainly included references to piggywiggies.

When the party arrived outside the shop George made a last game effort to prevent his aunt from entering. He thrust himself between her and the door, barring her way.

'Look, don't go in! If you do, something – something terrible will happen!'

'What?' she demanded. 'Get shot in the eye by an arrow, you mean?' and giggled.

'Worse!' said George darkly.

'Come back home and I'll let you look through my microscope,' urged Pip.

'Pooh!' returned that lady. 'Pooh, fiddlesticks and rot!'

George was dodging desperately from side to side to block her path.

'Chuck it, will you!' she exclaimed in exasperation, pushed him rudely aside, and marched in. George groaned and followed her. The others, rolling up their eyes and expecting catastrophe at any moment, waited.

'Oh, Miss Marchmont!' cried the shopkeeper. 'I do so 'ope that wool was to your satisfaction? I told this young gen'leman 'ere – '

'Bother wool!'

'I – er – haven't given it to her yet,' said George, in an attempt to delay the evil hour.

'Tole 'im yesserday, I did, biggest stitcher in the place, you are, and my bes' customer – oh yes, not a doubt of it . . .'

Her voice trailed off as she watched Aunt Marchmont eagerly scanning and poking among the rows of bottled sweets and toffees.

'Oh – them! I'll have a dozen of 'em!'

The shop lady stared, astounded, as Aunt Marchmont busily un-screwed the jar.

'Gobstoppers!' and she thrust one into her mouth and the rest into her pockets. 'Therthooarethanks!'

She slammed her sixpence down on the counter and waltzed out. George, with a desperate, pleading look at the pop-eyed wool lady, bolted after her. Aunt Marchmont was already doling out the gobstoppers. The children, mesmerised, obediently popped them into their own mouths, though this was certainly unwise, since it rendered them virtually speechless at a time when there was much explaining to be done.

'Cuth on, leth geth home,' said Aunt Marchmont thickly and set off, to their enormous relief, in the direction of home.

'Thank gooneth tha that!' said George in a heartfelt voice through his gobstopper.

'Fath ath you can!' agreed Pip.

They hurried homeward, and as they left the village behind heaved sighs of relief as deep as the chewing balls in their mouths would allow. This relief, however, was short-lived. In life, as you will have noticed, one disaster quite often leads to another, troubles never come singly and lightening often strikes in the same place twice.

They were already in the lane and approaching Dawkins' cottage when an alarming sight met their eyes.

'Oh Thiminy!' groaned Pip. 'That torn ith!'

They saw little Lil cowering on the step, and standing over her a strange young man – and a policeman! Their worst fears, it seemed, were to be realised.

'Come on, Connie – quick – let's hide!' cried George, manfully spitting out his gobstopper in the interests of clear speech.

'Oh, don't leth him lock her up!' wailed Lucy.

'Whoth afraid of the big bath wolf!' retorted the unquenchable Connie, and she marched straight on. Ellie, seeing this, ran swiftly ahead.

'Oh Ellie, Ellie!' Little Lil saw her and burst into tears.

'What's happening, what's happening?'

'Poaching, that's wot,' said the policeman. 'Poachin' and hunlawful possession.'

'S'right, hofficer,' said the young man, who was seen to have a pasty complexion and small, rapidly moving eyes. 'I only done my dooty reportin' it.'

'My Pa – ain't done – nuffin'!' sobbed little Lil. 'Oh don't send 'im to prison, sir, don't!'

'Hush,' said Ellie gently, and put an arm round her. She looked boldly up at the policeman. 'I'm sure Mr Dawkins has done nothing wrong.'

'Hi'll be the judge of that, young lady,' he replied. 'The Law's the Law.'

'Whath going off?' demanded the gob-stopped Aunt Marchmont.

The policeman turned. He seemed, for the moment, to see nothing amiss.

'Ah, Miss Marchmont. Arternoon, miss.'

'Whyth the crying?' Connie indicated the sobbing Lil.

The policeman cleared his throat.

'It's like this, Miss Marchmont – '

'Oh do sthtop calling me that!' she snapped.

'Dawkins 'as been reported for poachin', miss,' volunteered the pasty young man. 'I done it as my dooty.'

Connie stared at him.

'And who're you when you're ath home?'

The young man twisted his cap between his hands and shuffled his feet.

'Dobbs, miss, Albert Dobbs, and a nevvy of Mister and Missis Dobbs and glad to be of service miss!'

The children looked at him with undisguised hatred. This sly, dough-faced youth looked exactly as you would expect of a nephew of the detestable Dobbses.

'This 'ere young gen'leman 'as laid hinformation,' said the policeman. 'And I've a come to give doo warning. Warnin' first, then, warnin' not dooly taken – prosecution!'

Lucy let out a little shriek and the policeman proceeded to unroll a poster, bearing the legend:

POACHERS WILL BE PROSECUTED

'See that!' he waved it before the tear-stained face of little Lil.

'I – I can't read,' she stammered. 'Nor me Pa neither – 'e can't read!'

The policeman seemed momentarily flummoxed by this revelation, but rallied himself to pronounce solemnly, 'Hignorance is no Defence!'

Little Lil started to cry again.

'Don't sent my Pa to prison, don't!'

Connie stepped forward. First, very deliberately, she spat out her gobstopper, and it landed neatly at the officer's feet.

'What does it feel like to be a policeman?' she enquired.

He look startled, opened his mouth, then closed it again.

'What does it feel like to be a big – fat – bully of a policeman making little girls cry?'

'B-but Miss Marchmont, miss, I – '

'Don't you Miss Marchmont me!' she retorted. 'You clear off and take your beastly poster with you! No – here!' and she reached out, snatched the poster and calmly tore it in half. She then dropped it and trampled it under foot. 'There!'

She stood triumphant, hands on hips. The children gazed at their usually prim and strait-laced aunt with a mixture of admiration and terror. They reminded themselves that although she looked like a grown-up, she was in reality Connie, and a child. The two men, of course, had no such knowledge.

'She's gorn orf 'er nut!' whispered Albert Dobbs hoarsely. He put on his cap, lowered his head and slunk off into the trees.

'It's not against the Law to tear things!' cried Lucy, fearful that the aunt would be arrested in place of Dawkins.

But the Law was already in retreat, almost tripping over its own boots in its haste to put distance between itself and a lady who had clearly gone mad and was, amongst other things, chomping and spitting out gobstoppers.

'Hurray!'

'Good old Connie!'

'There,' said Ellie, hugging little Lil. 'Don't cry – he's gone now.'

'And that other beastly Dobbs,' added Pip.

'Fank you, Miss Marchmont,' said Lil timidly, gazing wide-eyed up at this gorgon of a lady.

'Oh, don't *you* start!' said Connie. 'Come on – it must be nearly supper – I'm starving!'

She ran off.

'Come on,' said George wearily. 'Oh lor, where's sunset got to?'

'Must be nearly,' Pip said. 'She'll be changing back any minute. But how'll we *know*? She doesn't *look* any different.'

They pondered this undoubted truth. From one moment to the next the real Aunt Marchmont would slide invisibly back inside that head.

'Will she remember?' Lucy asked.

'Don't know,' George told her. 'But mind you don't go calling her Connie.'

They had nearly reached the house now, and saw that Dobbs was working on the flowerbeds again. George caught up with Connie and grabbed her arm.

'Better not let him see us!'

'Whyever not? Who cares?'

And she danced off, and the children watched, aghast, as she snatched up Dobbs' cap from the cane where he had hung it.

'Yooee!'

''Ere!'

Dobbs turned, and when he turned he did not know he was looking at a child, he was seeing his employer, a haughty and impeccable lady whose word was law. That bedraggled person now plonked his cap on her own head and grinned. Dobbs stared. His mouth opened.

'Er – er – evenin', Miss Marchmont,' he stammered.

'Evening, Miss Marchmont!' she mimicked.

Dobbs fairly boggled and the children watched, breath held.

'Those dandelions!' she said, indicating a dug up clump of the flowers by his spade. 'You've been digging up *dandelions*?'

'I – jus' weedin', miss,' stuttered Dobbs, for whom the children were almost beginning to feel sorry.

'My favourite flowers! You just put 'em back again, you hear?'

'Y-y-yes, 'm.' The bewildered Dobbs picked up his spade.

'Y-y-yes, 'm,' she mimicked again.

'*Plant* 'em? Dandelions?' He evidently disbelieved his own ears, as well as his eyes.

'Now! Do it!' She stamped her foot. Then, quite deliberately, she stuck out her tongue.

Dobbs gasped. It was too much. His employer had clearly taken leave of her senses.

'I'm off!' He dropped his spade and ran.

'Hurray!' cried the children as one.

'And don't come back!' shrieked Connie after him.

'Master George, Miss Ellie!'

They whirled about to see Bessie on the steps.

Aunt Marchmont snatched Dobbs' cap from her head and threw it up into the air, and at that moment the sun set. If the children had happened to blink at just that moment, they would have missed the visible workings of magic. But they did not blink, and they saw an extraordinary blurring and shimmer about the person of their aunt. As Dobbs' cap fell unheeded to the ground, the ragtag Connie seemed to dissolve and fade, and in her place stood the outstandingly neat and starchy person of Aunt Marchmont. She regarded the children, who were staring at her open-mouthed.

'Do close your mouths,' she told them. Then, 'Whatever have you done to Dobbs?'

He was still running, in the distance now.

'He seems to have left his cap.'

'I – I think he's had some kind of fright, Aunt Marchmont,' George said.

'But not because of anything we did,' said Ellie hastily.

'You – you haven't by any chance got my magic thimble, Aunt Marchmont?' piped up Lucy, and was dug in the ribs by Pip.

'Your . . .?' Aunt Marchmont looked puzzled, then slowly uncurled her right hand and stared down in disbelief.

'However . . .?' she murmured.

'You borrowed it,' Pip said.

'Did I? I don't remember . . .'

'For your sewing, I expect.'

'Ah yes . . . my sewing.' She drew a deep sigh. 'Here, then, Lucy,' and she handed her the thimble, turned and went slowly into the house.

'She remembered my name!'

'And she *doesn't* remember being Connie!'

'Oh, there you are, ma'am,' they heard Bessie say. 'We was wondering where you was at dinner – at lunch time.'

'Oh. Betty, yes . . . I am feeling rather strange, I'm afraid. Dizzy . . .'

'Oooh, ma'am, and so'm I – least, I was! 'Ad one or two ever such funny turns!'

'Yes, that rather describes it,' murmured Aunt Marchmont. 'A funny turn . . .'

'Must be 'fectious,' said Bessie. 'You go in and sit down and I'll bring you a nice dish of soup.'

'Pooh!' responded Aunt Marchmont defiantly, whirling her mallet.

. . . she reached out, snatched the poster and calmly tore it in half.

'Thank you, Betty. Yes, I think I will.'

Aunt Marchmont passed through the door and into the house and the children let out long held breaths of relief.

'Well, then, is it near nuff sunset for your suppers, then?' Bessie enquired.

'Spot on,' George said. 'We're ravenous.'

'Oh Bessie, we've had a lovely day – and wouldn't it be lovely if that beastly Dobbs has gone forever, and – '

But Bessie was only half listening. She was looking beyond them, and they turned to see Dawkins, without either dog or gun, striding towards them, as though there were no such person as Miss Marchmont, who had first dismissed him and then threatened to turn him out of his cottage.

'Evenin', miss!'

'Oh – Mr Dawkins – evenin', I'm sure!'

Bessie screwed up her apron and looked flustered, as she did when she saw the milkman in Islington who was sweet on her.

'Compliments, miss!' He gave a mock half bow and brought from behind his back a dangling pair of rabbits.

'Oh!' gasped Bessie. 'Oh, you shouldn't reely!'

'Those from the sand-pit?' asked George.

'Ask no questions . . .' Dawkins grinned and winked and tapped his nose.

'It's ever so kind of you, Mr Dawkins.' The blushing Bessie took the rabbits. 'Oooh, and ain't they fat 'uns!'

'Sam,' said Dawkins, raising his cap. 'Sam Dawkins, miss, at your service.' He looked at the children. 'Warn't that Dobbs I see jus' now, a runnin' as if 'e was afeared of missin' the last trump?'

'Yes, it was,' George told him. 'And we just hope he doesn't come back.'

'Ah. Well,' Dawkins scratched his head and replaced his cap. 'You reckon you've seen the both of 'em off now, then?'

'Not *exactly*,' said the truthful Ellie. 'But we're glad they've gone – though Dobbs didn't exactly give his notice.'

'Cross-grained old badger,' added Pip.

'Ah. Well. Could've done me a good turn there,' said Dawkins.

'Oh, I hope so!' said Ellie. 'I do hope so!'

Dawkins grinned again, tipped his cap to the furiously blushing Bessie, and wished them all good evening.

Later, the children went into their aunt's room to say goodnight, somewhat quaking in their boots. As they filed in their eyes went straight to her face, to see if there was any sign that she remembered that only hours before she had been spitting out gobstoppers and cheeking Dobbs. She was sitting in her usual place, and it was a moment or two before they realised that there *was* something different – only a small thing, to be sure, but – different. As they entered she closed her book and placed it on the table.

'You're not sewing!' gasped Lucy.

'I beg your pardon?'

'You're not sewing!' she repeated.

Aunt Marchmont smiled then, a strange, satisfied smile.

'Bother sewing!' she said.

The children blinked. Had the child in Aunt Marchmont survived sunset?

'It has occurred to me,' she said, 'that I do not care for sewing.'

'I don't blame you!' said Ellie with feeling. She herself was quite hopeless with a needle.

'And it has occurred to me that there is no law that says I must. I think I have been sewing merely out of – habit. It is very easy, of course, to form habits – good or bad.'

She surveyed the children.

'Remind me of your names again.'

'George.'

'Ellen.'

'Philip.'

'Lucy.'

'And have you had a good day, George, Ellen, Philip, and Lucy?'

'Yes, thank you, Aunt Marchmont,' they chorussed, and Pip, at least, was tempted to add, 'Thanks to you!'

'You are lucky to have one another. When I was a child I was quite alone.'

'We know,' said Lucy, before she could stop herself. Her brothers and sister gave her fierce looks, and Aunt Marchmont looked at her curiously, but made no remark.

'Do you play croquet?' she enquired suddenly.

'Yes', 'No', and 'Sort of', they replied, mystified.

'Tomorrow I shall teach you how to play. Goodnight!'

'Oh, thank you, Aunt Marchmont! Goodnight, Aunt Marchmont!'

'It's as if she does half remember,' Ellie told Lucy as they got ready for bed. 'Why else should she suddenly decide not to sew any more?'

'Or teach us how to play croquet,' agreed Lucy. 'Good old Sammyadd! Oh!'

She clapped a hand to her mouth and so did Ellie, as the same thought struck them both at once.

'It's still out there in the summerhouse!'

'In the dark, away from its sand-pit! Oh poor Sammyadd!'

'Oh, let's go and fetch it in! It could share my bed.'

Ellie shook her head.

'It needs sand. You heard what it said – it said it'd die without it.'

'But it only had two bucketsful!' wailed Lucy.

'We'll have to leave it. But the minute we wake up tomorrow we'll go and see it.'

'I'm going to wish on my magic thimble for it to be safe and sound. And don't you dare say one word about it not being really magic!'

'I won't, Lucy lamb, promised Ellie, and Lucy shut her eyes and wished with all her heart, then placed the thimble carefully under her pillow, to guard her dreams.

Chapter XI

SMUGGLERS

Ellie was the first to wake the following morning, after a night full of dreams about the Psammead. And the moment she opened her eyes she remembered that poor fairy, shut in its hamper in the summerhouse, and probably despairing of ever seeing its own dear sand-pit ever again. She dressed swiftly, then left the slumbering Lucy, tiptoed down the stairs and opened the door.

'Oh no!'

Down came the rain in long silver needles out of a dark sky.

'Oh *no*!'

How in the world were they to get the Psammead back to its sand-pit, when at the first hint of wetness it might catch cold and die, like all the other Sand-fairies before it?

She stood on the step and hesitated, but only for a moment. If she ran to the summerhouse and back she would get a drenching, and a good scolding from Bessie. But that poor beast had lain in that hamper alone through the long dark hours of night, and was now doubtless listening to the steady drumming of rain on the roof, and wondering if its last hour had come.

Ellie ducked her head and ran. She gasped as the cold rain stung her cheeks and eyes, and the world went into a green blur. Over the squelching lawn she ran and reached the summerhouse and pushed open the door.

'Sammyadd!' she gasped. 'It's me!'

Her eyes went straight to the hamper. The lid was open. She ran and peered in, to see only a heap of sand, and here and there glimpses of the cloth beneath.

Ellie screamed.

'Gone! On no! Sammyadd! Sammyadd?'

She threw open the lid of the other hamper – empty. She feverishly tossed aside the jumble of dusty objects and scrabbled at the heaps of netting that lay in the furthest corner. But she knew in her heart that it was hopeless. She rushed to the door and scanned the garden.

'Can't be out here! The rain! Its poor whisker! Oh Sammyadd!'

Bang! Ellie let out a shriek.

'Oh no!'

Back she ran through the pouring rain and up the stairs and into the boys' room.

'George! Pip! Wake up!'

She ran from one to the other, shaking them, and the boys came to, blinking and dazed.

'What's up?'

'Stow it, can't you?'

'It's gone! Oh, the Sammyadd's gone!'

'What?'

'Strewth!'

The boys jumped out of bed and started to pull on their things.

'It's no good – it's raining – it's *pouring*!'

They looked at their sister and noticed for the first time her dripping hair, her face, hands and clothes grimed with a mixture of rain and dust that had formed a most unholy mud.

'Look at you! You'll catch it!'

'I know,' said Ellie miserably. 'But I had to go!'

'Go and get Lucy,' said George, with an attempt at manly firmness, 'and we'll hold a parley and see what's to be done.'

So this is what happened, but they found that there was little that *could* be done. The Psammead had disappeared, it was pouring with rain, and someone was out there shooting.

'It must be somewhere out there in the garden,' said Pip.

'But the rain! It'd never willingly go out in the wet! Its top twelfth left whisker, remember!'

'Oh dear, what if it's got wet and died!'

'Shut up, Lucy,' George told her kindly. 'So two things might have happened. Either it escaped in the middle of the night, before the rain started, or – or – '

'It's been itnapped!' exclaimed Pip.

'But who *by?*'

'And what about the shooting?'

'Oh dear – and it looks rather like a rabbit, I s'pose, from a distance . . .'

'Master George! Miss Ellie!'

It was Bessie. And Ellie, needless to say, got a tremendous wigging and was made to have a bath and change her things before she was even allowed breakfast.

Most of the morning was spent willing the rain to stop. They stared fiercely at it through the streaming windows, and Pip remembered an African rain chant he had come across somewhere.

'A rain chant's no good, duffer,' George told him. 'It's an *anti* rain chant we want!'

So Pip tried saying the chant backwards, though no one really believed in the possibility of its working, and of course it didn't.

At dinner Aunt Marchmont remarked on their unusual silence, and even made an attempt at conversation herself, but it fell on stony ground. The children were fairly hunched in misery. Each though its own doomy thoughts about the fate of the Psammead.

After dinner they went gloomily back upstairs. They started to play a game of brigands, but nobody had the heart. It is hopeless to try any kind of game of make believe when half of yourself is not there at all.

So George and Pip went off to the attics in search of some decent pastime that would not be rowdy enough to disturb the aunt. They had little hope of this. If a game is even halfway decent it is usually rowdy too.

'I'm going to make the Psammead a present,' Lucy said. 'It won't have had one for thousands of years – how can it, when there's no one to remember its birthday?'

Ellie fetched her Journal. She did so partly out of duty, because when her parents had given it she had promised to write in it every single day. But she fetched it, too, because her Journal was the only thing in the world to which she could tell her true feelings. It held secrets that not a single living person knew. She guarded it at least as jealously as Lucy her silver thimble. It seemed to her to be almost part of her own self.

'What will you make for the Sammyadd, Lucy lamb?' she asked as she arranged her things.

'I want to give it a big surprise,' Lucy told her. 'I expect what it would really like is a whisker warmer.'

'I expect so,' Ellie agreed.

'The trouble is, I don't know how to make one.'

Over the years the young Garsingtons had made many and various presents for uncles and aunts and so forth, but had never yet been asked for a whisker warmer.

'I know!'

'What?'

'A portrait!'

'Who of?'

'*Itself*, of course! Important people always have their portraits done and put on tea caddies and such. But mine'll be a proper picture, and I'll frame it and it can hang it on the wall!'

Ellie did not imagine that there were any walls in the Psammead's burrow – or at least, not of the picture hanging variety. Wisely, she did not say so.

'And then . . . and then . . .' Lucy's voice wobbled ominously. 'If – if we don't find it again, we'll have the picture to remind us.'

'I think that's a splendid idea, Lucy,' said Ellie warmly. 'Do one like the one you did of Methusalah.'

So the pair of them settled down, and there was silence but for the drumming of the rain and Ellie's sighs as she searched for the right words. Lucy, because she was painstakingly trying to make a faithful portrait of that fabulous beast, was bound to have it very much in her thoughts. And in those thoughts there was a huge, unbearable sadness.

Lucy was eight years old, and believed in magic and wishes even before she had met the Psammead. She had credited her silver thimble with all kinds of small occasions of magic – such as Bessie agreeing to take them all to the zoo, or it not raining on the day of a picnic. But magic of a more spectacular order – doubles appearing out of thin air, travel into the far off future – she had never dreamed of. Now that it had happened, she felt that she simply could not go a single day without it. The ordinary world seemed unbearably insipid and flat.

The Psammead, for all she knew, travelled as slowly as a snail. It might not get back to its sand-pit for days – weeks even. In that case, she reasoned, it must still be somewhere in the garden – somewhere dry.

'And I could find it,' she thought. 'And if I did, I'd be the heroine of the hour. *And* I could ask it for a wish.'

The thought was irrisistibly appealing. She laid down her brush. She took a sideways look at her laboriously scribbling sister, and said in a voice that she earnestly hoped did not wobble,

'Just going to look for something . . .'

Which was perfectly true, of course.

'Good,' murmured Ellie absently, without looking up.

Lucy then tiptoed back downstairs, took a large black umbrella from the stand, and quietly let herself out.

It was raining steadily – the kind of grey, monotonous rain you know won't let up all day. Lucy had a fierce struggle with the umbrella. Her arms seemed scarcely long enough to push up the spokes, and when she finally succeeded the brolly all but swallowed her. She had the greatest difficulty in seeing where she was going, and several times ran into trees. But under the trees she had to go – because there it was dry, or partly dry – and so that was where the Psammead must be. Past the summerhouse she went, and a little way further. Here she stopped.

'If it does move slowly as a snail, this is about where it will be,' she decided. 'In any case, it'll be as dry as toast under here.'

She could hear the soft rustle of the rain on the leaves above, and thought how dreadful that sound must be to the ears of the Psammead. She drew a deep breath.

'Sammyadd! Sammyadd! It's me, Lucy!'

Silence, but for the whispering rain.

'Oh, if you are here I wish you'd come out!'

Now Lucy had guessed quite rightly – that fairy beast was not far away. At dawn it had crept out of the hamper, but had hardly started on the journey back to its own dear sand-pit when it had been frightened by Dawkins, out early with dog and gun. It had burrowed down deep as it could in the soft, loamy soil. There it had snoozed a little, and by the time it awoke and poked its head out again, the rain had started.

'What's a day when you're thousands of years old?' it asked itself, and shrugged its fur and burrowed down again. There it was fitfully dozing when Lucy's whisper reached its delicate bat's ears, and having heard that wish, it was bound to respond.

Lucy was scanning this way and that as best she could under her tilting roof, when there came an ear-splitting screech, right by her feet.

'Eeech! Eeech! It's wet, it's wet!'

Lucy, overjoyed, saw the Psammead, wild-eyed and furious. She dropped to her knees and balanced the umbrella over it as best she could.

'Not under here!'

'Oh, my whisker! My poor whisker! I'll die, I'll die!'

'Oh don't, please don't!' begged poor Lucy.

'What do you want?' it demanded. 'You never expect a wish in all this wet!'

'Oh couldn't you? Please – it would only take a minute, and I've got the most marvellous – '

'No!' it screamed. 'No, no no!'

Then suddenly it stiffened.

'What's that?'

It was looking straight at Lucy's thimble, which she had worn for luck on so important an errand.

'Ask that!' it snapped.

'This? Oh, it only gives little wishes, like – '

'That ridiculous friend of yours – that grown-up one – she wished!'

Lucy was baffled.

'Wished – *what*?' she asked desperately.

'Duffer!' it told her. 'She wished the thimble could give wishes.'

At this, light dawned.

'You mean yesterday – when she grabbed it?'

'So now it can! Still can – because she never made one. I'm off!'

Lucy hardly heard. She was staring awestruck at the Christmas cracker thimble that now, it seemed, had powers as great as those of the Psammead itself.

Already it was whirling itself back into the ground.

'Only for one day, mind!' it warned, and was gone.

In the playroom the other three children were passing the time as best they could. George and Pip had had a fearful row in the attics over a game involving tin soldiers and hat boxes, and were now in a state of fruminous sulk. Ellie was writing a letter to the twins. Beside her was Lucy's unfinished portrait of the Psammead. This was coming along nicely, though there were problems with the whiskers, which are particularly difficult to deal with satisfactorily when the artist is wearing a thimble. George fidgeted by the window, looking for breaks in the cloud. Pip fetched out his paper and comb and tunelessly rendered *Danny Boy* and *Cockles and Mussels*. The others stood this for as long as they could, but finally George said, 'Stow it, can't you. Pipkins? It's driving me potty!'

'And me,' said Ellie. 'Don't be a piggywig, Pip dear.'

'I *feel* like a piggywig.'

'Then try feeling like a saint from heaven, instead,' Ellie told him. '*They* don't blow on combs.'

The door opened.

'Oh – there you are, Lucy. Did you find what you wanted?'

Ellie did not look up from her writing, and so did not see Lucy's suspiciously pink face and damp hair.

'Yes, thank you,' replied Lucy, biting her tongue to prevent it telling her adventure. As soon as she had her breath back, she intended to wish that they all had wings to fly with – it was one of her dearest dreams.

'This isn't a proper playroom at all,' said Pip, who at any rate could not blow and talk at once. 'No, fort, no soldiers – nothing!'

'Read a book,' suggested Ellie slyly.

'And so I would, if there were any decent ones, like *Treasure Island* or *Kidnapped*. Something with a bit of adventure.'

'Like that?' asked George, pointing.

It was a picture, showing smugglers in a cave. Pip went closer and peered at it. There was a glimpse behind of a greeny grey stormy sea and a rowing boat, and far away on the horizon, a sailing ship.

'Smugglers! Tip top!'

'Trouble is, there aren't any round here,' said Ellie, head bent over her letters.

'More's the pity. Don't I just wish there were! Don't I just wish we were there, with them, at this very minute!'

Chapter XII

A NARROW ESCAPE

The words were no sooner out of Pip's mouth than a queer ripple of magic ran through that room with its rainy windows and ticking clock. And the children gasped as the frame of the picture seemed to stretch and open, and all at once the sound of the rain lashing the window and the ticking of the clock faded, and in their place was the crash of waves and the rough, low voices of men.

'What's happening?' cried Lucy, feeling herself pulled into the picture, and the wind streaming through her hair.

'Oh help!' Ellie too found herself being drawn from the safe cocoon of the playroom into the cold harsh world and weather of the picture.

'Hurrah!' she heard Pip yell, and 'Oh I say!' from George.

Then they were there, in that cave, as Pip had wished them to be. Mercifully, they found themselves behind a huge boulder, out of sight of the smugglers.

'I say – what . . .?'

'Ssshhh!' hissed the others, and George did so. They crouched there and tried to hear what the voices were saying.

'Best get back now, and warn 'em, Lijah.'

'Sunset, tell 'em!'

'And send word fast if there's news of the Revenue.'

'There'll be no King's men tonight, never you fear – we've foxed 'em proper, this time.'

'Mind 'ow yer go, lads. 'Lijah and me'll stop 'ere – '

'We've a barrel of French brandy to keep us warm!'

There was a burst of rough laughter, and the sound of footsteps ringing on the rocky floor.

'Sunset, mind!'

'And them 'orses' 'oofs well muffled!'

'The sign's three winks of the lantern!'

Behind the rock the children gazed at one another wide-eyed. They could hardly begin to guess how they had found themselves in this fix (or at least, three of the four of them could not) but fix it was, and no mistake.

'Reckon we'll 'ave a clear run, 'Lijah?'

A grunt.

'There's folk in the village as blab, curse 'em!'

'Aye, and if I knowed oo they was, I'd 'ave their tongues out!'

'They reckon the Revenue's about. Reckon they're on to us?'

'One thing to rumble us, 'nuther to catch us, eh, 'Lijah?'

'Never done yet, John. 'Ere, give us another drop o' that brandy, and – '

'A – shoo!'

George simply could not help it. He had felt the sneeze growing, from a tiny tickle at the back of his nose, and had fought to suppress it till his eyes watered. The children stiffened, and more than one of them crossed its fingers.

''Ere!'

'Oo's there?'

'You come on out – and 'ands up, as we can see yer!'

George thought fast.

'You stop here,' he whispered to the girls. 'If you see your chance – run!'

He tugged at Pip, and they edged fearfully round the boulder.

'Well!'

'Upon my sacred!'

'A pair o' kiddies!'

The smugglers were standing, one with knife drawn, the other with blunderbuss raised.

'Don't shoot!' said George faintly.

'Shoot!' The bearded man roared with laughter. 'The day 'Lijah Rowe shoots at kiddies'll be the day the hocean turns to raw brandy! On the other 'and, on the *other* 'and, little eyes can snoop and spy as well as big 'uns, and little tongues can *blab* as well!'

The other man peered at them in the gloom with his one good eye (there was a black patch over the other) and with his knife still drawn, its wicked blade flashing.

'Ain't from round these parts,' he growled. 'Leastways, not as I know. Spies!'

'We're not!' said the two boys together.

'Jus' you look at them fancy togs!' John walked round them, knife at the ready. 'Little present from the Revenue, was they?'

'No, honestly, they're ours!'

'I *like* smugglers,' said Pip, and so he always had – in books. It is, of course, one thing to admire the exploits of pirates, brigands and smugglers in a book, and quite another to find yourself face to face with them in a very awkward situation.

'Likes! 'ear that, 'Lijah – *likes* smugglers!' Then his laughter stopped abruptly, and he thrust his face forward, his one eye glaring. 'And oo said anything 'bout smuggling? Eh?'

'Er – well – we just thought – '

'We've never actually met any smugglers before,' George explained, 'but in the pic – '

He broke off short. Any stories about walking into picture frames were going to be given short shrift here, he could tell that.

'Ho, never hackcherly met any smugglers before, eh?'

'But we've always wanted to,' Pip assured him.

'We're jolly pleased to meet you!'

'His they a kidding of us, 'Lijah?'

'Can't rightly say, John. But what I say is this. If they *is* a kidding of us, they'll wish they 'adn't afore the night's out!'

'Oh, we shan't be here tonight,' said George, though of course he could not be certain of this. He felt strongly that a mere thimble could not have worked this particular magic, but on the other hand could not for the life of him work out how the Psammead had.

'Look 'ee 'ere,' growled 'Lijah. 'You know oo's out there, ridin' the tide and a waitin' for the dark?'

'Er – no.'

'No, sir.'

'Abr'am Cox, that's oo!'

'King of the contraband!'

'Gosh!' said Pip and 'Golly!' said George, feeling that this was expected of them.

'And 'e's a lookin' for sailor lads, bain't 'e, John?'

'That 'e be,' nodded John.

'And if they don't come willin', 'e trusses 'em up and *takes* 'em!'

''Ow should *you* like to serve under Abr'am Cox and sail the 'igh seas, me little 'earties?'

'I don't think I'd be any good!' George stammered. 'I'd get sea sick.'

'And Mother wouldn't like it,' added Pip.

'Mother wouldn't like it!' John roared with laughter and slapped his thigh. ''Ear that, 'Lijah?'

'*Mother* ain't a goin' to be arsked,' said 'Lijah. 'Abr'am Cox is payin' five gold guineas – five *guineas* for every lad 'e gets.'

'Five for you, and five for me.'

'Right you are, John.' 'Lijah grinned wickedly.

Neither boy liked the sound of this at all – even Pip, who had always longed for adventure. He was rapidly coming to the conclusion that adventure was best when it was safely contained between the covers of a book.

'Look here, we're not really spies, you know,' George said. 'We're just – just sort of visitors.'

'Then you've made one visit too many, me darlings,' said 'Lijah.

'If we don't watch out, they could make a runner for it,' said John in a low voice.

'Right you are, John. And we can't be a 'aving of young spies with sharp eyes and long tongues a runnin' straight off – '

'An' blabbing to the Revenue.'

'So – what says you we truss 'em up, John?'

The two smugglers looked at one another, nodded, and next minute the boys were being seized and their arms pinioned. They yelled and struggled in vain.

'Let me go! Let me *go*!'

'Help!'

Ellie and Lucy, still crouched behind the boulder, were terrified. Now, if ever, was the moment to make a run for it as George had instructed them.

'Quick!' shrieked Ellie, and seized Lucy's hand, and together the pair bolted for the mouth of the cave. As they ran they heard a great bellow of rage and a shout.

'They've seen us!'

'Run! Run!'

And run they did, out of the dim cave and blinking out into the daylight, and over the sand and under the cliff's edge.

'Look!' There was a rough flight of steps cut into the rock and the girls clambered up it. It was steep going, and stones and earth slipped under their feet. At last, just as they were beginning to feel that they could not go another step, they were suddenly at the top. They collapsed, panting, onto the rough grass.

'They – they can't catch us now!' gasped Ellie.

'But – oh Ellie – the boys!'

'Well, now,' came a man's voice. 'What have we here?'

The girls, horrorstruck, slowly lifted their heads. They saw first horses' hoofs, then boots and spurs, and then last of all, two men, dressed in blue uniform.

'The King's men!' gasped Ellie.

'And where might you be going in such a hurry, my pretties?' asked the one with the gold braid, and peaked hat.

Lucy and Ellie scrambled to their feet and stood, still panting, gazing up. They were, it seemed, out of the fat and into the fire.

'In a *mighty* great 'urry, cap'n,' said the other, the one with a wide, curving scar on his cheek.

'True, Saunders,' murmured the captain. 'You'd think there was someone after them. Was there, I wonder?'

'Or sent of a message, cap'n. A *hurgent* message.'

'True . . . well?'

'Please, sir, we were just playing!' blurted Lucy.

'And we haven't any message, truly we haven't.'

'And we've never even heard of Abraham Cox!'

At this Ellie almost bit out her own tongue on Lucy's behalf. Eight year olds are not very reliable accomplices in games of cat and mouse. They have not yet learned to dissemble.

'Abe Cox, eh?' murmured the captain. 'Well, well!'

'But cap'n,' Saunders lowered his voice. 'Word is, it's Porchester as 'e's runnin' tonight!'

'Then word may be wrong,' the captain told him. 'As likely as not, word has been put about by his own men, to fox us.'

'Aye – they don't call 'im the Sea Fox for naught!'

'I – I think we'd better be going now, sir,' said Ellie.

'It's tea time,' added Lucy, taking Ellie's hand.

But Saunders moved his horse to block their path.

'Oh no, my pretties, not so fast.' He looked at his captain. 'Little birds sing, sir.'

The captain nodded slowly.

'Take them!' he ordered, and himself swung suddenly down and snatched up Lucy, who screamed 'Help! Help!' In the same instant Saunders scooped up Ellie. Next moment the men were spurring their horses and galloping away from the cliff edge and away from the cave where their brothers were at this very moment being trussed and gagged by the smugglers.

All four children were now captive, and three of them, at least, were thinking desperately about the Psammead, and wondering how they had come to be in such a dreadful plight. If it *were* the Psammead who had granted their wish, where had it been, and how had it heard them? If it were not, how did they know that this wish would wear off at sunset, as the Psammead's did?

At the end of their ride, which was not a long one, the girls were taken into a long, stone building which they supposed was the Customs House. It was filled with smoke and laughter, and swarming with men in uniforms, preparing for the night's work ahead.

'This night we'll have the fox's brush!'

'Abr'am Cox – at last!'

'But they were going to sell the boys to Abraham Cox!' whispered Lucy. 'They'll be taken prisoner too!'

'But they won't set off till dark, and the wish will wear off at sunset, remember.' Ellie was not herself certain of this, and said it only to comfort her sister.

'But how do we know? What if . . . what if it wasn't the Psammead at all – what if it was my thimble?'

'Oh Lucy – you can't really believe that!'

For a moment Lucy was tempted to tell all – of her visit to the garden under the umbrella, and her secret meeting with the Psammead.

'But I'll tell when we're all safely back home,' she decided, and hoped earnestly that they would be, when the sun set. She held her tongue, and the waiting was the more terrible because of that guilty secret.

The hours dragged by for all the children. They were helpless to do anything, prisoners as they were, and their only hope of release was with the Psammead. But that magical beast seemed far away from the wet, echoing cave and the smoke-filled Customs House. They could only conjure up pictures of it inside their heads, and wish harder than ever before.

The worst time was had by the boys, trussed and gagged in the cold, echoing cave. They had trussed and gagged one another many times before in the interests of a good game, but never before in earnest, and this, they soon realised, made a difference. Ropes and knots that are tied in real earnest cut into your flesh, and are certainly not of an order that can be loosened with your teeth. Their teeth, in any case, were lost in the evil-smelling cloth the smugglers had used as gags. Moreover, the darkness of the cave was such that they could not judge the time of day by the sun, and guess how much longer they must endure. Both George and

Pip had separately had the same gloomy thoughts as their sister. If this were not a wish given by the Psammead, they were doomed. (Perhaps fortunately, they knew only that they themselves were soon to be pressed into the service of Abraham Cox, the Sea Fox. They knew nothing of their sisters' meeting with the King's men, and the ambush being prepared.)

Only once did they manage a sort of communication. The two smugglers left the cave, saying 'Back soon, lads!' and 'Don't you be a runnin' off while we're gone!' and John hugely winked his one good eye, with horrible effect.

At once the boys began a frantic exchange of rolling eyeballs and strangled sounds. They writhed and squirmed in the hope of loosening the hard ropes.

'Ith hopeleth!'

'The bruth needn't have thied uth tho tight!'

'Thith with – thith thtupid with – what if it doethn't – wear off – at thunthet!'

'We're thunk!'

'The – girlth! Whath – happended – to them?'

They had no idea. Each tried to imagine a scene where the girls returned, triumphant, with some kindly fishermen, who would free the boys and send the smugglers packing. But neither really believed in such a scene. This, they well knew, only happened in books.

Just before sunset the captain of the Revenue gave his men their orders – as, doubtless, hidden somewhere on the cliffs, one of the smugglers was also doing. Somewhere a horse with muffled hoofs was waiting, and a man with a lantern to give the signal.

Ellie and Lucy clung tightly to one another, and stared fearfully at the swords and blunderbusses. The captain and his man strode to where they cowered in the shadows.

'Well, my dears, are you aready for another ride?'

'Oh no, please!' begged Ellie.

'It is necessary, I fear. We have you as hostage. No harm will come to you.'

'If yer keeps yer mouth shut!' growled Saunders. 'One squeak out of you, and – ' he leered menacingly and drew his hand across his throat. Lucy squealed and clapped her hands over her ears.

Next minute the girls were up on the horses again, and set off in the twilight over the cliff-top path. The girls were fairly stiff with terror. They could not be certain that sunset would release them all. And with so many guns and knives about, how could they be sure that no one would be hurt? The boys, for all they knew, were already being taken, trussed and gagged, to sail with Abraham Cox on the high seas.

They rode in file, in silence but for the soft thud of horses' hoofs, and all the while the sun was sinking over the sea, half blinding in its red blaze. All at once the look-out reined in his horse, and the others followed suit.

'Look, cap'n!' came a hoarse whisper. The look-out was pointing, and away down below they saw the flash of a lantern.

'One – two – three!'

'The signal, sir!'

'We've got 'em cornered!'

The captain made a sign and a group of the men split away, and the girls realised that the smugglers were being encircled, with no hope of escape. Still they waited and then, suddenly, the captain raised his arm.

'Forward!'

They spurred on their horses, and down below the girls could hear shouts, and the crack of guns, and as the horses leapt forward the sun dropped behind the horizon. In that moment the sounds all faded, and again there was the crash of waves and cold pull of the wind, and then they were tumbling onto the rug, and the air was warm and still.

'Back!'

'Hurray!'

'Oh Ellie!'

'Are you safe?'

'Phew, that was a near thing!'

And as they scrambled to their feet in a daze they could hardly believe that somewhere, at this very moment, a deadly encounter was taking place between the smugglers and the Revenue men. They stared up in awe at the picture that had been the start of it all, and it looked so still and harmless in its gilt frame that it was almost unimaginable that within it lay locked such secrets.

'My legs are all wobbly,' said Lucy, and so were everyone else's though they did not admit it. A Garsington, as a rule, was a stranger to wobbly legs.

'We were captured by the Revenue men,' Ellie explained.

'We thought we were a goner!' admitted Pip.

The door opened.

'Supper,' said Bessie. 'And you've been good children today, that I will allow. Not a sound 'ave I 'eard since you 'ad your dinners.'

'What's for supper? I'm starving!'

'You allus is, Master Pip,' said Bessie reprovingly. 'It's a rabbit stew, as a matter of fack.'

'Good old Dawkins!'

'An' guess what?' Bessie lowered her voice. 'You'll never guess oo she's 'ad in 'er room all arternoon!'

'Who? The sainted aunt?'

'Li'l Lil!'

'I don't believe it!'

'But why?'

'What do you want?' it demanded. 'You never expect a wish
in all this wet!'

They yelled and struggled in vain.

'As I live and breathe! A teachin' 'er to read, can you believe!'

'Oh, wonderful!'

'I just hope she coughed and coughed, so's the aunt can see how poorly she is!'

'Oh, she been a coughin', all right. I've 'eard 'er. Oh – and Miss Ellie . . .'

'Yes, Bessie?'

'I've been meanin' to 'ave a word. Your 'andkerchiefs. I'm two short, and looked everywhere. They can't 'ave gone into thin air.'

'Can't they just!' muttered Pip under his breath, and they all giggled. Bessie looked at them severely.

'It ain't no larfin' matter. Two good cambric – '

'I lent one to Lil, and she thought I'd given it, and I didn't have the heart to ask it back,' Ellie said.

'Ah. Well. That was real kind of you, Miss Ellie. The other'll turn up, I s'pose. Come along now, all of you, sharp!'

Off she went.

'Oh bliss to be back at sunset to rabbit stew!' said Pip.

'Yes, it was sunset . . .' said Ellie thoughtfully. 'So it must have been the Sammyadd that gave the wish. But how . . .?'

'Thank goodness it wasn't that thimble!' said Pip.

The idea of living with a thimble that might come up with unreliable wishes at any hour of the day or night, was alarming. Even wishes are more enjoyable if they are kept within proper bounds, and have proper rules.

'All we've got to do now is *find* it again,' George said. 'If the brute's gone off in a sulk, we're sunk.'

'As a matter of fact . . .' began Lucy. The time to confess had come.

That night they went in to say goodnight to Aunt Marchmont quite eagerly. Now that they had met her as a child, and she had started playing croquet and – wonder of wonders – teaching little Lil to read, the prospect was not so daunting as it had once seemed. Also, they no longer felt the need to do all kinds of 'buttering up' – had indeed been expressly requested not to do so.

'Ah!' She put down her book and looked at them. There was fortunately nothing in their appearance to suggest that they had spent the afternoon in the company of smugglers. 'George, Ellen, Philip and Lucy!'

'Spot on!' said George encouragingly.

'We knew you'd learn them all in the end,' Lucy told her. 'Is it true?'

'True?' repeated Aunt Marchmont. 'Is what true, Lucy?'

'That little Lil's been up here, and you've been teaching her to read?'

'Certainly,' replied Aunt Marchmont calmly. 'Though of course I have not done so in a single afternoon.'

'It's jolly kind of you, Aunt Marchmont,' George said. 'And that's not buttering up!'

'It is my duty,' she told them. 'There is no virtue in illiteracy. I cannot sit idly by when on my own doorstep there is a child who can neither read nor write.'

'Does Dawkins know?'

'I should hardly think he will object.'

'He's a very nice man,' said Lucy. 'He brought some rabbits for Bessie, and we've just – *owch*!'

She looked reproachfully at Pip, who had delivered a sharp kick to her ankle.

'Today I have received a letter from your mother,' Aunt Marchmont said.

'Hurray!'

'What does she say?'

'It appears that Edward and Fergus are very much better.'

'Edmund and Felix, actually. Oh topping!'

'Has all their skin peeled off yet?' Lucy asked with interest.

'How very disagreeable. She does not say. She merely says that she will write to you all shortly, and asks me to tell you that your stay will not be so long as was expected.'

'I expect you're glad,' said Lucy.

Aunt Marchmont regarded her thoughtfully.

'I don't believe I am as glad as I had expected to be,' she said.

'We have tried to be good – '

'Honestly – '

'On our very best behaviours – '

'And we're truly grateful – '

'You are doing it again,' Aunt Marchmont interrupted. 'That dreadful "buttering up"!'

The children immediately ceased their protestations.

'There's no need now, anyhow,' George said.

'We thought you had a heart of stone,' explained Lucy, while the others groaned inwardly.

'Did you, indeed . . . ?' murmured Aunt Marchmont. Then, almost as if to herself, 'Many grown-ups have, I suppose . . . almost as if they had never been children themselves . . .'

'But *you* have,' George said. 'We know that for a fact.'

The others tittered, and Aunt Marchmont regarded them curiously.

'Have you noticed anything about the room?' she asked. 'I had rather expected you would.'

They look around, and each realised as one and at the same time that the room was, indeed, strangely bare, and that there seemed to be more wall than usual.

'The samplers!'

'Your sewing!'

'I took them all down!' Aunt Marchmont sounded triumphant, as if she had achieved some splendid victory. 'Hateful things! Samplers! Ugh!'

'What have you done with them?' cried Ellie, who ever since the young Connie had told of the trick she had played, had been dying to look and see if it were really true.

'They are in the cupboard under the stairs, waiting to go to the next bazaar,' replied Aunt Marchmont happily. 'Good riddance! Now, who's for croquet tommorrow?'

Usually there would have been an eager chorus of acceptance. But tomorrow there were pressing matters to attend to. The Psammead must be found. The children averted their eyes and shuffled uncomfortably.

'I see.' Aunt Marchmont sounded disappointed, even hurt.

'It's not that we don't *like* playing with you, Aunt Marchmont,' Ellie said.

'You're a sport,' added Pip.

'It's just that we have an important mission – '

'A Quest . . .'

'Ah, a Quest. I see. How very interesting. I rather wish I had one myself. There seems rather a lot of time to fill, now that I no longer do any sewing.'

'You could take up science,' suggested Pip helpfully. 'It's jolly interesting.'

'For some,' said George.

'You could ask for a magnifying glass for your birthday, like I did.'

'Nobody knows my birthday,' said Aunt Marchmont.

The children gazed at her in horror. It had never even occurred to them that she was as lone and lorn as the Psammead itself, which had had no family to remember its birthday for hundreds, if not thousands of years. It seemed the saddest thing imaginable that she should have birthday after birthday with no presents to open, no special tea with iced cake and jelly, and no one even to wish her Many Happy Returns.

'Many Happy Returns!' said Lucy.

Everyone looked at her, startled.

'That's for *last* year's, she explained.

They all laughed, and even Aunt Marchmont managed a smile.

'When's your next one, please?'

'As a matter of fact it is quite shortly – in a few days.'

'We'll have a party,' said Ellie.

'And an enormous cake and sausage rolls, and stuff,' said Pip.

'And play charades and Blindman's Buff and such . . .'

'Oh, will we really?' Aunt Marchmont looked positively excited, her cheeks were pink and her eyes shone. It occurred to Ellie that perhaps even as a child Aunt Marchmont had never had proper birthdays – especially as she had no brothers or sisters to plan surprises.

'Won't we just!' said George. 'Just you wait and see!'

And so the children went to bed that night quite happy, despite the knowledge that the Psammead was missing, and might never again be found. They had the kind of warm glow that comes out of being kind to others. When Mother told them that it was better to give than to receive they never quite believed her, but had often found, to their surprise, that it was perfectly true.

Chapter XIII

THE MILKMAN CALLS

At breakfast next morning none of the children was hungry. Each was thinking of the Psammead, and what awful fate might have befallen it. To make matters worse, they felt guilty, too. After all, if it were not for them the Psammead would still be slumbering peacefully in its own sand-pit, where it had spent all the thousands of years of its life. And no one had even gone out to the summerhouse to say goodnight to it, and see if it was comfortable. They were miserably aware that in keeping the Sand-fairy shut in the summerhouse they had been behaving out of their own selfishness, just as Stella had when she tried to keep them. They had treated it not as the magical and lordly beast that it was, but like any common or garden hedgehog.

Needless to say the minute breakfast was over they flew down to the sand-pit.

'Oh let it be there, let it be there!' cried Lucy as they dropped to their knees by the heap of stones. Ellie drew a deep breath.

'Sammyadd, dear Sammyadd – we're sorry we left you shut in the hamper and never even came to say goodnight. And Sammyadd – we wish you'd forgive us and come out!'

They waited, and all secretly crossed their fingers, though naturally they did not really believe that this would help. Nor did it. The sand by the heap of stones lay quiet and unruffled as any other patch of sand in the world.

'Oh *please*, Sammyadd,' whispered Lucy. 'We wish you would!'

Again they waited.

'No good,' said George dully.

'Not there,' said Pip. 'Now what?'

'Back home, I s'pose, and all spread out and comb the garden.'

Which is what they did, but as they went they were unusually silent. The children were all thinking the same thought – that the most magical thing they had ever met, or were ever likely to meet, had slipped through their fingers through their own carelessness.

'It must still be in the garden somewhere,' said Lucy at last. She, at least, had seen the Psammead yesterday.

'If Dawkins hasn't shot it,' said Pip gloomily.

'Oh don't, don't!' Lucy's hands went to her ears.

'So it must,' said Ellie, 'so all we have to do is search.'

'Oh yes,' said Pip with heavy sarcasm. '*You* ever tried finding a needle in a bottle of hay?'

'Nothing's impossible,' said Ellie stubbornly. 'Not to a Garsington, anyway.'

'She's right,' said George, summoning up his own spirit. 'We don't give up – no fear. Now everybody – spread out – and search!'

But there were so many wild acres of garden that they could hardly think where to start. Here and there they wandered, calling its name. They went to the corners of the garden they had never even visited, they looked in the hot-house, the vegetable garden and even amongst Dobbs' precious flowerbeds. By dinner time they were hot and tired and almost ready to give up.

But steak and kidney pudding followed by raspberry pie had a rejuve-
nating effect on their spirits, and afterwards they went back out into the
garden to discuss their next tactics.

George asked Lucy exactly where she had seen the Psammead the day
before, but she shook her head dolefully.

'I couldn't see. The brolly was too big. All I know is it was under the
trees.'

'And so is three quarters of the garden,' said Pip. 'You are hopeless,
Lucy! Why didn't you mark the spot?'

'Oh yes, in the pouring rain and with a brolly to hold!'

'Girls!' said George contemptuously. 'Well I'm going to carry on
looking. *Nil Desperandum*!'

'And me, and I may as well look for a fox at the same time,' Pip said.
He had been looking for a fox ever since he read about Spartans keeping
foxes under their jackets and letting them gnaw at them, to test their
courage. Unlike his sister, he did not believe everything he read in
books, and he thought this an unlikely story. Pip was not much interested
in testing his courage, but nonetheless thought this would be a worthwhile
experiment. If the fox bit, he meant to drop it, fast.

'Wait!' said George. 'Now listen. What the Sammyadd needs is sand.
Right?'

'Right!' they chorussed.

'And the only sand round here is at the sand-pit itself, and in that
hamper. Right?'

'Right!'

'So it's bound to make for one of those two. So here's what we'll do. Pip
and me'll carry on searching the garden. You girls, stay in the summerhouse and keep watch.'

This was generally agreed to be a sound idea. The boys armed themselves with rakes and set off again. The girls fetched their work – Ellie

her Journal and Lucy her portrait, to keep them occupied.

'Let's take Methusalah,' suggested Lucy. 'Birds've got sharper eyes than human beings. *He* might spot the Sammyadd.'

'And *tell* us, I suppose,' said Ellie. 'Do be your age, Lucy.'

'Eight isn't much of an age to *be*,' said Lucy. 'Everyone's always expecting me to be older than I am.'

Anyway, they took the parrot, and cleared a space in the dusty jumble of the summerhouse, and settled down.

'Let's not even *think* about the Sammyadd,' said Lucy, 'The best things always come up on you when you're not looking.'

'That's true,' agreed Ellie, remembering how that very thing had happened to her on that first, magical meeting in the twilit sand-pit.

And so each became lost in its own thoughts, one busily writing and the other painting, and the parrot, as usual, silent and unblinking on its perch. In the end, though, someone was bound to speak.

'I think this portrait's going to be my best ever,' Lucy said. 'Even better than the one I did of Methusalah.'

She looked over to where that bird sat, shut-eyed now, and silent.

'You liked that, dicky ducks, didn't you?' she asked.

The parrot, needless to say, ignored this question entirely.

'Pity he can't even say "yes",' Lucy said. 'I thought *all* parrots were meant to talk. I wish this one did. Just think of the things he might say!'

'Look, Lucy, I want to write my Journal. Just paint your portrait, and then we'll have another try at teaching him.'

'He's hopeless,' Lucy said. 'He can't even say "boiled beef and carrots"!'

'*Boiled beef and carrots!*'

Both girls jumped. They knew that it was quite impossible that this dunce of a bird should suddenly come out with this remark after a life-time's silence.

'Let alone . . . let alone . . . round the ragged rocks the ragged rascals ran!' Lucy faltered.

'*Round the ragged rocks the ragged rascal ran!*'

Ellie put down her pen, staring.

'Did you hear that?' Lucy whispered.

'*It's rude to whisper! Mind your manners!*'

It *was* Methusalah – unless another more loquacious bird was concealed in one of the hampers, which seemed unlikely.

'My thimble!' Lucy stared at her finger with awe. 'I put it on to wish the Sammyadd would come back and then – just now, I wished Methusalah could talk!'

'*Old Aunt Marchmont's a Sunday School Prig!*'

The girls stared at the bird with horror. The sly thing had evidently been listening to all their private conversations.

'Hush!' they cried. 'Don't say it!'

'*Fruminously Foe!*' said the bird with relish.

'Oh do be quiet! She might hear you!'

'*What a silly cuckoo!*' remarked the parrot. '*You're the one who wished me to speak!*'

'Ah, there you are!'

The girls whirled round to see Bessie's head poking round the door.

'*Whoops-a-daisy!*' said the parrot.

Bessie looked startled for a moment, then, 'I've jus' come back from that poor l'l Lil,' she said, '*ever* so lonely, she is. Get down there, there's good girls, and keep 'er company a bit.'

'Oh we will, we will!' cried the girls, eager that Bessie should leave before the parrot made another of its utterances.

'Good gels!' She disappeared.

'*Bessie's had another of her funny turns!*' screeched the parrot.

Bessie's face reappeared frowning now.

'What was that?' she demanded.

'Nothing, Bessie!'

'Nothing at all!'

'I should 'ope not, indeed!' and again she disappeared.

'Oh *now* what?' cried Lucy. 'We can't go to the cottage and leave him here talking his head off. What if Bessie comes in, or Aunt Marchmont!'

'*A Golden Deed a day keeps the doctor away*,' observed the irrepressible bird.

'Yes, and much good Golden Deeds will do us if you go and *un*do them,' Ellie told him severely.

'We'll have to take him with us,' Lucy said.

Ellie nodded slowly. The parrot simply could not be left swinging there and saying anything that came into his head.

'You're going on an outing, Methusalah,' she told him.

'*Hip hip hooray! Absolutely ripping!*'

'Oh no!' cried Lucy suddenly. 'Look!'

There, on the lawn beyond was Aunt Marchmont, and with her the boys. She had evidently rounded them up for a lesson in croquet.

'Oh no! And they're supposed to be searching!'

No sooner were the words out of Ellie's mouth than a thought struck her. 'But they don't need to!'

'Why?'

'Don't you see? You wished Methusalah to talk, and he can! So the Sammyadd must be somewhere near.'

Lucy stared at her, round-eyed.

'Oh so it must! Darling Sammyadd!' But some stubborn and hopeful part of her still believed that her thimble might have played a part.

'The trouble is,' said Ellie slowly, 'it's dangerous.'

'Why is it?'

'Because the boys don't know. What if they let slip a wish and it comes true? What if they wish the aunt would disappear off the face of the earth . . .'

'Or the earth would swallow her up . . .'

'Or that we were all back home in Islington . . .?'

The possibilities were endless. It is perfectly possible, as you know, to wish for anything at all on the spur of the moment. And usually such wishes, especially if they are mean and horrid, are not meant at all, and are in any case harmless – because which of you has a Sand-fairy at hand to grant them? You can say to your brother 'I just wish you'd go away and never come back!' or 'Tell tale tit, your tongue shall split – and I jolly well wish it would!' – without the least danger of it happening. Here, the case was very different.

'It's no use,' said Ellie. 'We can't warn them. We'll just have to keep our fingers crossed. The main thing is to get past them with the parrot without the aunt hearing.'

She covered his cage, and they edged out of the summerhouse, though a muffled voice could be heard coming from under the cloth, '*Help! Murder!*'

They sidled away, hoping thus to make themselves invisible, but inevitably there came a shout.

'Hey! Where are you going with that?'

'Just taking him for a walk!' called Lucy.

'To keep Lily company!' added Ellen, on a sudden inspiration. 'True, anyway,' she told herself.

'*Two's company, three's a crowd!*' came the muffled voice of the parrot, mercifully unheard by the croquet players. '*Aunt Marchmont's a –* '

'Hush!' screamed the girls and ran, and did not stop until they were well out of earshot, and Dawkins' cottage in sight. There sat little Lil, as usual, with her doll. They waved, and she waved back.

'I think she's looking fatter already,' Lucy said.

'That nice lady brought me some cake,' Lil told them. 'I like her. Is she your Ma?'

Lucy giggled at the notion, but Ellie frowned, and said, 'No, Lily. Our mother's at home – but Bessie looks after us while we're here.'

'I ain't got nobody to look after me. 'Cept Pa.'

'We know,' said Ellie gently.

'What's that?' Lil pointed at the cage.

'*What's that, what's that?*'

'It's *alive!*'gasped Lil.

'It's a parrot,' Ellie told her. 'We thought he'd be company for you.'

'A real live talking bird!' Lil's eyes opened wide.

'Well, only since this morning,' Lucy said.

Ellie lifted the cover from the cage and little Lil gasped.

'Oh, ain't 'e pretty?'

'*Pretty poll, pretty poll!*' boasted the parrot.

'An' look at 'is nice little eyes!'

'*What a pretty girl, what a pretty girl!*'

''E *likes* me!' Little Lil was ecstatic, her eyes shone. 'Oh, is 'e reely to stop wi' me, reely and truly?'

The girls hesitated and exchanged glances.

''Arf a pound of tuppeny rice,' said Lil.

'*Half a pound of treacle,*' supplied the parrot obligingly.

'Oh, ain't 'e clever!'

'*Eat your cabbage and make your hair curl!*' said Methusalah.

'That's jus' what my Ma used to say!'

Ellie could see the boys coming towards them through the trees, their croquet lesson evidently over. She did not wish to explain Methusalah's sudden talkativeness in front of little Lil.

'Look, we must go now. We'll leave him with you, to get to know each other.'

Little Lil seemed hardly to hear, enraptured as she was with her new friend. Lucy and Ellie left them and ran to meet the boys.

'Look here, what's going off?' demanded George.

'What's the parrot doing out here?'

'You'll never believe us,' Ellie told them, 'but he's talking!'

'I don't believe you!' said George.

'There! I said you wouldn't! But he *is* – he's talking like anything – '

'And making rude remarks about Aunt Marchmont and Bessie – '

'So we simply had to get him away from them.'

'But why?' asked Pip. 'Why's he talking?'

The girls exchanged glances again. Neither really wished to be the one to tell their scientific brother what had happened, because it seemed impossible, even to themselves. Lucy was beginning to wonder whether her wish had been overheard by the Psammead, or whether her thimble had something to do with it. Yesterday it had apparently taken them into the picture of the smugglers. The Psammead had warned her that its powers would last only for that one day. But she had been believing wholeheartedly in her magic thimble ever since it had rolled out of her cracker, and to her it seemed not altogether impossible that it had rendered talkative the stubbornly dumb Methusalah.

'The Sammyadd must be somewhere about,' Ellie said, 'and over-heard us.'

'Or my thimble,' put in Lucy.

The boys hooted, as she had known they would.

'Strike me pink!' said Pip. 'The thimble, she says!'

'And pigs can fly,' added George.

'Well I had it on my finger, and I wished he could speak.'

'The silly thing's never worked before,' Pip pointed out.

'Till yesterday!'

'That's different. That was because of the Sammyadd.'

'Either that, or – could it be something to do with this *place*?' asked Ellie.

'There could be magic in the air!' exclaimed Lucy.

'Magic, my elbow!' said Pip. 'It's not – '

'If you say "it's not scientific" once more, I shall scream!' said Ellie.

The others were startled by this outburst from their usually calm sister.

'All right, all right, no need to get waxy,' said Pip.

Tempers were frayed. An all out row would almost certainly have developed had not a startling sight then met their eyes. It was Lucy who first spotted it.

'Look!' She pointed, and they all turned.

At first sight an oversized bunch of flowers on legs appeared to be approaching. But as this walking bouquet neared them there were glimpses of a figure behind it, and about this figure there was something vaguely familiar, and when it was seen to be crowned with a tuft of ginger hair –

'Arfur!' exclaimed George in weak tones.

There is something oddly shocking in seeing a familiar figure in unfamiliar surroundings. Back in Islington the children were well used to seeing that small, ginger-headed figure running up and down steps, feeding his horse, even on occasion sitting in their own kitchen, his lashless eyes fixed adoringly on Bessie. Their nurse was not exactly walking out with Arthur, but he could certainly be described as a follower. Now, here he was in that leafy place far from the doorsteps of Islington, and his very person was made odd and foreign, as if a dinosaur had suddenly appeared, or an Indian tiger.

'Arthur!'

They ran towards him. The enormous bunch of flowers was lowered, and there was that freckled face, though more than usually shiny and well scrubbed. He was dressed as if for church, in a suit that seemed to have been made several sizes too large – either that, or the milkman had since shrunk. His boots shone like glass.

'What on earth?'

'Mornin', miss! Mornin'!'

'But what are you *doing* here?'

A tide of scarlet swept Arthur's face and neck, it went among his gingery whiskers, where it clashed horribly.

'Jus' 'appened to be passing,' he mumbled.

The children gasped at this palpable fib. They were not, as it happened, particularly fond of Arthur. He shouted at them when they patted his horse, and cursed when they threw harmless snowballs. Furthermore, they did not admire his gingery appearance. In short, he was not worthy of Bessie, and they had even hinted as much to her. At which she would turn pink and say, 'Get along with you!' or 'Cotton must serve while you wait on velvet!' or some other such thing.

'Did you just happen to pick that bunch of flowers?' enquired Pip. 'Or were they for anyone in particular?'

'You mean you just happened to go to the station and get on a train and it just happened to come down here?' asked George. 'We're not dummies, you know.'

The milkman took a swipe at him with the flowers, but George jumped smartly back and the others tittered. The flush darkened.

'Little beggars!' observed the milkman. 'Don't know 'ow she puts up wiv yer, and that's a fack.'

'She likes us!' piped up Lucy. 'So there!'

'Then more fool 'er,' growled Arthur.

'And she only puts up with you while she waits for velvet!'

Lucy had only the vaguest idea of what this might mean, but it seemed to serve as an insult of sorts.

'I've 'ad enough of your cheek! Hout my way!'

The milkman pushed past them and they watched the bouquet march on its way towards the house.

'Does Bessie know he's coming, I wonder?' said Ellie.

'She had a letter,' Lucy said. 'I saw her open it and she went all pink.'

'Good Lord!' said George disgustedly. 'Now look here, are you sure that bird's talking?'

'Come and listen for yourself,' Ellie told him.

George could not resist this invitation. He had spent many hours vainly coaching that beaktied bird.

'And then let's go back to the house and see what Bessie's doing,' Lucy said. 'Does she *really* like Arfer, d'you think?'

'Shouldn't think so,' Pip told her. 'Though she may turn soppy when she sees the flowers.'

The four of them went over to where little Lil was holding rapturous conversation with her new found friend. As they did so, a shot rang out.

'*Help*! *Murder*!' said the parrot.

'Dawkins!' exclaimed George. 'And the aunt's about!'

Another shot. Another.

'She stuck up for Dawkins the other day with that policeman,' Ellie said, 'so perhaps her heart of stone is already melting.'

'She was a *child*, then duffer!' Pip told her.

George went over to the parrot and gave it a playful poke.

'Say "Hello, George," if you can, dunce!' he said.

'*Hello George if you can dunce*!' responded the bird obligingly.

'Crickey, it's true!'

'Can he read as well, d'you think,' said Pip. 'And that reminds me . . .' he dug in his pocket and fished out a book and handed it to Lil. It was a lavishly illustrated Alphabet that had evidently belonged to Aunt Marchmont in her youth.

'Did that nice lady send it? That Bessie?'

'Not her. The aunt. She'll have you doing algebra next, if you don't watch out.'

'I quite likes Miss Marchmont now,' said Lil. 'But she's not so nice and pretty as Bessie. Who was that man with the big flowers?'

'Arfur,' George told her. 'Arthur, I should say – our milkman from Islington. He's sweet on Bessie.'

'I wish my Pa was,' said Lil wistfully. 'I wish my Pa was sweet on 'er, I do. Then they could get married and live 'appy ever after. I'd like that, I would.'

Chapter XIV

LIL MAKES A WISH

Little Lil spoke those words, she made that wish, and it did not occur to one of them that the wish was granted as soon as spoken. The Psammead, you see, was bound to grant a wish whenever it heard one. It was still making its snail-like way back home to the sand-pit. When it had told the children that all it ever did was sit, it had been speaking the truth. It hated the tangle of grass and flowers and nettles, and it moaned 'Sand, sand!' just as a thirsty traveller in the desert cries 'Water, water!' Yesterday it had barely escaped from the hamper at dawn when it had been terrified by Dawkins' dog and gun, and burrowed its way into the ground. There it had stayed till Lucy found it, and by then, it was raining.

This morning it had nervously poked its head out again, testing the air with its top left twelfth whisker. Almost at once it had heard Lucy's wish about the parrot, and had granted it, however reluctantly. Then, inching its way through the long grass, and scrambling through thickets, it was passing quite close to Dawkins' cottage when it heard a second wish.

'Selfish, inconsiderate child!' it muttered, but blew itself out all the same, and granted it. It was right in the middle of this when it heard another crack of the gun.

'*Help! Murder!*' screeched the parrot.

The Psammead tried desperately to burrow its way down again, but it was right in the middle of a bramble patch. So it concealed itself as best it could amongst the leaves, and sat there fairly quaking with fright. (It had been easy enough to sound brave and careless about dogs and guns when it was safely at home in the sand-pit. Here, in this strange world of grass and thicket, that fairy was as out of place as a fish in air.)

'Look here,' said George, ignoring Lil's soppy remark, and not even noticing that it contained the fatal word 'wish', 'that man – Dobbs's nephew, the one who sent for the policeman – did you know him?'

''E's a bad man!' said Lil. 'My Pa says 'e's after 'is job, and our 'ouse.'

George whistled.

'So that's it!'

'An' 'e goes shooting, so's Miss Marchmont'll 'ear, and think it's my Pa. Look!'

She pointed, and there, propped against the wall, was Dawkins' gun.

'So that wasn't him just now!'

Lil shook her head.

'But *she* finks it is.'

The children were aghast.

'A plot is afoot,' said George darkly.

'Of deep dyed villainy!'

The children exchanged meaningful glances. It seemed that now there was not only a Quest to pursue, but a plot to be foiled into the bargain. They cheered somewhat at the thought – it is not often in life that children are faced with the exciting prospect of unmasking villains.

'Look out – Bessie!' said Lucy suddenly.

'Quick – hide the parrot!' Pip snatched up the cage and placed it behind a convenient shrub.

'And Arfur!'

Trotting at Bessie's side was the bunch of flowers. It had evidently met her on her way to the cottage with provisions, and it had turned back to keep her company. She herself looked uncommonly pink and flustered, and would doubtless have been twisting her apron had not her hands been otherwise engaged in carrying baskets.

''Ere we are, then!' she gasped, setting them down. She said not a word to explain the escorting bouquet, rather as if she hoped no one would notice it. Little Lil pounced on the baskets and uttered joyous cries at the sight of pies and pastries, cheeses and jams.

'Morning again, Arthur!' said George.

'*Arfur's ugly, Arfur's ugly,*' remarked the parrot from behind his redcurrant bush.

Bessie looked startled. The children all began talking at once in the hope of drowning out any further utterances.

'They look jolly nice!'

'Cook's a trump!'

'Why don't you go for a nice walk with Arthur now?'

Bessie's hands, free of the baskets, were now twisting her apron.

'I honly got a coupla hours,' said the milkman. 'I come a long way to see you, and Hislington's a 'orrible place wivout yer.'

'Oh, go on!' muttered Bessie, in agonies of embarrassment.

'I've 'ardly got the 'eart to do me rounds wivout a sight of yer!'

Bessie's apron went into a feverish bunch.

'*'Orrible yourself, 'orrible yourself!*' came the parrot's new found voice.

Bessie, bemused, looked about her, but at this moment there came a welcome distraction.

'Look!' shrieked Lucy.

Advancing at a very fast rate was a second giant bunch of flowers, a Goliath of a bunch.

'Strewth!' exclaimed George.

Arthur turned, and at the sight of this rival floral offering his face went into a scowl the children knew only too well.

'It's Pa!' cried little Lil.

It was indeed. Dawkins strode forward, thereby almost knocking over the milkman, gave an awkward half bow and thrust the flowers at the astonished Bessie.

'For you!'

She did not take them. She looked from one to the other of her admirers, uttered a shriek, turned on her heel and ran back towards the house as fast as ever her charges had seen her go. Lucy, enchanted by this turn of events, hopped from one foot to the other.

'Go after her, Mr Dawkins! Go after her!'

Dawkins, after a moment's hesitation, made as if to do so, but the milkman stepped in his path.

'And oo might you be?' he demanded menacingly.

Dawkins lowered his bouquet.

'And who might you?'

'Hi'm from Lunnon, Hislington,' replied Arthur. 'And me'n Bessie's engaged to be married.'

'Oh you never!' gasped Ellie.

'*Wot a whopper, wot a whopper!*' supplied the parrot.

'Don't you go calling me a liar!' said Arthur.

'I never did!' said Dawkins hotly.

'*Liar!, Liar!*

'There – you did!'

'*Some*one did,' said Dawkins, 'an' p'raps you are!'

He brandished his flowers and the milkman did likewise. But Dawkins was the bigger by half a head, and by now Arthur was looking jumpy and licking his lips. He turned and made to follow Bessie, but now it was Dawkins' turn to block his path.

'There'll be a fight if that bird doesn't shut up!' muttered George.

'*Fight*! *Fight*!' screeched Methusalah.

'If it's a fight you want, a fight you'll get!' Dawkins brandished his bouquet like a sabre.

'*Cowardy cowardy custard*! *Daren't eat mustard*!'

'Right you are!' roared Dawkins. He threw down his flowers and raised his fists. The frightened milkman took one look and fled.

'Bessie, Bessie! Help! Help!' he yelled.

Dawkins hesitated, then picked up his own flowers and ran after him.

'Jiminy!' exclaimed Pip. 'What's got into Dawkins?'

'My Pa is sweet on Bessie!' Little Lil's eyes were shining. 'I wished 'e was, and 'e is!'

A silence fell. The four of them stared at her, light slowly dawning. George beckoned the others.

'Here – we'd better have a parley!'

They went into a huddle out of earshot of little Lil and the incorrigible Methusalah.

'She *did* wish it!' said Ellie.

'The Sammyadd!'

'It's somewhere about – must be.'

This seemed incontestable. Dawkins had certainly in the past displayed a certain softness for Bessie, but nothing so extreme as this.

'Come on – we must find it!'

'Wait!' George looked in the direction of little Lil and frowned. 'We don't want her seeing. What if she blabs?'

'She would, you know,' Pip nodded. 'Girls do.'

'There is one thing,' said George slowly. 'I supposed we could always try *wishing* it back to the sand-pit.'

'So we could! Not so dusty, Jaws!'

'But we don't know for sure it'd work. And another thing . . .'

'It's *done* two wishes today, already.'

'Even more, for all we know . . .'

'And it's been out of sand for ages . . .'

'So it could be weak. It might be dangerous . . .'

'It rained yesterday, and all the other Sand-fairies caught cold and died . . .'

'We daren't risk it,' said George decisively. 'If we leave it where it is, anyone could wish for *any*thing.'

'You girls, you take Lil off somewhere, then me and Jaws'll look.'

'But *we* want to find it!' cried Lucy.

'No, Lucy lamb, he's right. Come on – else perhaps *none* of us'll ever find it – ever again!'

At this dire prospect Lucy allowed herself to be led away, and Ellie said, 'Look, Lil, let's take the parrot for a walk. I think he's tired of being behind that bush.'

'*Walkies*! *Walkies*!' sqauwked the parrot.

'Parrots like a change of scene,' added Lucy obligingly.

Ellie picked up his cage, and the three of them set off, Lucy and Lil hand in hand.

'He saw Arfur off, anyhow,' said Pip grinning. 'So it wasn't a wish wasted! Right – the Sammyadd!'

They really did not know where to start, and rather hoped it would give itself up.

'Sammyadd!' they called. 'Sammyadd, where are you?'

The Psammead, still quaking in its bramble patch, heard those calls and was inclined to respond. It was still furious with the children, certainly, for itnapping it and then going off so carelessly, leaving it in the hamper. On the other hand, there was still a long way to go to its sand-pit, and guns were out.

'Here!' it called faintly. 'Here!'

'If it's a fight you want a fight you'll get!'

And so Pip's clothes obligingly began to perform a jig.

'There!' cried George triumphantly, and they trampled through the undergrowth in the direction of the voice.

'Sand, sand!' moaned that familiar voice.

George drew aside a hanging bough and there, sitting reproachful-eyed amongst the brambles, was the Psammead.

'Thank heaven!'

'Sammyadd!'

'Sand, sand!' it whimpered. 'I shall die without sand!'

'Wait here!' ordered George. 'Come on, Pips!'

He tore off in the direction of the summerhouse, followed by his mystified brother.

'Where are we going?'

'Sand, idiot!'

The nearest sand was that in the hamper. George had some vague idea that they could drag that down to where the Psammead was, and then on to the sand-pit. It was too risky, he decided, simply to snatch up the fairy and run, as he had on the first occasion. By now it had been out of sand for ages, and for all he knew, it *might* die. George had ambitions to go down in history, all right, but not as the one responsible for the extinction of the last of the Psammeads.

By great good fortune he spied a wheelbarrow near the summerhouse.

'That's it!' he cried. 'The very ticket!'

He seized the handles and pushed it into the summerhouse, where he began feverishly scooping sand into it from the hamper. Pip followed suit, and soon the barrow was half full.

'There's not much,' said George dubiously. 'But it should be enough to keep it going till we get to the sand-pit.'

He snatched up a feathered headdress from the other hamper, tossed it into the barrow, and started to wheel it back towards Dawkins' cottage. Pip grabbed at his arm.

'Look out! The aunt!'

George looked up and saw Aunt Marchmont, Dobbs beside her, advancing over the lawn. He swerved violently aside into the shrubbery, thereby almost tipping the barrow and its precious cargo. There the pair of them crouched, each shutting its eyes, as one does when one hopes to be invisible.

'Are you sure, Dobbs?' they heard Aunt Marchmont say. 'And why should you think it is Dawkins?'

'It's 'im, all right,' said Dobbs grimly. 'Oo else would it be? You 'eard 'im shooting jus' now . . .'

'Well, yes,' agreed Aunt Marchmont. 'But I rather think I can overlook that, now. After all, the poor man has no wife, and that little girl to feed . . .'

'That's as mebbee. But jus' you wait till you sees my hot-'ouse. Not a peach left, miss, nor a grape either. It's my belief he's been robbin' 'em and selling 'em!'

'Disgraceful!' cried Aunt Marchmont.

It was all the boys could do to restrain themselves from rushing out of their hiding place and challenging Dobbs to his face. Had there not been the more urgent matter of restoring the Psammead to its sand-pit, they would certainly have done so.

Then George sneezed.

'Oo's that!'

Dobbs was into the shrubbery in a flash, and they were discovered.

''Ere – where you going with my barrow!'

'George! Philip!' exclaimed their aunt.

'We – we're just having a game!'

'Cowboys and Indians!'

'The barrow's the stage coach!'

The aunt, to their huge relief and amazement, laughed.

'I remember doing the very thing myself! Off you go, then.'

'But – my barrer!' spluttered the furious Dobbs.

'I'm sure it's perfectly safe with them – you are going to show me the stolen fruit . . .'

The boys were already making good their escape.

'You and your beastly sneezes!' said Pip. 'That's twice you've nearly done for us with 'em!'

'Can't – help – it!' panted George, running and pushing like anything.

'You should learn to *swallow* 'em! There's no need to go sneezing like the last trump!'

(Later, Pip would give George a lesson in the art of suppressing sneezes, but to little avail. George simply could not get the hang of it, and had to resign himself to going through the rest of his life an explosive sneezer.)

As they raced along on their mission of mercy, further shots rang out. They knew for a fact that Dawkins was armed only with a bunch of flowers, and that little Lil had been right. Dobbs and his pasty nephew were in conspiracy, out to lose Dawkins his job and his home, so that Albert could take both.

Back at the bramble patch they found the poor Psammead quaking fearfully. It sat hunched, its skinny arms wrapped round its head, looking not in the least like the most powerful fairy left on earth.

'We're – back!' gasped George.

It let out a little whimper, but did not look up.

'Right!' George leaned over, scooped up the furry bundle and plonked it in the barrow.

'Sand! Sand!'

There was at once a furious working of arms and legs and sand flew out in a shower.

'Steady on! You'll spill it all!'

When the sandstorm subsided there sat the Psammead, still only half covered.

'Where am I? Where am I!'

'In a wheelbarrow,' replied George, taking the handles again and starting to push. 'We're taking you back to the sand-pit.'

'In a wheelbarrow?' echoed the Psammead in tones of deepest disgust. 'The last of the Psammeads – in a wheelbarrow?'

'Better chuck the feathers over it,' George muttered to Pip. 'Someone might see it.'

So Pip threw the great, feathered headdress of Big Chief Someone-or-other over the disgruntled Psammead, which at once began complaining loudly and struggling to throw it off.

It was at this point that Arfur came pounding up behind them.

'Strewth!' exclaimed George. 'What happened?'

The unnaturally spruce and Sunday-best appearance of the milkman was quite undone. His shirt and collar were pulled awry, his jacket torn and one of his eyes was puffed and turning a delicate plum colour.

'Jiminy!' said Pip. 'You've had a proper pasting!'

'I ain't runnin' after 'er no more,' said the milkman through gritted teeth. 'Never you fear. Come 'ere wiv a *ring*, I did, and – *that* to the pesky thing!'

He plucked a small, glittering object from his pocket and hurled it to the ground with such force that anyone could see that this was exactly what he wished to do to Dawkins. The boys grinned, and their grinning served only to infuriate him further.

'An' – an' you stop that sniggerin', else I'll, – I'll – ooh, I wish – '

'*No!*' cried the boys as one in an almighty shout, and 'No!' screamed the Psammead in the barrow, at that very moment hurling aside the feathered headdress. The milkman boggled at the sight of that strange beast, with its tangled fur and glaring eyes. He shut his good eye, then opened it again, as though hoping thereby to convince himself that everything had been a horrible nightmare from which he was now waking. The boys closed their eyes, too, and held their breath.

When they opened them the Psammead had drawn itself up with as much dignity as it could muster in such humiliating circumstances, and was pointing a skinny finger at the terror-struck milkman.

'I solemnly warn you . . .' it began.

But the milkman had had enough.

'It's a mad'ouse! I'm orf!'

He took to his heels while the boys fairly hooted.

'*That* was a shaver,' said Pip, when their mirth and subsided.

'What was he going to wish, d'you think?'

'Search me. Good old Sammyadd – you certainly saw him off.'

'I did, rather,' agreed the Psammead, with a glimmer of its customary smugness. Then, with an abrupt change of manner, 'Now – take me home, and look sharp!'

The boys obeyed with a will. Off they set again with the wheelbarrow and its occupant.

'You're perfect noodles, of course,' observed the Psammead.

'Why?'

'All this fuss. Why didn't you simply *wish* me back to the sand-pit?'

'We did think of it,' George told it.

'But we didn't want to risk it. You'd been out of sand for such ages.'

'And we thought you'd be quite worn out . . . especially your whisker . . .'

The Psammead gave a huge yawn.

'I suppose I am, rather,' and it closed its eyes.

They reached the safety of the sand-pit without further incident. There, George lifted the Psammead down and no sooner had he done so than it starting whirling itself down.

'No – wait!'

They had the merest glimpse of its furious face through the flying sand.

'And don't you dare wish! Don't you dare!' And then it had gone.

Later, the children held another parley. The boys told the girls what they had overheard when they were fetching the sand.

'He was trying to make out Dawkins was stealing fruit from the hot-house, and selling it.'

'Oh, and just as the aunt's heart was melting! Should we tell her, do you think?'

George shook his head.

'Not yet. We can't *prove* it. It'd be just our word against his.'

'And no one ever believes children against grown-ups,' said Ellie bitterly.

'We'll have to come up with something,' Pip said, 'or that brute Dobbs will scupper us yet.'

'And our Quest will have failed.'

Just then Bessie poked her head in.

'Supper!'

'Another of Dawkins' rabbits?' enquired Pip, mainly for the pleasure of seeing her turn pink again. Today, she had been in an almost permanent state of pinkness.

'That'll do from you, Master Pip!' she told him.

'He's definitely gone on you,' George said. 'Lawk – you should've seen Arfur's eye!'

'I don't want to 'ear another word! I never did know such vexing children.' Then her expression softened. 'Though I will say this. It was a reel kind thought, giving that parrot to that poor little gel.'

'Where is he?' demanded George, who had last seen his parrot in the custody of the girls.

''E's down at Dawkins'. I tole you, it was a right kind thought, you giving 'im.'

'But we didn't – ' began Pip.

'And 'er that lonely, bless 'er 'eart. She's that lonely – you know what she tole me?'

They waited, half knowing what would come.

'She tole me that bird 'ad been a talking to 'er! Talk! Can you believe?' The children, of course, could. 'Oh dear me – talk! – that bird! Come along now, your suppers is on the table and Cook'll be fretting. Talk! That blessed parrot, as 'as never . . .'

She was away and halfway down the stairs, her voice fading.

'Won't be talking now,' said Pip. 'Gone sunset.'

'And the Sammyadd's back in its sand-pit and all's right with the world!' said George. 'Come on – supper!'

Chapter XV

VILLAINS UNMASKED

Next day, straight after breakfast, the children set off for the sand-pit.

'We don't know for absolutely positive certain that it'll be there,' said Ellie. 'It might be afraid that we'll itnap it again.'

'You can't just chuck up living in a sand-pit if you've lived there thousands of years,' pointed out George reasonably enough.

'Oh darling Sammyadd, I do hope it's there,' said Lucy. 'Isn't it funny that Dawkins' name is Sam? I'm going to ask the Sammyadd if I can call it Sam – it sounds much friendlier.'

'*Sam?*' echoed George. 'The Sammyadd? You can't do that, Luce old thing.'

'Why not?'

'The Sammyadd is a lordly and ancient beast, you can't just go calling it Sam as if it were a milkman or something,' Pip said.

'It'd be like calling a unicorn . . . Janet,' said Ellie.

'Or St George, Georgy Porgy!'

'Or Long John Silver, Peg Leg!'

They had reached the cottage in the lane. There sat Lil, but as well as her doll she had a book on her knee, and on the step beside her, Methusalah.

'She thinks she's got that parrot for good,' said George. 'You girls are idiots – why did you give him to her?'

'We didn't – at least, we just lent it to her, didn't we Lucy?'

'Well, it's going to be jolly awkward getting him back,' George said.

'Leave him now,' Pip told him. 'Come on, we've got to get to that sand-pit, quick!'

Little Lil saw them and waved.

'I'm reading!' she called 'C-a-t!'

'We know!' called back Ellie. 'I'll come and help you, later!'

The two boys, fearful that their sisters might be sidetracked, broke into a run, and so they all reached the sand-pit out of breath. They stopped and stared down at the familiar heap of stones. Under that harmless sand there might lie buried a creature of mystery and power – or there might not.

'Well. Right. Better do it,' said George.

They dropped to their knees.

'You do it, Ellie,' whispered Lucy.

'And lay it on thick,' advised Pip. 'Give it a good buttering up.'

Ellie hesitated, drew a deep breath, and began.

'O great and mighty Sammyadd, O wise and powerful fairy!'

'Good stuff, Ellie,' George whispered. 'Keep it up!'

'Last of the Sammyadds, greatest of the Sammyadds, wisest and best of the Sammyadds – '

'Don't overdo it!' warned Pip.

'We have come to crave an audience, O Mighty One . . .'

'And we do wish you'd come out!' burst out Lucy, unable to contain herself a moment longer.

They waited breath held. And then – a fountain of sand! The children cheered, they could not help it. George actually threw his cap in the air.

'Hurray!' cried the children, as the familiar, whiskered face of the Psammead emerged in a halo of sand.

'What time is it?' it demanded crossly. 'I was having the most marvellous dream, about a Brontosauri. Those were the days . . . ah me!'

It heaved a deep sigh, as if to reproach the children for not themselves being Brontosauri or Pterodactyls or other such interesting beasts.

'It's gone breakfast – we've already had it,' said Pip.

'Then you must have bolted it down most unwholesomely,' the Psammead said. 'Was it Pterodactyl?'

'Er – no – toast, actually,' George said.

'Oh Sammyadd, don't be cross with us,' Ellie pleaded. 'We're dreadfully sorry we never came to say goodnight to you in the summerhouse, the other night.'

'And I'm making you a lovely present,' added Lucy.

'Present!' The Psammead looked pleased despite itself. 'That is very thoughtful of you, dear child. I can't remember how many thousands of years it is since I last had a present. I suppose you mean a token of esteem?'

'Rather – we esteem you like anything!' Pip said. 'But look here – what went off exactly? Not yesterday, the day before?'

'Went *off*?' repeated the Psammead. 'It's none of your business!'

'But is it really true that it was Lucy's thimble that gave the smugglers wish?' persisted Pip.

'In a way,' it replied. 'That silly grown-up person certainly wished that the thimble could give wishes.'

'And you did your puffing up and *made* it work!' exclaimed George.

'Puffing *up*?' echoed the Psammead witheringly. 'I *expanded*, I performed the difficult and powerful work of a Sand-fairy. I granted the wish.'

George whistled.

'I get it now. So the next time anyone wished on the thimble – '

'But not now.' said Pip. 'The silly Christmas cracker thing's back to normal now.'

'I hope you have not come to complain,' said the Psammead. 'If people make absurd wishes, they must take the consequences.'

'Well, we did have rather a close shave,' admitted George.

'But we had a perfectly splendid day,' said Ellie quickly, with a warning look. 'And *thank* you, dear Sammyadd.'

'I try to please,' it said.

'But how did you get out of the hamper?' asked Pip, who liked to have all his I's dotted and his T's crossed.

'I merely raised the lid,' it replied calmly. 'It was not fastened.'

'You gave us the most dreadful fright,' Ellie told it. 'But it all turned out well in the end, and you really are most frightfully clever, dear Sammyadd.'

The Psammead preened itself and assumed an expression of sublime superiority. It was the kind of expression that, if you saw it on a human face, you would wish to wipe off immediately, but one that was forgivable on the last of the Psammeads.

'I suppose you've come for another of your silly wishes,' it said.

'Oh crikey!' exclaimed Pip.

'We never even thought – '

'We just came to find *you!*'

'But let's think of one,' begged Lucy.

'I advise you to think before you wish,' it told them 'Wish in haste, repent at leisure.'

'That's true,' said George. 'And we shan't be getting many more wishes, now.'

'We'll be going home soon, you see,' Ellie explained.

'Well, I haven't got all day,' it said. 'If you want a wish, you had better make it quickly.'

The children racked their brains, but not one of them could come up with an even halfway decent wish.

'Do come on, everybody!' cried Lucy. '*Think!*' (She was a fine one to talk, having for the moment quite forgotten her own idea about wings.)

'My brain won't work,' said Pip.

'As usual,' said George, who then had an inspiration. 'Look here, old – ' he was about to say 'old thing', but realised in time that this was a highly unsuitable form of address to the last of the Psammeads. 'Look here, Sammyadd, do you think that, just for today, you could give us a wish whenever or wherever we happen to think of it?'

'Then we could go away and think of something absolutely first class,' said Pip.

'Oh *please!*' begged Lucy.

'Some other children asked me that once,' it told them, 'and lived to wish they hadn't.'

'*Other* children?' exclaimed Ellie jealously. 'Who?'

'Oh, it doesn't matter,' it said airily, 'It was some time ago – don't ask me when.'

All the children, who had thought of the Psammead as being their very own, secret fairy, were much put out at discovering that this was not so.

'I expect those other children thought up all kinds of stupid wishes,' said Pip.

'No sillier than yours,' replied the Psammead. 'It sounds like the easiest thing in the world to make a wish, but as a matter of fact there is quite an art in it.'

'It's a pity wishing isn't a subject at school, then we could learn it,' Lucy said. 'But I don't s'pose it ever will be. When I told my teacher I thought daydreaming should be on the timetable she just laughed at me.'

'And told you you did it all the time anyway,' Pip said.

'Do you want me to make that wish of yours, or not?' demanded the

Psammead. 'I shan't stay much longer, you know.'

'Nor shall we, now,' said Lucy sadly. 'Just think – this will be one of our very last wishes. Oh Sammyadd, would you mind if I stroked you?'

The Psammead looked at her. She edged closer.

'Oh Sammyadd!' Lucy put out her hand and touched it, gingerly at first, then stroking it as if it were a dog, or cat. Had it been the latter, it would certainly have purred, judging by the expression on its face. Instead, it uttered several little sighs and whimpers of pure pleasure. The others watched, and rather jealously wished that, just for this once, *they* were the youngest, and entitled to such soppy behaviour.

'Oh, you're so nice,' said Lucy softly. 'Much, much better than a thimble.'

'Thimble?' it exclaimed in tones of withering scorn. 'So I should hope! I'm off!'

It began to dig itself back into the sand, but George cried, 'No! Wait! I'll do it! I wish that today we may have our wish whenever and wherever we think of it!'

The Psammead stopped scrabbling and at once began to blow itself out, while the children watched with their usual fascination. Pip watched particularly carefully. (Later, in the secrecy of his room, he would try to perform this blowing out himself, as a scientific experiment. He tried it several times, I need hardly tell you with what result.)

'There!' it said, after the last, shuddering gasp. 'That's done. Remember what I said – look out! Good day!' And then it was digging with its skinny arms, and the next minute gone.

'Well, that's that, then,' said George. 'It was rather a decent wheeze of mine, don't you think? Now we've got time to think of something absolutely prime.'

'We must think of something truly splendid,' agreed Ellie.

'Something perfectly rapturous!'

'It'll be no good wishing once we're back in Islington,' agreed Pip.

'We may as well go back to the house now,' Lucy said. 'I don't like the sand-pit when the Sammyadd's not here.'

And far away down in its sand the Psammead heard those words, and smiled drowsily.

The children dawdled back to the White House, pondering wishes. Lucy wanted to be queen for a day, but the others promptly vetoed this. There would not, they pointed out, be much fun in this for themselves – particularly as they would doubtless be ordered about left and right by their own younger sister. Pip suggested going back to prehistoric times, but was the only one at all keen on encountering a Pterodactyl or Brontosaurus Rex. George pointed out that they had had enough frights of this kind with the smugglers, and said that they should think of something that would be fun, but safe.

They were leaving the wide, sandy dunes when they saw a man, head bent, hurrying ahead of them on the road.

'Where's he sprung from?' said George.

'And where's he going?'

It was Albert, Dobbs' whey-faced nephew.

'You don't think he was following us, and saw the Sammyadd?'

The thought was almost too awful to contemplate. They could barely begin to imagine the kind of dreadful wishes he might make.

'Not he,' said George. 'But he's up to no good. What's he hatching up now, I wonder . . .'

'Perhaps we should give the wish a miss today, and concentrate on catching him and Dobbs out,' suggested Pip.

'Look – there he goes, skulking under the trees – daren't take the lane in case he's seen, I suppose.'

But as the children themselves turned into the lane they were met by a sight that put both skulduggery and the thought of wishes right out of their heads. Coming towards them was the trap, and in it sat Aunt Marchmont, wearing a decidedly floral hat, and next to her, holding the reins – Dawkins!

'Look!' gasped Lucy.

'Here's a go!' exclaimed George (whose mother did not like him to use this vulgar expression).

They stood and stared. Aunt Marchmont smiled and waved. Dawkins gave them a grin followed by a wink. The trap rolled on by and turned into the road towards the village.

'Am I seeing things? I thought I saw the sainted aunt with Dawkins!'

'Hurray!' cried Ellie and Lucy together.

'Come on – let's find out what's gone off!' said Pip.

They had not gone much further when they were met by another surprise. Hearing the furious beating of a carpet, they looked towards Dawkins' cottage. There, to their amazement, they saw Bessie mercilessly whacking a tattered rug in a storm of dust. Little Lil, instead of being on the doorstep as usual, was enthroned in a chair that stood on the grass, and eating buttered scones while turning the pages of a book. The children gaped at this extraordinary tableau.

'Bessie!' they called, and ran over.

'What's gone off?'

'We just saw the aunt with Dawkins!'

'I'm playing at queens on thrones,' said Lil proudly.

'Bless yer 'eart, you *be* queen, my ducky,' said Bessie fondly.

'But what are you doing?' persisted George.

'I'm giving Sam's 'ouse a good go through, that's what,' returned Bessie, resuming her task. 'You get along, there's good children, and don't 'inder me.'

She scooped the rug from the line and bustled back into the cottage to finish the cleaning, while the children exchanged looks of extreme puzzlement.

'Come on,' said Pip. 'Seeing those scones's made me ravenous!'

'Let's go and ask Cook!'

This seemed an excellent idea. Cook was happy to provide them with both scones and an explanation of what was happening.

'Them blessed Dobbses!' she said indignantly. 'I *knowed* it was them at the back of it all!'

'What about them?'

'Such fairytales as you'd never believe! If *they* was to be believed, Dawkins 'ad robbed the crown jools, let alone a rabbit or two!'

The children exchanged glances. Perhaps they need no longer worry about that scuttling figure they had seen earlier.

'So has Aunt Marchmont forgiven him?'

'And can he and little Lil stay in their cottage?'

'Your aunt,' said Cook, ''as been as nice as pie, now she knows the truth of it. And I reckon you kiddies 'as 'ad to do with it, I do. You've fair brought 'er on.'

They positively beamed at this tribute.

'Our Quest has succeeded!'

'We needn't do any more Golden Deeds,' said Pip.

'You didn't anyway,' George told him. 'Not that I noticed.'

'None of us did,' said Ellie. 'And we didn't need to – Aunt Marchmont *hadn't* a heart of stone.'

'Just a splinter of ice, like little Kay's in *The Snow Queen*', said Lucy. 'And now it's melted.'

'Bessie's down at Dawkins' cottage kicking up a fearful dust!' Pip said.

At this Cook smiled knowingly.

'She's fair took to that poor little gel,' she said. She lowered her voice confidingly. 'And it's my belief she's took a liking to Dawkins, and 'im to 'er!'

'Good grief!' said George disgustedly.

'What – like in a fairytale?' said Lucy.

'Are there any more scones?' asked Pip. 'Don't be such a muff, Lucy. We're not in a *book*, you know.'

'I don't know about fairytales,' said Cook. 'I only says what I sees plain as the nose on your face. Now, *hout* my kitchen, or there'll be no dinner today!'

At this threat they willingly left, and wandered out into the garden again, still agog at the amazing turn of events. They went and sat under a wide cedar to hold council.

'Is Bessie really sweet on Dawkins, d'you think?' asked Lucy. 'Even without the wish?'

'Search me,' replied Pip, 'But he beats that Arfur – and *he* hasn't even got a gun!'

'And he had ginger whiskers – ugh!' said Ellie.

'Do you think . . .' Lucy giggled. 'D'you think they kiss?'

'Shut up, Luce,' George told her good humouredly. 'Little girls should stick to their dolls.'

'I'd give anything to know,' Lucy sighed. 'If only I were invisible . . .'

'If I were invisible, I'd think of better things to do than spy on *them*!' said Pip scornfully. 'In fact, I wish I *were* invisible, and then for a start I'd go straight back to that kitchen and polish off those scones, and then – '

'Pip!' shrieked Lucy and Ellie together.

They all watched as Pip visibly dissolved. One minute his funny, freckly face was there, lit up by the prospect of scones, the next it had gone. But, horror of horrors – his *clothes* were still there on his invisible body. The effect was so uncanny that, as Ellie said afterwards, it was far worse than if Pip had vanished entirely, clothes and all.

'Oh Pip!' said Lucy in a small voice.

'What's up?' demanded Pip's voice, from somewhere above his jacket collar.

'P'raps he'll come back in a minute, like the Cheshire cat,' said Lucy.

'Oh no he won't,' George told her. 'The idiot's gone and blown our special wish!'

'I wish you'd all stop gaping as if I were a circus freak or something,' said Pip, who was evidently still blissfully unaware of his own invisibleness.

'You *are* one,' George told him. 'Pity you can't see yourself.'

'Look at your hands,' suggested Ellie.

'See if your fingernails are clean,' added Lucy.

There was a longish silence, during which they supposed their brother was obeying these instructions, finding that he *had* no fingernails, clean or otherwise, and scaring himself into giddy fits.

'Oooh – I *can't* be!' came his voice at last.

'What price scientific experiments now!' said George.

'But – but my clothes are still here!'

'So at least we know where you are!' and George gave him a playful poke in the ribs, but the jacket jumped back, affronted.

'Stow it, will you!' it said.

'I don't like it when your voice comes out of nowhere,' Lucy said. 'You should have wished for your *voice* to go invisible, as well!'

'And your clothes,' added George. 'You don't half look a dog's dinner, Pipsqueak!'

'And if anyone sees you they'll die of fright,' said Ellie. 'I know I would.'

'You certainly can't go after those scones,' George agreed. 'Cook'd give notice like a shot.'

'I think you're mean and selfish, wasting a wish like that,' said Lucy.

'You're a fine one to talk!' said Pip. 'Wishing from morning to night on that silly thimble. If anyone – '

'You can just shut up 'cos I'm not listening!' and Lucy covered her ears.

'Do a dance!' said Ellie suddenly.

'A *dance?*' came Pip's disgusted tones.

'Oh do – a Scottish reel or jig – it would look so comical!'

'Be a sport,' said George. 'It's the least you can do to be a sport.'

And so Pip's clothes obligingly began to perform a jig, and the effect was so comical that the rest of them went into fits of laughter, and even Lucy removed her hands from her ears and joined in. The dance ended abruptly.

'It's all very well for you!' said the jacket. 'And anyway, what's the use of being invisible if I'm not really invisible at all?'

'You should have thought of that before you went wasting our wish,' George told him.

'Wait!' said Ellie. 'Listen – you *are* invisible – all over, I expect, not just your hands and face. All you've got to do is take your clothes off!'

There was a silence.

'What – go round *starkers?*'

Lucy giggled, but Ellie frowned and went on.

'You won't really be starkers, because no one can see you.'

'Just invisible as air!' said Lucy.

'She's right, you know, Pip old chap,' said George.

'You'd all laugh,' came Pip's sulky voice.

'We won't,' they assured him. 'We shan't see anything to laugh *at.*'

'Just think, it'd be like the *Emperor's New Clothes*, only the other way round,' urged Lucy. '*He* got laughed at 'cos people could see him, and not his clothes – '

'And with you, it'd be vice versa,' finished George. He then added cunningly, 'I don't see how you'll get any dinner, looking like that.'

'Oh Philip dear, where is your head today?' Ellie mimicked Aunt Marchmont.

This settled the matter. An invisible body could evidently feel as ravenous as a visible one.

'All right,' came Pip's grudging voice, 'but – but I'm not doing it here in front of you lot. I'm going behind a bush.'

His empty suit (except that it was not empty at all, as they knew) turned and ran off into the shrubbery.

'Oh bother!' said Lucy. 'I was dying to see that!'

'I still think it's a rotten waste of a wish,' George said.

'It was your idea,' Ellie told him, in the interests of fairness. 'You were the one who asked to have a wish whenever or wherever we thought of it.'

'Yooee!' they heard Pip call. 'I'm putting my whole arm out from behind the bush.'

They stared.

'Can you see it?'

'No!'

'I'm coming right out.'

They waited.

'There!'

'You *sure* you're there?' asked George.

All three of them stared into the shrubbery till their eyes ached.

'Over here!' came Pip's voice, now from quite another direction.

'Where?'

Next minute Ellie's hat was invisibly plucked from her head – she shrieked and clutched at it, but it went dancing off, followed by their popping eyes, until it finally dropped to the ground.

'I see you but you don't see me!'

This was true, and rather unnerving for the rest of them.

'Pick a flower,' suggested Ellie. 'Then we'll see where you are.'

They waited.

'Look – there!' cried Lucy, and sure enough, there was a lupin spike, seemingly waving in thin air.

'I *am* invisible! Hurray! I'm off!' and the lupin went prancing off. Lucy ran to the bush where Pip had hidden, and there in a heap were his clothes and boots. The others followed her and stared down, still hardly able to believe that somewhere their brother was running around starkers and invisible.

'It's all very well for him,' said George at last. 'Wasting our wish like that!'

But magic moves in a mysterious way, and this wish, like others before it, turned out not to be wasted at all. Just as a seemingly silly wish about the parrot had helped to see off Arthur, so this equally thoughtless wish was to work most powerfully for good.

As Pip danced off, delighted now by his new-found invisibleness, his eye was caught by the figure of Dobbs among the trees. As Pip watched another figure appeared.

'His nephew!'

He dropped the lupin and ran over. To be invisible is an open invitation to become eavesdropper.

'Our last chance, I tells yer!' he heard Dobbs say. ''Er ladyship's got that kid of 'is up at the 'ouse – and 'e took 'er out – look, 'ere they are now!'

Pip turned to see the trap pulling up by the house.

'Now's our chance! 'E's well out the way. 'Ere – get an eyeful o' this!'

Pip then saw that lying by him, concealed amongst the undergrowth, was a sack. He gasped. From it Dobbs was taking a large silver teapot – one that Pip recognised because it stood in place of honour on the dresser. It was followed by a jug and dish, flashing in the sunlight.

'There's candlesticks 'n all! Nuff to put 'im in jug for life!'

'Strewth!' exclaimed Albert. Then, nervously, ''Ad we better? Wot if we're caught?'

'It's *'im* that'll get caught,' said Dobbs with a malevolent leer. 'Look sharp – we'll get 'em to 'is place afore 'e's back!'

His pasty nephew was nodding now.

'And bob's yer uncle!'

Pip listened with horror. If the stolen silver were found at Dawkins' cottage, all was lost. Their Quest to melt Aunt Marchmont's heart, that seemed to have succeeded, would be foiled at a stroke. Dawkins would not only lose his home and job, but be sent to prison as well. And what would become of little Lil?

He hesitated only for a moment, then sped back to where the others were still scanning about them for sight of a walking lupin.

He snatched up a delphinium (much he cared now about Dobbs' flowerbeds) and waved it, calling,

'Here! Here!'

'Look out, idiot!' said George. 'The aunt's back.'

'Listen – I've just seen something!'

He told them, and Lucy started to wail and George kept muttering 'The bounder! The beastly bounder!' and Ellie cried 'But what can we do?'

'Listen, here's what we'll do . . .' and Pip told them his plan, which had come straight into his mind ready made, as if by magic.

'But quick as you can!' he told them. 'I'll do my best – but I can't promise!' and with that he dropped his spike and raced off.

Fortunately, Dobbs was a slow plodder, even when on an evil errand, and soon Pip caught up with the pair, moving stealthily through the trees. He took a deep breath. Everything was up to him now.

'I spy with my little eye!'

The two of them stopped dead in their tracks.

'Wot was that?'

They turned, and Pip, who could even now hardly believe in his own invisibleness, held his breath. It is a very curious feeling, that you do not exist, and he felt himself break out in goose pimples, all over.

'Get be'ind 'ere!' Dobbs grabbed at Albert and they dodged together behind a large tree, pressed hard against its trunk, eyes darting fearfully left and right.

'All clear?' said Dobbs hoarsely at last. Slowly, very slowly, they edged out from their hiding place. On they went, from time to time taking nervous looks over their shoulders.

Now Pip very much prided himself on his impression of an owl. He had it off to a fine art. Neighbours in Islington often remarked how rare it was to find that bird in town (especially one that frequently hooted in daylight, winter and summer alike). One of them even wrote a letter to *The Times* newspaper about it.

There are few occasions when such an accomplishment serves any useful purpose, but now, it seemed, was just such a one. He cupped his hands to his mouth.

'*Whoohoo! Whohoo!*'

'Hst!'

'A *owl?*' ejaculated Dobbs, and he raised his eyes skywards as if in expectation of seeing that nocturnal bird in flight.

'In broad day?' said his nephew. 'I don't like it. 'T'ain't nateral.'

They stood, heads cocked. Pip, delighted with his success, hooted again.

'Well, there *is* owls round abouts righ 'nuff,' said Dobbs at last. 'Least it warn't a cuckoo. If we was to 'ear a cuckoo, mid August, that would be a go!'

It was irresistible. Much the same skills are needed to imitate both owls and cuckoos. Again Pip cupped his hands.

'*Cuckoo! Cuckoo!*'

The men froze and stared at one another mouths agape.

'We – we're a bein' 'aunted! Let's drop it and do a runner!'

'Nah!' growled Dobbs, much to Pip's relief. That was not his plan at
all. 'It's only bloomin' birds. Fine gamekeeper you'll make, if you're frit
o' birds. Come on!'

Pip waited till they were within sight of Dawkins' cottage before he
played his next trick. He found a long, snapped off branch, and crept up
behind them. Then, very lightly, he scratched the back of Dobbs' neck,
just where his cap ended. Dobbs' free hand clapped the spot, but Pip had
whisked the stick away. On they went. Again Pip tickled. Dobbs stopped.

'Albert . . . Albert . . .' he quavered.

'Wot?'

'There's – there's something a scratchin' at my neck!'

Quick as a flash Pip dropped the stick. Next moment Albert had turned
and was looking, it seemed, straight through him.

'Nah . . . you're gettin' jumpy, Uncle.'

Dobbs rubbed the back of his neck hard.

'There was, I tell yer! If you'd a felt it you'd a knowed!'

'Well I didn't!' snapped his nephew. 'Look sharp, will yer, else 'e'll be
back!'

The men hurried on. Pip grinned invisibly. Next minute Albert
yelped and was clapping a hand to *his* neck.

He whirled round, glaring.

'There! Tole yer!'

'We're b-b-bein' 'aunted!'

'I ain't a feared o' no ghosties!'

'Well I am!'

'It's broad day! Wot 'arm can it do? Let's get this stuff dropped and
scarper!'

. . . he was just in time to see the back of Pip, starkers,
disappearing into the shrubbery.

Not once did it cross their minds that what they were seeing was children with wings.

The two men hurried off towards Dawkins' cottage. Pip followed, and as he did so, saw that his delaying tactics had worked perfectly. Luckily, the villains were so bent on carrying out their plan that they looked neither left nor right, and did not see what he saw.

Advancing fast down the lane were several figures. There were George, Ellie, Lucy and Aunt Marchmont, all carrying croquet sticks. Behind them came Dawkins, followed by Cook and Bessie, both armed with brooms.

'Swelp me!' breathed Pip. 'It's worked!'

Then, because the scheming pair were now at the very door of the cottage, he quite forgot his invisibility and yelled 'Quick! At the double!'

The rescue party broke into a run and hollered and screeched and brandished their makeshift weapons.

Dobbs and his nephew froze. They turned. Their jaws dropped and so did the sack.

'Gotcher!' screamed the decorous Bessie, picking up her skirts and running, broom raised aloft. Next moment the pair were cornered. Whichever way they looked there stood a grim-faced person armed with broom or mallet. Albert groaned and made as if to run for it, but Aunt Marchmont twirled her mallet menacingly and he stepped smartly back.

'It's no use your trying to bolt!' cried George.

'Let's 'ave a look what's in that sack, shall we?' said Dawkins.

The pair gulped and swallowed and rolled their eyes.

'Come along!' ordered Aunt Marchmont, and fetched them a swipe with her mallet.

'Game's up!' muttered Dobbs. 'Go on!'

Albert, grimacing horribly, tipped up the sack and out spilled the stolen silver.

'Oooh, they oughter be 'anged!' shrieked Cook.

Just then there came a tiny voice, 'Wait for me! Wait for me!'

They all turned to see little Lil, staggering under the weight of an axe almost as big as herself.

'Oh my gawd!' groaned Dobbs. 'We're done for!'

His listeners could scarcely believe that he was referring to this small child – she could barely drag the axe, and would certainly not be able to swing it. They all swivelled in the other direction and saw, to their utmost astonishment, a policeman!

'We're nicked! 'Ow did 'e get 'ere?'

'I sent for him,' said Aunt Marchmont calmly. 'You told me yourself that fruit was being stolen. I saw him in the village and asked him to come up.'

'Hurray! Hoist with his own petard!'

'Surrender, blaggards!' shrieked Lucy, whirling her croquet mallet.

And so they did. There was no help for it. The pair were marched off to the village by the Law, with Dawkins and his fists in attendance. The sack of stolen silver was towed back up to the house by George and Ellie, and the triumphant rescue party marched to a rousing chorus of *Men of Harlech*. Even Aunt Marchmont joined in.

Pip himself felt left out of all this triumph and rejoicing. This was rather thick, he thought, considering that he had been the one to overhear the plot, and to delay the villains long enough for them to be caught in the act. It is a bitter pill, to be unthanked and deprived of the glory that is one's due.

'I'll get up to some real devilry this afters, won't I just!' he promised himself, kicking stones with his invisible feet.

As things turned out, at dinner time matters took another unexpected twist. The children arrived promptly at table to find Aunt Marchmont already sitting there, looking uncommonly pleased with herself.

'Ah, there you are, George, Ellie, Lucy and – ' she stopped, 'Where is Philip?'

'You've really got our names off pat now, Aunt Marchmont,' said George encouragingly, avoiding this unanswerable question.

'He – he asked to be excused, Aunt Marchmont,' said Ellie, who had already decided on this small untruth.

'Is he not well?'

'He – he's not quite himself,' replied Ellie, this time with perfect truth.

'I have observed,' said Aunt Marchmont, 'that as a rule he eats a great deal.'

'Not half, he does,' agreed George.

'And so missing a meal will scarcely harm him.'

'Shall I run up and see 'ow 'e is, miss?' asked Bessie.

'No!' cried all the children at once.

'I shouldn't, Bessie. He won't want to be reminded he's off his grub,' advised George.

'It might make him worse,' added Lucy.

'Bless 'is 'eart,' said Bessie absently. 'Now, oo's for steak and kidney?'

They all were, including the invisible Pip. His usual chair was suddenly pulled out from the table, as if by magic. Fortunately this was unnoticed by the grown-ups, but the children saw it and exchanged anguished glances.

'Er – has Dawkins definitely come back to work for you, Aunt Marchmont?' asked George.

'Wasn't he *brave*!'

'Certainly he has,' she replied. 'I cannot imagine how I allowed Mr and Mrs Dobbs to turn me against him so.'

'They were beasts!' said Pip warmly.

'And now they've got their just desserts!' added George swiftly, to cover for his invisible brother.

Aunt Marchmont did look somewhat startled, but evidently decided she must have mistaken the voice – after all, she had only just learned to recognise the names. At the same time a bread roll transferred itself from Lucy's plate to Pip's. From then on the children worked frantically to distract the grown-ups from such interesting phenomena.

'All he did was shoot a few rabbits to feed poor little Lil,' said Ellie.

'Precisely,' nodded Aunt Marchmont. 'The child's reading is coming along splendidly. I have taught her the entire alphabet,'

'Good for you!' said George.

'You're a brick, Aunt Marchmont,' said Ellie.

'With a heart of gold,' added Lucy.

'I appreciate your remarks,' Aunt Marchmont told them 'but feel bound to point out that bricks cannot have hearts, either of gold or anything else.'

'What we mean is that you're a real trump,' explained George.

'And brave as a lion!' said Lucy.

'You certainly whacked 'em one with that mallet!'

Aunt Marchmont looked pleased by these fulsome compliments, evidently realising that on this occasion they were sincere, and not merely 'buttering up'.

During this exchange several forkfuls of steak and kidney transferred themselves from George's plate to Pip's invisible mouth.

'All you need now is a new housekeeper,' said Ellie, one eye on the floating fork.

'And if poor little Lil had a mother then everything would be perfectly perfect, and everyone would live happily ever after,' said Lucy.

At this Bessie went into a paroxysm of nervous coughing, and hurried from the room, muttering something about Cook and the pudding.

'I rather like the idea of people living happily ever after,' said Aunt Marchmont unexpectedly.

'S'only in *stories* they do,' came Pip's voice. The rest of the children winced, and Ellie said hurriedly, 'Oh, so do *I*!' and 'They're my very favouritest stories of all,' added Lucy.

'*Favourite*,' corrected Aunt Marchmont. 'Grammar, Lucy.'

She looked round at them all.

'Do you regard me as part of your family?' she enquired.

They were somewhat startled by this abrupt query.

'Er – of course, Aunt Marchmont,' said Ellie.

'After all, you're Father's aunt,' said George.

'We don't *see* you very often,' said Lucy. 'In fact we've never seen you till now.'

'I have never felt part of a real family before,' said Aunt Marchmont. 'But now, I believe I really do. You are my family.'

'But we'll be going soon,' Ellie reminded her.

Aunt Marchmont sighed.

'I know, child.' Then, quite suddenly, she brightened. 'But do you know what I have done this morning?'

They shook their heads, each with one eye on the eerily floating food.

'I have visited the photographer! And this afternoon at three o'clock he is coming to take a photograph!'

Chapter XVI

A HARD BARGAIN

The children gaped.

'Then, when you are gone, I shall have something to remind me of you. Remind me that I have a family, after all.'

'It – it's a jolly good idea, Aunt Marchmont,' said George faintly. 'But don't you think tomorrow might be better?'

'Tomorrow?' she echoed.

'It – it looks like rain,' said Ellie quickly.

'Then we shall pose indoors,' said Aunt Marchmont. 'I don't think it looks like rain. In fact, I was rather looking forward to this afternoon. Who's for croquet?'

Silence. Fortunately Pip, in his invisibility, was sufficiently sensible not to say 'Me!'

'We – er – we have to go and see someone,' said George (meaning the Psammead. If a photographer was coming at three, Pip must be made visible again at all costs).

'Who?' asked Lucy, puzzled.

'You know . . .' he said meaningly. '*Thingy* . . .'

Her brow cleared.

'Oh – yes. Yes, we do.'

At this Aunt Marchmont looked so down cast that Ellie was smitten with pity for her. She heaved a deep sigh.

'I suppose you think me rather dull, and don't care to play with me.'

'Oh no, we don't, we like you, truly we do! We didn't at first, but we do now!' cried Ellie. 'And George and I will play croquet with you. Lucy can go by herself to see the – the person.'

Aunt Marchmont perked up instantly.

'Splendid!' Then, wistfully, 'I wonder who I shall play with when you are gone . . .?'

The rest of the meal passed without incident, or rather, without either of the grown-ups noticing such trifles as floating spoons and forks, and crumbs on plates at empty places. Once outside. the children held a hasty council.

'We've simply got to get Pip visible by three o'clock,' said George.

'What, just for a silly photograph?' came Pip's voice. 'I *like* being invisible, it's a real lark!'

'Pick a flower again, or something, can't you?' said George irritably. 'It's a bit much expecting us to talk to thin air.'

A hollyhock obligingly appeared in mid air.

'It's *rather* queer talking to a hollyhock!' said Ellie, and the girls giggled.

'But I thought the Sammyadd said you couldn't unwish wishes,' Lucy said.

'Not in the ordinary way,' agreed George. 'But this is a time of direst need. There must be some way it can bring it off.'

'If it doesn't, and Pip's missing, I shouldn't wonder if Aunt Marchmont doesn't send for the police again,' said Ellie.

'So it's all up to you now, Lucy,' George told her solemnly. 'You must explain what's happened, and ask the Sammyadd to undo the wish.'

'Beg it,' said Ellie. '*Implore* it.'

Lucy, as youngest, was rarely entrusted with important errands, and was naturally pleased. On the other hand, it was a dreadfully heavy responsibility for such young shoulders.

'I know,' she said. 'I'll take it my portrait. That should put it in a good mood.'

'Not so dusty, Lucy,' George told her.

She ran to fetch it, and Ellie, to whom a splendid idea had just occurred, ran after her.

George then addressed the hollyhock.

'And you, Pip old chap, had better get your things on, if you don't want to be caught starkers!'

Ellie's idea was simple and perfect in that it killed two birds with one stone. Lucy's portrait of the Psammead would be seen to better advantage if it were in a frame, and Ellie was dying to have proof that they all had really met Aunt Marchmont as a child. In the cupboard under the stairs were all Aunt Marchmont's old samplers and tapestries, waiting to go to the jumble.

It was the work of a moment to sort swiftly through them and find the one she guessed Connie had told them about. She snatched it up and ran upstairs after Lucy.

They pulled the cover from the back of the frame with trembling fingers. They gazed down in awe. There, neatly stitched, was the legend 'Norah is a cross-eyed piggywiggy', and a stout pink pig with deliciously curling tail.

'True, then!' breathed Ellie at this incontrovertible proof of magic. 'Oh, I wonder . . .'

Already she was having the beginnings of another perfect idea. Now, however, was not the time for it. She placed the sampler in a drawer and set about replacing it with Lucy's portrait.

'There!' she said. 'Now it looks like a real present!'

As Lucy went down the lane carrying her portrait she met Dawkins, carrying little Lil pic-a-back.

'Art'noon, missy!'

'Good afternoon, Mr Dawkins,' replied Lucy, rather enjoying being greeted singly, as a person in her own right, instead of as just one of a crowd.

'My parrot don't talk any more,' Lil told her. 'P'raps he's homesick.'

Lucy knew that this was not at all the reason for the parrot's lapsing into his customary dumbness, but naturally did not say so.

'P'raps I could teach him,' Lil continued, '*And* to read!'

'I'm glad you got your job back,' Lucy told Dawkins.

He grinned.

'Truth will out, missy!'

'My Pa's not a thief!' said Lil indignantly.

'I know,' said Lucy. 'It was those beastly Dobbses. They've gone to prison, you know. I must go now – I have a burning mission!'

On she went, and the nearer she came to the sand-pit the more nervous she felt. 'But if I do it, I'll be the heroine of the hour,' she told herself, and 'Stout heart!'

She reached the heap of stones and stared doubtfully down. The sand-pit stretched about her, enormously bare and lonely.

'Stout heart!' she muttered again, dropped to her knees and drew a deep breath.

'Sammyadd!' she called timidly. 'Sammyadd!'

Nothing. Silence.

'Dear Sammyadd, it's me, Lucy – the one who stroked you this morning. Please come out. I wish you would!'

The Psammead, slumbering in the sand, heard that urgent wish and was bound to grant it. It stirred, and started to dig itself out. Lucy saw the whirling sand and rapturously cried 'Hurray!'

Then it was there. It gave the most prodigious yawn, as if in reproach.

'Oh, it's you again, is it? Where are the others?'

'They're back at the house. Sammyadd – I've brought you a present – I mean token of esteem. Look!'

The Psammead gazed at the portrait as she held it aloft.

'It's a portrait of you!'

'Is it?' said the Psammead dubiously, tilting its head this way and that.

'All important people have their portraits painted,' she told it.

'Ah, well, I am certainly that,' it agreed. 'But I hardly think you have done justice to my whiskers.'

'They're dreadfully hard to do, they're so fiddly. But do you like it?'

It nodded slowly.

'I like it, and I like *you*,' it said surprisingly.

'Oh, do you?' she said eagerly.

'A kind heart is a rare thing,' it told her.

'Have you got one?' She asked. 'Because I want to ask you a very special favour.'

'I expect it's something to do with that wish you made this morning,' said the Psammead. 'I did warn you. I suppose someone has ended up in a besieged castle, or with eyes in the back of its head or ten feet high?'

'Invisible, actually,' said Lucy humbly.

'Hmm. What – all of them?'

'Just Pip.'

'I see no harm in that,' it told her. 'He is a mere – absence.'

'But Aunt Marchmont's sent for a photographer and he's coming at three and if Pip's not there she'll send for the police!'

'And so you wish me to make him visible again before sunset?'

'Oh yes, yes!'

'It is against the rules, of course,' it told her.

'I know, and I'm dreadfully sorry! But isn't there just the chanciest chance that you might?'

The Psammead surveyed her thoughtfully.

'I *could* . . .' it said.

'Oh, thank goodness!'

'But the unwishing of wishes means working the most powerful and dangerous magic. Even I have only ever done it once or twice. I may even have forgotten how.'

Lucy stared aghast, and prayed fervently that it had not.

'If I do it, all the magic will drain out of me.'

'What? Forever?' cried Lucy, horrified.

'Not forever,' it replied. 'But I shall be exhausted. You will have to promise not to come asking for wishes for at least three days.'

'But we're going home soon! And I was going to wish for all kinds of things, and the very best wish I've thought of is wings to fly!'

'You must decide,' it told her.

Poor Lucy was in a dilemma. She knew that Pip must be there for the photograph at three o'clock, but hardly dared think what the others would say when they learned of the price that had to be paid.

'Oh, what shall I do?'

'It will do my top left twelfth whisker no good at all, of course,' remarked the Psammead.

'Oh dear!'

'But I can do it, if you wish.'

'Oh, my head's all muddled! I don't know, I don't!'

Meanwhile George and Ellie were playing croquet with Aunt Marchmont, though their thoughts were not on the game at all. They were with their little sister, alone at the sand-pit, parleying with the Psammead. Even so, they did notice that curious things were happening to the ball. It would roll, fall short of a hoop, and then mysteriously move again, of its own accord, it seemed, and roll cleanly through. They knew, of course, that this was the work of their invisible brother. It was not their own balls that were being assisted in this way, but those of their aunt, who appeared not to notice, but moved here and there whacking her ball and thoroughly enjoying her success.

'Oh, splendid!' and 'Oh, I am enjoying this!' she kept crying.

'What's his game?' George muttered to Ellie, after their aunt's ball had taken a particularly spectacular swerve.

'Trying to put her in a good mood by making her win, I expect,' whispered Ellie.

'Where *is* the blighter?' George took out his watch. 'Hmm! Not *far off three*!' he exclaimed loudly.

'Come along then, quickly, I've almost won!' cried Aunt Marchmont.

'*I* shouldn't like to be caught starkers!' said George loudly.

'What *are* you talking about?' exclaimed Aunt Marchmont.

'Ooooh!' gasped Ellie faintly.

She was looking horrorstruck at something behind George. He, guessing what it might be, whirled about, so that he was just in time to see the back of Pip, starkers, disappearing into the shrubbery. Aunt Marchmont was so occupied in working out her next move that she mercifully missed this interesting spectacle.

'Phew!' George let out a breath of relief. 'Good old Lucy! She's done it, then.'

Aunt Marchmont struck a winning ball.

'There!' she cried triumphantly. 'How's that?'

'I think you're getting mixed up with cricket,' George told her, 'but jolly good, anyway.'

Dawkins and little Lil emerged from the house, where Cook and Bessie had been plying them with food. The invisible Pip had managed nothing like his usual helpings, and there had been plenty of steak and kidney left over.

Aunt Marchmont brandished her mallet.

'I won!' she called. A thought struck her. 'Do *you* play croquet, Dawkins?'

'No, miss, I can't say as I do.'

'Then I shall teach you,' she announced. 'I shall require you to play with me as part of your duties.'

'Yes, 'm!' said Dawkins smartly.

'An' me, an' me!' cried little Lil.

'When you are stronger, Lily,' Aunt Marchmont told her. 'Oh, won't we have jolly times!'

'*There* you are, Master Pip!' exclaimed Bessie, and they all turned to see him stroll coolly out from the shrubbery. 'I thought you was poorly!'

'I was,' he replied, 'sort of. I felt as if I was there, but *not* there, if you know what I mean.'

'Oooh, 'e's 'ad one of them funny turns like you and me 'ad, ma'am,' said Bessie. '*Must* be fectious!'

'It certainly was a strange feeling . . .' murmured Aunt Marchmont.

'Now come along, all of you, and get yourselves tidied to 'ave your pictures took!'

Lucy arrived huffing and puffing back from the sand-pit, and was mightily relieved to see Pip, clothes and all.

'Well done, Lucy!' whispered George.

'Was it dreadfully hard?' asked Ellie.

Lucy shook her head.

'Tell you later!'

Best togs had to be fished out and changed into, faces washed and hair brushed. There was no time to explain the bargain Lucy had struck with the Psammead in return for the unwishing of a wish. When they came down they were surprised to see that even their aunt had changed out of her customary black, and was wearing a dress of violet, with ruffs at the neck.

'Oh, you do look nice, Aunt Marchmont!' Ellie told her, and was not, on this occasion, accused of 'buttering up'.

The photograph was taken, while Dawkins, little Lil and Bessie looked on.

'I wish I could have my picture took,' said Lil wistfully.

'Then you shall,' Aunt Marchmont told her. 'We *all* shall!'

'Oooh!' cried Bessie. 'And me in me second best pinny and 'air like a cuckoo's nest!'

'Cuckoos don't *have* nests, Bessie,' Pip pointed out, and 'Then take your pinafore *off*, Bessie,' said Aunt Marchmont.

And so Dawkins, Bessie and little Lil had their photograph taken too, standing stiff and straight and staring nervously at the camera, yet pleased, too.

When the photographer had gone and the group dispersed the children gathered for a parley.

'Come on, Lucy,' said George. 'Tell all.'

'Was it cross?' asked Ellie anxiously.

'It wasn't exactly cross,' Lucy told them. 'But it was most fearfully difficult. It blew and blew and blew itself up till I honestly thought it would burst!'

'But it didn't!'

'No – o. But – ' she paused. She could hardly bear to tell them.

'But what?'

'But – it used up all its magic!'

'Not forever!'

'No – but it said it was 'zausted, it just sank down in a little crumpled heap!'

They waited.

'And – and it said we mustn't ask for any more wishes for three whole days!'

'Strewth!'

'Oh *no*!'

'And we're going home soon!'

'I know,' said Lucy miserably. 'But you said I had to get Pip visible again and I didn't know what to do!'

Her face crumpled.

'Oh don't start blubbing!' Pip told her.

Ellie put an arm round her.

'Never mind, Lucy lamb. It's not your fault.'

Chapter XVII   (and last)

THE LAST WISH

Even if a thing is not someone's fault it can still be a sore trial. And the Psammead's having to unwish a wish *was* someone's fault — Pip's. As soon as they had had time to realise that three whole bleak days without wishes lay ahead of them, the others were bound to remind him of this. Pip then reminded them that it was George who had asked for their wish to be granted whenever and wherever they thought of it, and George hotly pointed out that he had meant a *proper* wish, a decent one that everyone could join in. Pip then retorted that had he not been invisible, the Dobbses would doubtless have planted the stolen silver, and Dawkins would now be in prison. I am sorry to tell you that the pair came very close to fisticuffs and were only prevented by the peace-loving Ellie.

'Stop it!' she cried. 'We shall be too busy for wishes, anyhow.'

'Busy?' echoed Pip, who did not much like the sound of that word. It seemed to imply toil and trouble, rather than decent activities with microscopes or games of bandits.

'Aunt Marchmont's birthday,' she reminded him.

'The party!'

'And presents,' supplied Lucy. 'We must all make presents and they must be absolutely secret!'

'A surprise!'

All the Garsingtons were fond of surprises – of the pleasant variety, at any rate. And once their disappointment had been nobly swallowed they set to with a will on the work of making the aunt's birthday the most splendid occasion ever. The party, they decided, should be a picnic.

'And listen,' said Pip, 'the sainted aunt's birthday's in three days . . .'

'So straight after we can go to see the Sammyadd!'

This prospect was bound to cheer them. The three following days were so busy that it was hard to see how they could have managed to have their usual wishes *and* give the aunt an even halfway decent party. Lucy decided to make a portrait and frame it.

'But you usually make needle cases, Lucy,' Ellie told her.

'But she *hates* sewing now,' Lucy reminded her. 'She's a reformed sewer.'

George said that he would make a bookmark and Pip volunteered a spill holder. Ellie, however, was very mysterious about her own intended offering.

'Wait and see,' was all she would say, sounding exactly like a tiresome grown-up.

The children then drew up a mouthwatering list of goodies for the picnic and went to see the Friendly Cook.

'Why, bless your 'earts!' she cried when she was shown the list, which was as long as your arm, and would have been longer had Pip not been restrained. 'She ain't never 'ad a birthday before!'

'She must have *had* them,' Pip pointed out, reasonably enough. 'It's just that no one remembered them.'

'So we're trying to cram all her lost birthdays into one,' explained George.

'And it's going to be a picnic.'

'So better not make the jellies too wobbly,' Pip advised.

'There'll 'ave to be a cake!' cried Cook, thoroughly entering into the spirit of the thing.

'With her name on it in pink sugar – oh, can *I* help?'

'You're proper little ducks,' Cook told them, beaming, 'and your aunt's turning into a duck, an' all, as fast as she knows 'ow!'

'Our Quest has succeeded!' said Lucy proudly.

'And I daresay Bessie'll miss you with all 'er 'eart!'

The children stared.

'Oh lawks!' exclaimed Cook. ''Adn't you guessed?'

In their heart of hearts, the children had guessed. Dear Bessie was to stay behind and marry Dawkins, and be a mother to little Lil. And she and Dawkins would look after the aunt instead of the beastly Dobbses.

'And live happily ever after!' said Lucy ecstatically. 'Just like a fairytale!'

And so it was. The wishless days passed in a fine frenzy of secret preparations and when the aunt's birthday arrived the skies were as blue and cloudless as in any fairytale. (Not that the young Garsingtons would have been daunted by rain. Unlike the Psammead they had no top left twelfth whiskers to cosset, and would simply have had the picnic under as large a tree as they could find.)

The day started with the giving of the presents and a pink cheeked Aunt Marchmont opened each in turn and declared each the fulfilment of her dearest wishes. She announced her intention of making sure to read several pages each day, to light fires and lamps continuously, and to hang her portrait in place of honour above the mantel shelf. Ellie saved her mysterious parcel till last.

'Now, what . . .?' murmured Aunt Marchmont, pulling at the ribbons. 'Another portrait, I wonder . . .?'

It was certainly something in a frame. She gazed down at it, and the most curious expression came over her face. It was an expression the children half recognised from that moment in the dusty summerhouse when the hidden Psammead had granted her wish.

And then she smiled. And then she laughed! And the children crowded round and saw that there, framed back to front, was that carefully stitched sampler that had hung in the drawing room for over forty years. But now there was a fat pink pig with prodigiously curly tail, and the neatly worked legend 'Norah is a cross-eyed piggywiggy'.

Her delight was such that nobody minded that Ellie's gift was clearly the aunt's favourite of all, despite the fact that it had been made by the recipient rather than the donor, as is usual in the case of birthday presents.

At three o'clock a procession set out from the White House carrying hampers and rugs and bats and balls and all the ingredients of a first class picnic. Bessie, Dawkins and little Lil were so splendidly turned out that it seemed a shame there was no photographer present. Aunt Marchmont wore her pretty violet frock and the young Garsingtons were as spruce as Bessie had been able to make them, given that they were unable to stand still for a single moment.

The site for the picnic had been carefully chosen for its proximity to the sand-pit.

'Then, as soon as we've played games and had tea we'll go straight to see the Sammyadd.' said Pip.

'And take it a piece of cake,' added Lucy.

'And ask it if we can have just one more absolutely last wish,' said Ellie.

'And listen – I've had the most perfectly splendid idea . . .' said Lucy.

And she whispered it, and the others nodded their heads in agreement.

The picnic passed as swiftly as all picnics do. Time is a very curious thing – rather like elastic, and not very friendly to humans. It is provokingly short when all is jollity and exitement, and stretches out long as long when there are sums to be worked or dentists to be visited. The feast vanished rapidly and endless bottles of ginger pop were drunk. Little Lil was seen stuffing her pockets with buns and biscuits, evidently still unable to believe that the whole world had changed since the coming of our heroes and heroines. Methusalah (who by now had been handed back to his rightful owner) became so excited that he seemed almost in danger of saying something, without benefit of the Psammead.

There were games of Blindman's Buff in which matters were complicated by trees and shrubs, and Pass The Parcel was played to the accompaniment of Pip and his paper and comb. A game of Hunt The Thimble was slyly proposed by George, but promptly vetoed by Lucy.

At last they were all breathless and tired out and collapsed to the ground.

'I really think this has been the best day of my whole life!' said the aunt.

'An' me,' said little Lil, who had had to give up the games early on, floppy as a rag doll. 'I'll be that lonely when you're gone. I wish you was stopping forever, I do!'

'Here – take him!' and George impulsively lifted the parrot's cage and put it down beside her. (Methusalah was strictly his, having been a present given on his sixth birthday, in the vain hope that the parrot would prove more communicative than his stuffed owl.)

Little Lil's eyes stretched wide in disbelief.

'For me? Reely for me?'

'You might be able to get him talking,' said George gruffly.

'That's fair 'andsome of you, Master George!' exclaimed Bessie.

It was – but it must be said that George, in giving the bird, had known in his heart of hearts that he was *meant* to do so. He had been to the future and back, remember.

All the time the shadows were lengthening and the birds were now whistling their special evening notes. Now and again the children would look to see where the sun was beginning to sink in a red glow behind the tree tops. At last, as Dawkins and Bessie began to stack the plates and repack the hampers, George said,

'Er – we've just got something to do.'

'Something we want to show little Lil,' added Ellie.

'Then off you go,' Aunt Marchmont told them. 'But mind you don't tire her.'

Little Lil entrusted the parrot to Dawkins, who solemnly swore to guard him with his life. Then she was hoisted on to George's back and the five of them set off to the sand-pit. They went at a fast lick. The sun was sinking and time was short. Lucy ran ahead, crying,

'Oh do hurry! This is the bestest wish ever and there'll be no time for it!'

The sand-pit looked more than ever a place of mystery, bathed in the evening glow. Even little Lil, who knew nothing of the magical beast that inhabited the place, was awed by the deep, powerful silence.

'I ain't never been 'ere before,' she whispered.

George set her down, and they stood staring at the familiar heap of stones.

'Now – just you wait!' Ellie whispered to Lil. 'We're going to introduce you to something . . .'

'And when we've gone, it can be your friend,' Lucy said.

Because this is what the children had decided. It would be pure selfishness, they thought, to go back to Islington without passing on the secret of the Psammead to some other lucky child. They had not, to tell the truth, performed many Golden Deeds during their Quest, but this was truly a shining Golden Deed.

George dropped to his knees.

'Sammyadd! Sammyadd!'

Silence. Little Lil, mystified, looked all about her.

'We wish you'd come out, dear Sammyadd!' said Ellie.

They all watched for the last time that spurt and flurry of sand, and saw with delight the familiar whiskered face of the Psammead.

'Oh!' gasped little Lil. 'What is it? A monkey?'

The Psammead stiffened.

'Five of you?' it snapped. 'Who's this? Monkey indeed!'

'It's little Lil and she's going to be your friend when we've gone and don't be cross,' begged Lucy. 'Look – here's some cake!'

'Oh, aren't you nice!' and Lil put out a hand to touch it, and it was easy to see that its heart was won by this simple gesture. It squirmed, rather, with pride and embarrassment.

'Hmm. Well. I suppose none of you is going to enquire after my health?'

'How are you?' asked George quickly.

'We hope you're feeling better,' added Ellie.

'People shouldn't ask for the unwishing of wishes. I have scarcely opened my eyes these last three days. And as for my poor top left twelfth whisker . . .'

It rolled its eyes and shuddered.

'It was terribly clever of you to do it!'

'And we're eternally grateful!'

'Thank you, thank you, dear Sammyadd!'

They were buttering it up. Unlike Aunt Marchmont, it did not seem to notice, and merely accepted these remarks as no more than its due.

'We're going home tomorrow,' George told it.

'And shan't see you again.'

'And so I suppose you have come for a last wish?'

They stared.

'How did you guess?'

'Folk generally do. The last lot did.'

'So – so could we have one?'

'The very bestest wish ever . . .'

'You had better hurry up! Do you want those wings or not?'

They fairly goggled then. Without a word being spoken that magical and ancient beast had divined their wish.

'You – you knew!'

It assumed an air of sublime smugness, and waited.

'Oh yes – yes, please – I wish we all had beautiful wings to fly with!'

The Psammead nodded. It drew an enormous breath and they saw for the last time the extraordinary puffing and grunting that went with the granting of a wish. And just as all the air went rushing out of it the Psammead gasped the one word 'Goodbye!'

Then the sand was flying again and it was gone. The children stood there, feeling a fearful mixture of sorrow and delight – sorrow that they would not see that fairy creature again, and delight because, already, they had wings!

'Hurray!'

'Wheeee!'

'Watch me!'

Ellie seized little Lil by the hand and pushed on her toes and next minute they were airborne, up, up, up with little Lil's skinny legs dangling and her mouth a perfect soundless O.

And that is where we had better leave them, flying through those last precious minutes before sunset, over the sand-pit, over the trees, free as birds.

Dawkins and Bessie, laden with rugs and hampers, were trudging after Aunt Marchmont back to the White House. Thinking they heard faint, familiar voices, they looked about, but realised that those voices, impossibly, seemed to be coming from overhead. Aunt Marchmont, too, stopped in her tracks. Dropping their baggage they stood, all three of them, shading their eyes against the sun's last beams, and saw, or thought they saw, a flock of exotic, strange plumaged birds. Not once did it cross their minds that what they were seeing was children with wings.

'Rum birds, them,' remarked Bessie, and picked up the rugs again.

The last of the Psammeads, deep, deep down in its sandy burrow, heard those words with its sharp bat's ears, and smiled drowsily. Its secret was safe – from the grown-ups, at any rate.

EXPLICIT